RED'S ALPHAS

WOLVES OF CRIMSON HOLLOW BOOK ONE

M. H. SOARS

MICHELLE HERCULES

ISBN: 9781726822022

For those who never cease to seek their happily ever afters.

Coming Soon!

Wolves of Crimson Hollow Series:

Wolf's Calling (Book Two)

Pack's Queen (Book Three)

RED'S ALPHAS

WOLVES OF CRIMSON HOLLOW BOOK ONE

Website:
www.mhsoars.com
www.michellehercules.com

Editor: Cynthia Shepp

Cover Design: Rebecca Frank

CHAPTER 1

RED

"All right. Stop everything." Kenya brings the palms of her hands up. "It's midnight, and you know what that means." Her lips curl into a wicked grin, and I shake my head.

Here we go.

Kenya had been more excited about my upcoming twenty-first birthday than I was, but only because it meant I could officially join in on my best friend's escapades. I didn't have the heart to tell her I could have already tagged along on those wild nights way before what Kenya calls my *Freedom Day*, thanks to my fake ID. It was a rite of passage to procure one at my old high school in Chicago, and I've had mine since I was sixteen.

When I moved to Crimson Hollow to take care of my grandmother two years ago, I left my party days behind. That's why I never told Kenya about my illegal document. It had been an adjustment for sure—not forsaking the parties, but leaving life in the big city. I missed the noise, the chaos, and my friends. But most importantly, I loved how my busy life kept me from being stuck inside my own head for too long. Strange thoughts roamed freely in my brain when there was no other stimuli, thoughts that felt like they belonged to someone else. And that scared me.

"I'm not drinking twenty-one shots," I say loudly enough so

everyone in our group can hear me over the loud music in the bar. There are six of us in total—four friends from Crimson Hollow's community college, Peter, who is my coworker at the hardware store, and me.

"Aw, come on. You don't turn twenty-one every day." Kenya pouts.

"True, but if I want to live to see another birthday, I'd better stick with one shot."

Kenya opens her mouth, but Peter cuts her off. "One shot is fine. Don't be a pusher, Kenya. Not everyone can guzzle down alcohol like you do and survive."

Peter winks at me from behind his thick-rimmed glasses before turning to the bar to order the shots. I appreciate the support, but I suspect it comes with expectations. I'm fairly certain Peter's friendly feelings for me have evolved to more. I caught him staring at me several times at work in a wistful manner. Even Kenya has noticed he acts differently around me. It sucks because I don't see him that way. He's a nice guy and cute, but there's no chemistry between us. At least not on my part. In reality, the only time I came close to that blissful feeling people in love gush about was with my ex, Alex.

No, I can't go there. Not on my birthday.

Peter returns with tequila shots in hand, then hands me a glass. "Need salt and lemon?"

"No. I'm good."

He raises an eyebrow while the beginning of a smirk blossoms on his lips. I'm beginning to think people in town believe I'm a boring wallflower, which couldn't be farther from the truth. *Whatever.* Let them assume that's the case. It's not like I talk much about my previous life in Chicago.

Once everybody has their drinks, Kenya raises her glass. "To Amelia Redford, the best friend I didn't know I needed. Thanks for coming to Crimson Hollow, girlie."

"Cheers!" the rest of the group shouts.

With a smile, I bring the shot glass to my lips and throw my head back, letting the fiery liquid go down my throat. It's been a while since I drank anything stronger than beer, and it burns. Shaking my head, I shudder, ready to put my empty glass back on the counter. But a tequila bottle materializes out of nowhere. Suddenly, my glass is full again.

Raising an eyebrow, I look at Peter. "What's this?"

"Sorry, Red. I think you need more than one shot." He smirks.

I narrow my eyes. "Traitor. I have to work tomorrow."

"No, you don't. I gave you the day off."

My jaw drops. As he's the owner's son, he can do that. But I'm annoyed he took away my shift without asking first. If I'd wanted to, I could have requested the day off. I hadn't for a reason—to have an excuse to bail on my birthday party early. I don't like leaving my grandmother alone for too long, but sometimes it's easier to say I'm tired or I have an early shift at work instead of explaining. The truth always leads to worried or pitying glances from my friends, and I'm tired of them. Cancer sucks, but Wendy Redford is putting up a hell of a fight.

I gulp down the second tequila shot with a jerky movement. Annoyance simmers low in my gut. For the rest of the night, avoiding Peter will be my goal. The background music cuts off abruptly, and a skinny guy hops onto the stage to introduce the band. The Howlers are playing tonight.

Kenya whistles, joining the cacophony of shouts and applause from the crowd. It's a popular rock band—especially among women—the reason being the lead singer Samuel Wolfe. He's the typical bad-boy rock star—tall, dark, and sinfully gorgeous. I usually scoff at those stereotypical men, but I can't deny the guy has a presence. When he saunters onto the stage in his beat-up leather jacket that does little to hide his ripped body and wide shoulders, something unfurls in the pit of my stomach.

Jesus, it's like when he came into the room, the air went out.

After he thanks the skinny guy, he gazes out at the crowd. His hair is shaved on the sides and longer on top, so when he tilts his head, a strand falls across his face. He smiles as he says good evening, revealing adorable dimples on his cheeks. Seriously? Like he needs another hot factor. His velvety voice makes my heartbeat kick up a notch, and my mouth goes dry. *Hell and damn.*

Music explodes, and everyone is into it immediately. Samuel doesn't play an instrument. Instead, he holds the microphone as if he's making love to it while he belts out lyrics I don't recognize in his raspy and addictive voice. Goose bumps break out on my skin, and I barely notice I'm inching closer to the stage. It's almost as if I'm in a trance. I'll berate myself later for my lack of control, but right now, I can't stop staring at him.

I'm in the thick of the crowd when my gaze collides with Samuel's electric blue eyes. He doesn't break the connection, but seems to sing only for me. I'm immediately ensnared by his intense stare. When he sends a wink in my direction, I feel like my heart is going to explode. What the hell? Since when am I susceptible to hot men in leather? I've always gone for the preppy boys.

My irritation snaps me out of whatever hypnotic spell Samuel put on me. Turning, I head back to the bar, elbowing whoever is in my way. Peter is talking to one of my classmates, but his attention quickly diverts to me. Shit, so much for avoiding him.

"More tequila?" he asks.

I don't want to get hammered, so I open my mouth to say *no* when my phone vibrates in my purse. Quickly, I fish the device out. It's a text from my grandmother.

"Is there something wrong?" Peter asks.

"It's my grandma. Apparently, Elliot has run away and she's freaking out."

"I'm sure he's fine."

"Yeah, but I should go home and look for him." I glance back at the crowd, searching for Kenya.

"What? Are you serious?" Peter sounds disappointed, his

eyebrows furrowing to match.

Too bad.

I find Kenya all the way to the front of the stage, ogling the sexy singer without shame. A spike of jealousy surges out of nowhere, making me see red, which is crazy. Why would I be jealous? The Howlers lead singer is nothing to me. The tequila is definitely creating havoc in my brain.

To be safe, I text Kenya. Slipping away without a goodbye is the smartest course of action. I doubt she'll let me go without a fight otherwise. It'll take a while for her to notice my text, and a sliver of guilt pinches my heart. She was super excited about tonight—way more than I was. I can be a sucky friend sometimes.

When I step outside the bar, I pause to take in a deep breath of night air. I still haven't gotten used to the clean and fresh smell of the forest that surrounds Crimson Hollow or the fact that thousands of stars can be seen in the midnight-blue sky.

The street is quiet, a far cry from the busy and loud music venue. Without the cacophony, it's easier to think straight. The tequila gave me a nice buzz, but as much as I'd like to blame alcohol, my insta-lust reaction to Samuel Wolfe can't be explained by drunkenness. Not that it matters. He's a notorious manwhore—at least that's what Kenya tells me—and I have no intention of becoming another notch on his belt.

I veer toward the main square, hoping to find an available taxi there. Crimson Hollow is too small for Uber. I knew I shouldn't have caved and let Kenya drive tonight.

Not a minute later, I hear hurried footsteps behind me. Looking over my shoulder, I grimace when I discover it's Peter coming after me. "What are you doing here? I thought you wanted to stay."

"Nah, I just came out tonight because it was your birthday. I'll give you a ride home."

Exactly what I don't want.

"Pete, are you sure? How many shots of tequila have you had?"

"Just two and lots of water as well. Don't worry. I'm good, Red." He taps my shoulder before lacing his arm with mine. "Come on, my truck is parked just around the corner."

I bite my lower lip. There's no way I can refuse Peter's offering without offending him. During the drive, he wants to chat about the store and some of the ideas he has to bring more customers in. I appreciate his dedication to his father's business, but I'm not in the mood to talk shop. So I turn on the radio until I find an upbeat song I can sing along to.

Grandma's house is out in the boonies. It's a chalet in the woods accessible only through a dirt road, and a fifteen-minute drive away from town. When I moved in, I begged her to consider relocating to the city and closer to the hospital, but Grandma is a stubborn lady. It took me a long time to get used to the isolation. In the first few weeks, I would jump at any sound coming from the forest surrounding the property. Now, I'm completely used to it. Kenya finds the forest creepy, but the peace and quiet have grown on me.

All the lights in the house are still on, which means our stupid dog hasn't turned up yet. It's past one in the morning. When I find that rascal, I'm giving him a tongue lashing. As crazy as it sounds, I'm sure the dog can understand every word I say.

"Thanks for the ride," I say, my hand already on the door handle.

Peter grabs my forearm before I can open the passenger side door. "Wait. I got you a birthday present." He bends across the gap between our seats to reach the glove compartment. I tense at the proximity.

"Here," he says. "I hope you like it."

A big lump gets stuck in my throat when I recognize the label on the small box Peter hands me. It's from an expensive jewelry store in town.

Peter, what have you done?

"You didn't have to get me anything," I say.

A wistful glint shines in Peter's eyes, and it's obvious he's gathering the courage to say something I don't want to hear. Quickly, I open the box, revealing a necklace with a beautiful heart-shaped pendant inside. The stone is dark red.

"Before you say anything, that's a crystal, not a ruby. But one day I'll get you a real precious stone."

Ah, hell. Peter's voice is shaky. I can't look into his eyes, so I keep staring at the necklace as if it will somehow give me a clue about how to let him down gently without breaking his heart.

"Thank you. It's a beautiful gift," I finally manage to say.

Inching closer, he touches my face with the back of his hand. I freeze, clutching the box tighter in my hands. He's going to try to kiss me. Crap, I need to go now. I pride myself for being courageous most of the time, but when it comes to hurting someone I care about, I'm a total chicken.

"Red, I've been meaning to ask you something for a while now."

"Pete, I-I have to go. Thanks for the gift." I'm out of the car faster than a speeding bullet. "I'll see you next week."

I run to the house without a glance back until the front door is open. Only then do I turn around and wave at Peter. I can't see his face, but I can imagine the look of disappointment in his expression.

"Amelia, is that you, hon?" Grandma asks from her bedroom.

Every time I come home, she asks the same question. I don't know who she expects to come through the door. A burglar wouldn't make the same noises I do.

"Yes, Grandma. Did Elliot come home yet?"

She walks into the living room, still wearing her day clothes. I frown, the irritation aimed at our stupid dog renewing. She should be sleeping by now.

"No. I suspect he caught the scent of a bitch in heat. He's probably still busy." She chuckles.

"Great. Well, I'd better end his party. It's late, and you need to go to bed."

"How was the birthday celebration?" She stares at Peter's box. "Is that a gift?"

I hand it to her. "Yes, from Peter."

Her eyes widen a fraction. When she opens the box, she whistles in appreciation. "Somebody has a crush."

"Yeah, it seems so." I let out a loud exhale. "But I don't like him that way. What should I do, Grandma?"

She returns the box, but now her eyebrows are furrowed and her mouth is pinched. "You need to tell him the truth."

I'm not surprised by her reply. One of the first lessons she ever taught me was that honesty is one of the greatest virtues in the world.

"I was afraid you were going to say that." Moving to the console table by the front door, I set the box there. I can't keep this gift.

"It's better than stringing the poor guy along, isn't it?" She arches an eyebrow, making my guilt double.

"I'm not stringing him along," I say, my voice getting a little harder as I go on defense mode. "I never gave him any indication I was interested."

With a shake of her white head, she says, "It doesn't matter. An infatuated heart sees what it wants."

My shoulders sag. I have to come clean to Peter eventually, but I can't worry about that now. I have a horny dog to find.

"Let me go look for Elliot. I'm tired, and I want to go to sleep."

I take off my high-heeled pumps, then replace them with sensible boots. Just as I'm about to head out with a flashlight in hand, a howl echoes.

Apprehension freezes me where I stand. "Crap. Was that a wolf?"

Grandma peers over my shoulder as her gaze goes out of focus. "Maybe. You'd better take the shotgun just in case."

Grumbling, I grab the weapon from its mount on the wall. It belonged to Grandpa. When he was alive, he taught me how to shoot. But it was only when I moved to Crimson Hollow that I finally understood his love for hunting. I took the sport of shooting as a distraction from being homesick, and I've already won several competitions. Grandma says I'm a natural. It's the only reason I'm not afraid to venture into the woods to search for Elliot while there's a wolf nearby.

With Grandpa's gun in hand, I'm the predator.

I search the perimeter near the house before I go deeper into the woods. Despite the summer night, a chill penetrates my light jacket. *That bitch better be worth it, Elliot.*

The foliage becomes denser the farther away I get from the house. Even with the full moon above, barely any silvery light streams through. It's only when I come near a creek that the trees turn scarcer, negating the need of a flashlight to illuminate the way. After I shut it off, I wait a few seconds for my eyes to adjust to the gloom.

"Elliot," I call out in a half-whisper, but all I hear is dead silence.

I continue searching until the sound of a twig snapping to my left makes my heart jump into my throat. A small furry animal skitters by. "Fucking squirrels."

I turn on my heel, then freeze mid-step. Only a yard away from me, there's a wolf partially hidden by shrubs and shadows. I swallow hard as my body's immediate reaction is to panic. But I quickly take control of my emotions like Grandpa taught me.

The wolf's low growl tells me it wants to make a meal out of me. *Not tonight, buddy.*

Slowly, I bring the muzzle of the shotgun up and take aim. The wolf moves forward, his growling much louder now. Despite the confidence in my shooting skills, I can't help the spike of adrenaline that shoots up my veins. It's the thrill of the hunt. My finger twitches against the trigger, ready, but I don't want to kill the animal. When the creature takes another step forward and howls, I move the aim slightly to its left and press the trigger. But instead of a loud bang, there's only the pitiful sound of a low click.

"Ah, hell," I say right before the wolf pounces.

CHAPTER 2
TRISTAN

The sound of my labored breathing rings in my ears as my fists crash against the punching bag. The gym is silent and empty, just the way I like it. I have lost track of time, but the soreness in my muscles and the sheen of sweat covering my skin tells me I've been here a while. I could go on for hours without stopping. Pain is something I learned to ignore at an early age, a necessary skill for an alpha's son.

The last thing I want is to think about the pack's hierarchy or the shit storm that will come when my father dies. I have more pressing problems occupying my mind. The company's biggest construction project has been on halt since that witch of a mayor decided she doesn't like our kind anymore. For two weeks now, my guys have been waiting for the signal to start working on Wolfe Corp's newest development. I don't want to lose them, so I've been paying the guys a salary for sitting on their asses. On top of that, all the house units have been sold. If the company doesn't deliver the final product by the deadline, we'll have to pay a huge fine. We're bleeding money.

I hit the punching bag harder. The relationship between the pack and Mayor Montgomery has always been difficult, but things changed for the worse after Dad went to a meeting with the woman a month ago. He never said what was discussed, but he must have pissed her off royally because now she's exacting her revenge on the company.

Wolfe Corp employs most of the pack. If it folds, our members will be in dire financial situations. I can't allow that to happen. Not everyone in Crimson Hollow is aware they live side by side with supernatural creatures. To keep the secret from spreading, the supernatural community runs their own businesses and employs their own kind. It's a solution that has worked since the town was founded centuries ago, but now the mayor seems keen on fucking it up.

I pull my arm back, then swing a punch so powerful it breaks the punching bag's chain, sending it flying across the room. The door to the gym opens, and Lyria stops under the frame. She eyes the punching bag on the floor before turning her gaze to me.

"What did that bag do to you?"

Not waiting for my answer, she waltzes in wearing skin-tight workout clothes that leave nothing to the imagination. I can't help how my body reacts to her. She's one of the most beautiful females in the pack and a beta, which makes her an ideal match. Even so, I've kept Lyria at arm's length despite her attempts to seduce me.

Giving her my back, I walk to the corner and grab a towel from my duffel on the floor. "The chain must have been loose."

"Yes, made loose by the way you were hitting the bag." Lyria stops behind me, touching my arm with the tips of her fingers. "You know, Tristan. There are other ways to relieve stress."

Knowing it's a mistake, I turn to face her. There's barely any space between our bodies, and the mating scent Lyria radiates is beginning to make my head swim. My will can only go so far before the animal instinct takes over. She watches me with a knowing glance, lips curling into a victorious smirk. I can't blame her; I'm on the verge of giving in. Fuck my reservations. My dick is already standing at attention. It has been weeks since I slept with someone. And by that, I mean a regular woman, not a member of the pack. In my position, I can't afford casual relationships with any female wolf.

Grabbing Lyria by the hips, I pull her closer. "What do you suggest, Beta?"

A glint of pride shines in the brunette's eyes. If she were a cat, she would have purred. "Come back to my place and I'll show you."

She brushes her hand against my crotch before squeezing my erection, making me growl. I narrow my eyes and lean in, ready to seal my fate and fuck Lyria right here on this gym floor.

"There you are. I've been looking all over you," Billy, the pack's omega, says from the door.

I let go of Lyria. When I step back, the distance sobers me up. *Shit. That was close.*

"What the hell are you doing here, Billy?" Lyria glares at the kid.

"Dr. Mervina wants to speak to Tristan." He shrugs. "She says it's urgent."

My mood changes instantly, the sense of urgency overriding the lust that clouded my judgment only a few moments ago. I head out of the room without a backward glance at Lyria, Billy following close behind. As the omega, he's the weakest wolf in the pack. There's no doubt Lyria will take her frustration out on him whenever the chance arrives. Probably sooner rather than later. Even knowing Billy is following orders, I can't and won't interfere. Every wolf in the pack has a role, and the omega's is to serve as a scapegoat for the rest of us. Wolves are aggressive by nature, and that anger must go somewhere. Otherwise, chaos ensues.

"Did my mother say what this is about?" I ask to distract him, knowing my mom, the female alpha, hadn't told Billy anything.

"Nope. Only that it was urgent."

After leaving the second largest building in the compound,

I cross the small square toward the main house where my parents live. My brothers and I still have rooms there, but we have our own places elsewhere. My apartment is in the city, above Wolfe Corp's office.

Bypassing the main double doors, I veer toward the side of the house where the entrance to my mother's clinic is. A veterinarian before she became a wolf, her profession came in handy when she married into the pack. She still has her practice in town.

As I predicted, I find Mom in her office. She's usually a calm person, but she's pacing back and forth in front of her desk with her eyebrows furrowed. She pauses when she sees me standing by the door. Her gaze shifts to Billy, who is still behind me.

"Thanks, Billy. You can leave now. Tristan, close the door, please." She moves behind her desk, but doesn't take a seat. Instead, she grabs the back of the chair and lowers her gaze.

I do as she asks, catching a glint of disappointment in Billy's eyes. Omega or not, the kid loves to be in the know. He's the biggest gossiper in the pack.

"What's wrong?" I ask after I hear Billy retreat.

She raises her gaze to mine. "There's a blood moon tonight. You need to patrol the Irving Forest area."

"A blood moon?" I clench my jaw hard, trying not to scoff at her statement. Mom has the sight just like my brother Dante does, and their sixth sense has helped the pack many times in the past. However, one thing I don't believe in is anything that has to do with hocus pocus BS like the blood moon myth. It's the sort of gibberish that only the witches in town take seriously.

Irritated, I continue, "Is that truly your emergency, or did you just call me in here because you saw what Lyria was up to?"

Mom narrows her eyes. Despite being a foot taller and stronger than her, I take a step back. I should know better than to cross Mervina Wolfe.

"I'm going to pretend you didn't say that. However, my intervention came in good time. You reek of her disgusting scent."

Crossing my arms, I grind my teeth. Mom has never liked Lyria, nor made any attempt to hide her feelings. I've always wondered if her animosity stemmed from the same source as my hesitancy did. Nevertheless, I'm a fucking adult. I don't need my mother meddling in my affairs.

"Why the Irving Forest? What's going on there?" I change the subject before I say something I'll regret.

Mom's angry expression morphs back into one of worry. She shakes her head, staring at a spot over my shoulder. "I don't know what's wrong exactly. All I know is that you have to get there quickly."

"Okay, I'll get Seth and a couple of enforcers."

"No!" Mom raises her arm, her eyes as round as saucers. "You must go alone. Your brothers will meet you there."

"I haven't seen Dante in days, and Samuel has a gig tonight."

Mom's stoic expression doesn't waver. It's like she hasn't heard a word I said. "They will be there. Now go!"

Dismissed, I leave her office. Billy sits on one of the benches in the hallway. The kid springs to his feet when he sees me.

"Do you need me to go fetch Seth?"

Shit. I doubt he overheard my conversation with Mom, but he must have read that something serious is going on from my expression. But I can't have him spreading rumors, so I stop in front of the omega and stare hard.

"You won't say a word about my mother summoning me. Is that clear?"

Billy blanches and nods. As the pack's beta, my command is to be followed in the alpha's absence or there will be hell to pay. The kid isn't stupid.

I continue down the hall, then exit the building through the back door. It leads to the forest surrounding the compound. I strip off my clothes, folding them neatly and placing them on a lonely metal chair by the door before summoning the primordial powers that course through my veins. My skin tingles, something that always happens before the shift. I feel my joints crack, then my muscles contract and expand. Closing my eyes, I take a deep breath. The change isn't as painful as it sounds, or maybe I'm used to it. Being a shifter is all I have ever known, unlike my mother who was turned into one by my father, the pack's alpha.

When I open my eyes again, I'm in wolf form. My senses are sharper, my emotions amplified. Everything is more when I surrender control to the beast.

Raising my snout to the moon, I howl, then take off in the direction of Irving Forest. By car, it would take ten minutes to get there, but cutting through the woods on the speed of four powerful legs, I can probably make it in five.

Halfway there, I catch the scent of another shifter. My wolf bristles while the man inside curses. It isn't one of us, but a wolf from the Shadow Creek pack. What the hell is one of those mutts doing there?

I barely finish the thought before I smell fresh blood followed by a woman's scream.

CHAPTER 3
RED

My instinct is to dodge out of the way, but I force myself to remain steady and use the shotgun as a bat. I almost don't have time to pull my arm far enough back to swing before the wolf is on me. A loud smack, the sound of metal slamming onto bone, then the animal lets out a whimper as it falls on its side.

Now I run.

Adrenaline boosts me forward, but I have no hopes of making it back home before the wolf catches up with me. I need to climb a tree, but I'm in the densest part of the forest. The trees are ancient, too tall for me to reach their lowest branches. It's almost impossible to see anything in front of me as well.

I'm so fucked.

I sense the wolf right behind me. As crazy as it sounds, I can almost hear its paws hitting the ground, getting closer and closer. *Think, Red, think.* Spotting a dark shape straight ahead, I veer for it. It's a large boulder. It's not as good as a tree, but I climb it just the same, slipping once on the mossy surface. I'm not safe by any stretch of the imagination, but at least now I have the higher ground.

I don't have time to catch my breath before the animal reaches me, stopping by the foot of the rock. Instead of trying to climb, the wolf begins to circle my useless island, snarling as it goes. I clutch the shotgun tighter, my muscles tense and ready.

"So you've learned your lesson, huh, buddy? How is the side of your head?" I ask, if only to keep the panic at bay.

The wolf's snarls sound angrier, as if the beast understands I'm taunting him. And yet, I can't stop doing it.

It's official. I've gone insane.

"Why don't you put your tail between your legs, so we can call it a night? I won't tell your friends."

The wolf decides it has had enough, and it jumps to my right. I move out of the way, only to realize the wolf is smarter than I thought. It changes course faster than I can blink, coming at me from the left. To avoid getting my leg stuck between the wolf's sharp teeth, I leap out of the way, but I overcompensate and lose my footing on the slippery rock. It's like everything happens in slow motion. I use the gun to keep my balance, leaving my back exposed. The wolf pounces on me before I can get out of the way. I let out a scream as I fall—for all the good that does. It's the middle of the night, and no one can hear me this far out in the woods. Before I hit the ground, the wolf bites my shoulder. It's like I've been punctured by a blazing rod.

Motherfucker.

The white-hot pain is sharp; it robs me of breath. It burns, almost blinding me. It gets worse as the wolf's teeth sink farther into my flesh, tearing my muscles. I have to get the animal off me or I'm dead meat. But as hard as I thrash, I can't dislodge the beast. A metallic smell reaches my nose. It's blood—my blood.

Impossible, a person cannot smell blood like that.

Sticky wetness drenches my clothes, and I feel the strength draining from me.

No! My name might be Red, but I'm not going to be eaten by the Big Bad Wolf.

Stretching my arm, I try to grasp the gun that fell not too far from me. I grunt as the wolf bites me again. Weirdly enough, the pain isn't as acute. Maybe I'm in shock. My fingers barely brush the end of the shotgun when another snarl joins the fray. In the next second, the wolf on my back is gone.

It takes me a couple of breaths to understand what's happening. There are two wolves now, fighting in a battle to the death. Inching forward, I pull the gun toward me and prepare to stand, but my eyes remain glued to the savage dance in front of me—or more precisely, on the new wolf. Even in the gloom, his white fur is a stark contrast to his surroundings. He's bigger than the darker wolf that attacked me, but the size difference doesn't stop his opponent. In fact, that son of a bitch seems to be winning the fight.

I'm snapped out of my stupor at the howling of another wolf in the distance. Shit, if I don't move, I'll become wolf chow for sure. But even faced with imminent danger, my body doesn't cooperate. My first attempt to rise is an utter fail. I crawl in the boulder's direction, the progress too slow for my liking. I need to get the hell out of here. My vision is getting worse by the second, and I'm also lightheaded. I'm going to pass out soon, and I can't allow that to happen.

Leaning against the rock, I slowly unfurl from the ground. The sound of wolves fighting continues behind me, but I'm afraid to look in their direction. Somehow, it'll signal that their prey—me—is escaping. Focusing on putting one foot in front of the other, I use the gun as a crutch. Of all the days for my beloved heirloom to fail, it had to be the one time I needed it to save my life. Isn't that ironic?

The dark forest looks the same in all directions, and I don't know which way Grandma's house is anymore. I begin to move at a snail's pace in the direction I think the stream is. It leads to Mr. Anderson's apple orchard. Maybe if I get wet, it will help disguise my scent so the wolves can't follow me. *Yeah, wishful thinking, Red.*

I'm grasping at straws, but it's the best solution I've got. It turns out I'm not too far from it. Without thinking, I stumble straight in the shallow, cold water. The problem is that I forgot how fucking slippery the moss-covered rocks are. It only takes me two steps before I lose my balance and fall on my ass.

A desperate sob bubbles up my throat, and tears prickle my eyes. I'm never getting out of this mess. I'm either going to bleed to death or be eaten alive by whichever wolf wins the fight.

No, Amelia. Don't you dare give up now.

The voice of encouragement in my head doesn't belong to me. It's similar to those other strange thoughts that have plagued my mind since I moved to Crimson Hollow. Weird or not, it works to snap me out of my panic. My shoulder burns when I try to get up again, but my legs won't hold my weight.

"God*damn* it," I say, immediately regretting my loud outburst.

I'm running out of fuel, so I decide to drag myself out of the water. If I'm seconds away from passing out, I most definitely don't want to drown.

Feeling extremely tired now, I rest my cheek against the muddy stream bank as my eyelids become unbearably heavy. This is it. I have nothing left in me. My eyes are almost completely shut when I see the shape of a white wolf materialize not too far from me. Instinctively, I know it's not the same wolf that was fighting in the forest. Either I have accepted my fate or the blood loss has affected my ability to feel anything because when the wolf approaches, there's not an ounce of fear in my body.

"I hope I'm tasty," I mumble.

The wolf stops just a few steps from me. It starts to vibrate, then shimmer, before it changes into a man. But not just any man.

Samuel Wolfe.

CHAPTER 4
TRISTAN

For fuck's sake, I can't believe I'm losing to a Shadow Creek mutt. I don't recognize his scent, but he's way too young and small to be an alpha. Where is all his power coming from? He doesn't have enough body mass to justify it.

Knowing the whys won't help me. I need to find an opening to end this quickly. But every time I believe I have the upper hand, the smaller wolf manages to break free to attack me. When he body slams against my side, I have to use all the muscle strength in my hind legs to keep from folding. If this crazed wolf gets on top of me, it's game over.

Something unnatural is definitely going on, but I don't have the luxury to dwell on it. Pissed off that this fight is taking longer than I anticipated, I snap my jaw when the other wolf glances away for a split second, managing to get some flesh. Blood fills my mouth, but it tastes wrong. Foul. It makes me slightly dizzy for a moment, enough to give the motherfucker an opening. Turning, he locks his jaw around my throat. He would have slashed it open if Dante hadn't appeared in the last second to save the night.

About fucking time.

My brother Dante was born two minutes after me. He's slender but much faster. He can even outrun our father. He's also much more vicious, a total contradiction to his nature in human form. With a strength only those destined to become alphas possess, he tosses the mutt against the boulder nearby. I hear a crack followed by a whine, and then everything goes eerily quiet.

I drop my mental shield, opening the telepathic link with my brother. Thanks to mainstream media and movies, there's a false notion that all wolves within a pack are automatically linked mind to mind. Complete bullshit. We aren't all reading each other's minds while in wolf form. If that were to happen, chaos would ensue. Wolves, as a rule, are short-tempered.

"Are you okay?" Dante's voice echoes in my mind.

"I've been better."

"You were losing pretty badly and to a Shadow Creek mutt to boot." He moves closer to the fallen wolf, and I decide to ignore my brother's taunt. Yes, Dante is nicer as a human.

"He wasn't a regular wolf. He was stronger than our father. Something was done to him."

"I noticed that, too. And his blood didn't taste right."

Now next to Dante, I catch something odd protruding from the dead wolf's head. *"What's that?"*

A second later, Dante shifts back to human and crouches in front of the carcass. Opposable thumbs are handy to inspect shit, but I don't dare change back yet. There might be other enemies nearby, which reminds me—the woman. She was bitten; I'm certain of it.

"Sam went after her," Dante says.

Fuck. I forgot Dante could keep the telepathic link up even in human form.

"Stop reading my mind when you are in your two-legged version."

"Quit bitching and check this out." Dante pulls a small metallic box from the dead wolf's head.

"What do you think that is?" I lean closer to smell the small object, getting nothing out of the ordinary besides the stench of death.

Dante rolls the box between his fingers before answering.

"I don't have a clue. We'd better show this to Dad when he returns."

"Let's find Sam, then get out of here."

Nodding, Dante unfurls from his crouch and looks over his shoulder. Following the movement, I sniff the air. Sam isn't too far, and he found the woman. She's marked, which means we now have a potential Shadow Creek wolf on our hands. Potential being the imperative word—only a small percentage of humans survive the transformation.

I follow Dante to the nearby creek where Sam is. He's cradling a blonde woman in his arms as if she were his lover or something. Ah, fuck. Maybe she is. I can't keep track of how many regular women my brother has screwed. If wolves weren't immune to human diseases, Sam's dick would have fallen off by now.

Since Sam has shifted back into human already and I can't scold him telepathically, I decide to shift back as well. I didn't pick up the scent of another wolf nearby, so most likely the fallen wolf was a rogue.

Once back on two legs, I glare at Sam. "What the hell are you doing?"

He frowns, pinching his lips. "I know her."

"Oh, great. She's one of your groupies." I throw my hands up in the air.

"Fuck off, Tristan. I haven't slept with her. She was at my show tonight celebrating her twenty-first birthday."

Knowing Sam didn't sleep with the woman makes me feel better. Less complications. I take a step closer to look at her. Strings of blonde hair frame her ashen face, but it doesn't hide the fact she's attractive. Too attractive, actually. My gut clenches painfully, and I don't know why.

Forcing my eyes away from her face, I notice the big gash on her shoulder where the rogue wolf almost mauled her to death. Well, death is still a probable outcome, and the idea makes me unbearably sad. Shit, what the hell is going on with me? I don't want an innocent person to die like that, but the sharp pain in my chest feels more like I'm losing someone I care deeply for. Nonsense.

"Let's get moving. She needs immediate medical attention. My truck is parked not far from here," Dante says.

Frowning, I turn to my brother. "Wait? You want to bring her into the compound? Have you lost your mind?"

"What do you suggest? Leaving her here to die?"

"Of course not. But if she survives the shift, she'll belong to those assholes up north."

No one speaks for several beats. If a human is attacked by a wolf, it's that pack's responsibility to handle the situation as they best see fit. Some ruthless alphas choose to just end the human's life without giving them the chance to shift. It doesn't matter, though. If we take the woman into our compound and help her through the transformation process, it would be considered a terrible slight. Our relationship with the Shadow Creek pack is already precarious as it is.

"I don't care about them. Their wolf breached our territory and attacked a human. He would have killed her if we hadn't intervened." Sam stands with the woman in his arms. "They don't deserve our consideration. Fuck the protocols. We're taking Red to the compound."

"*Red?*" Dante raises an eyebrow.

"That's what her friends call her. Her name is Amelia Redford. She goes to the community college, and works part-time at the hardware store."

Crossing my arms, I watch Sam through slitted eyes. "How do you know so much about this chick?"

Despite the grim situation, a grin unfurls on his lips. "I did my homework."

"You wanted to fuck her."

"Well…" He sucks his lips in, looking guilty as hell.

"Sam, I swear to God…" I ball my hands into fists with half a mind to take the woman from his arms.

"Jesus, will you relax? I'm not going to try anything. Unless she wants to."

RED'S ALPHAS

"He won't touch the girl," Dante chimes in. "Mom will rip his nut sack off if he tries."

I follow my brothers, muttering curses under my breath. Taking care of a gorgeous, newly made Shadow Creek wolf is exactly what we *don't* need.

Dante's truck is parked at the beginning of the trail that led to the spot of the attack. It will be another five minutes before we get back to the compound, and I honestly don't know if Red will make it. She's no longer bleeding, but loss of blood is not what kills humans attacked by shifters. It's the virus responsible for the mutation that the majority can't handle.

Once his truck comes into view, Dante sprints toward it. He grabs a pair of jeans from the backseat, then pulls them on fast.

"I have a couple of spare sweatpants in the trunk," he tells us.

"I'm good." Sam gets into the backseat with the woman without a glance in our direction.

Red. What a stupid nickname.

I have no issues with my nakedness. We have to undress before we shift or risk getting our clothes ruined. But out in the human world, I prefer not to be caught butt naked, so I take Dante up on his offer.

"How is Red?" Dante asks as soon as we begin to move, peering at the backseat through the rearview mirror.

"Her breathing is shallow, and she feels warm." His reply is laced with worry.

I turn on my seat in time to catch Sam brush a loose strand of hair off her face. Seeing my younger brother treat a mere stranger as if she were his beloved girlfriend doesn't sit well with me. I don't know why I'm getting this crazy feeling of foreboding. Maybe because if she survives, she'll still be the enemy. I've never heard of a match between wolves from different packs that didn't end in bloodshed or worse, isolation.

Shaking my head, I force myself to gaze at the road ahead.

I'm worrying over nothing. No way Sam feels anything more for this woman than lust. He's a notorious manwhore; there's no chance in hell he would imprint on her.

When Dante parks in front of the clinic's entrance, I'm not surprised to see Mom already waiting at the door.

Did she see the woman in a vision?

"Quickly now, I have the examination room ready for her." Mom turns on her heels, striding down the hallway with purpose. Her deep mahogany hair is pulled into a tight bun at the base of her neck, and she's wearing scrubs. She must have known what we would find in Irving Forest.

Sam puts Red on the bed while Mom sterilizes her hands. A metal tray with medical instruments is ready on the nightstand.

"What can we do?" Dante asks, hovering too close to her.

"Stay out of my way." Mom twists her nose. "What's that God-awful smell?"

"The other wolf's blood," we all answer at the same time.

"A rogue?" She arches both eyebrows.

"Maybe. We found this attached to the back of his head." Dante shows her the small square box.

"It looks like a tracking device of some sort." She narrows her eyes, studying it, but doesn't touch it.

"I know someone who might be able to tell us what this is," I say.

"Who?" Sam looks at me.

"A kid who works at the hardware store. He helped me before when I had computer issues in the office."

"Can he be trusted with this?" Dante asks.

"He doesn't have ties with the supe community. I believe he's safe."

Mom nods in agreement, then immediately returns her attention to the woman, who's lying so still it's like she's already gone. Her flawless skin is white as snow, but her plumps lips still hold their ruby color. It's not makeup. Maybe that's why her friends call her Red, because of her cherry-colored lips. She's indeed the most beautiful creature I've ever seen. With a groan, I look away. There's nothing for me to do here; I should leave.

"What are you doing, Mom?" Sam asks, and I glance at the bed again. She has a pair of scissors in her hand.

She doesn't answer my brother, but proceeds to cut open what's left of Red's top, revealing a sexy, black lacy bra. I suck in a breath while my blood begins to pump faster in my veins. I should be noticing the gore on her shoulder, not the swell of her breasts. Maybe I'm as bad as Sam.

Under the bright lights in the room, the gash looks much worse. Red was bitten in two spots on her shoulder. The second bite is much too close to her aortic artery. Another inch and she would have bled to death. Dirt is mixed with the torn muscle and blood, so Mom focuses on cleaning the wounds first. She dabs the area with a reddish liquid, making Red hiss and arch her back.

I trade a worried glance with Dante while Sam says, "I thought she was out cold. How can she feel anything?"

"I don't know," Mom answers.

As soon as she finishes cleaning the wounds, the torn skin begins to heal, as if it's knitting itself back together. Shifters have accelerated healing, but I've never seen anything like that and Red is not even a wolf yet. Mutation usually takes a month, and it's a messy and painful process.

"What the fuck?" Sam moves closer, eyes wide.

When Red starts to convulse, Mom orders us to hold her still. I grab Red's ankles while Sam and Dante each hold one of her arms. Her eyes fly open, revealing ember-colored wolf irises.

"She's shifting already? How is that possible?" I ask.

Mom doesn't answer. Instead, she holds a syringe in her hand, her eyebrows scrunched in concentration.

"What's that?" Dante asks.

"Painkillers."

Red screams at the top of her lungs when her muscles begin to spasm. I can feel the trembling under my palms. The wound on her shoulder has healed completely already, leaving behind only a light pink scar.

The petite woman flings her right arm with extreme force, managing to free herself from Sam's hold. Then she scratches Dante's hand with her claw. Holy shit. She partially shifted.

Knowing we can't stop what's happening to her, I let go of her legs and pull Dante out of her range. Restraining Red while she shifts will only make things worse. Mom steps back, and Sam gets in front of her. She can hold her own, but instinct tells us to protect any female in our family, even if she's stronger than we are.

Red rolls over and falls to the floor, curling into a tight ball. Her screams turn into whimpers. Her body is deformed, caught in mid-transformation, but her face remains human. It's scrunched in pain.

"We have to do something," Sam says, anguish lacing his words.

"It's too late now. She has to finish the process without sedation," Mom replies, and Dante shoots her a pinched look. Fuck. Why does he have such despair in his eyes?

It's the first time I've seen an infected human shift into a wolf for the first time. I knew the process was extremely gruesome, but I had no idea it was this bad. Mom went through it so she could be with our father, but she never talked about the experience with us. I have to wonder if Dad watched. And if he had, how was it possible he hadn't lost his mind? I don't think I have the same sorrowful glint in my eyes as Dante and Sam do, but I'm having a hard time watching a stranger go through the process.

Red's body begins to shimmer. Finally, she changes. The crying and whimpering ceases. The sudden silence is so thick it's almost unbearable. A small grey and white wolf lies all curled up on the floor. Her muzzle is hidden under her paws. For a minute, no one speaks. When the newly transformed wolf raises her head, the air is sucked out of my lungs. It feels like my entire world has tilted off its axis. Everything besides

the female wolf in front of me goes out of focus.
    Then, she attacks me.

CHAPTER 5

RED

I blink my eyes open, not understanding what's going on. For starters, there's something terribly wrong with my vision. The colors around me are muted, faded. I also don't recognize the place I'm in. The last thing I remember was being attacked by a wolf.

I try to lift my arm to touch my shoulder, but catch a glimpse of a furry paw. The scream I release sounds like an animal whine, and I jump back.

What the hell is going on?

It feels like I'm stuck in someone else's—something else's—head. My heartbeat increases as panic sets in. *Keep calm, Red. Just take a deep breath and think.* I was in a forest before, and now I'm in a room of sorts. Maybe someone heard my scream and saved me from the wolf, but now I'm alone. I can see a bed and a nightstand, but from my point of view, it seems impossibly high. Why am I on the floor? I try to call out to whoever rescued me, but I can't form words. Again, I hear the animal whine instead. Is it coming from me?

Freaking out now, I backpedal, bumping into something. A lamp falls to my right, shattering completely. A few shards land on top of my—*what the fuck*—paws? And is that the tip of a white tail? I must be hallucinating; it's the only explanation.

The door bursts open, and three very large men come into

the room, filling the small space. I immediately recognize Samuel Wolfe, the lead singer of The Howlers, but I have no clue who the other two are.

My heart thunders inside of my chest, and there's a rushing in my ears. I step back until I hit the corner of the room. Why am I so terrified? Nothing is making any sense. Without meaning to, I snarl. It's like there's a different will inside my head besides my own. A foreign presence that's savage and wild.

Samuel takes a step forward with an outstretched hand, but I snap at him in warning. No, not me—the beast occupying my head.

"I'm not going to hurt you," he says, but the wild presence refuses to believe him.

Looking beyond him, I notice they left the door wide open. I can make a run for it, which is what the beast wants. But if I do, I'll never find out what's going on. Slowly, my reasoning begins to crumble under the wild influence. My body tenses as it prepares to bolt. It's like it has a will of its own.

Then, I'm assaulted by flashes of another place, scenes that don't make any sense. I'm in a lab, and there are several men wearing white doctor coats. Their faces are covered by masks as they stare down at me. Fear and rage are all there is, and then unmeasurable pain.

I drop to the floor and howl while my body feels like it's splitting in two. My skin burns as if it were doused with acid, and liquid fire courses through my veins. If I still had my voice, I would be begging for death.

Strong arms hold me, and then a soothing voice tells me everything will be okay. The beast rebels, but there's no strength left in my body, or the beast's body. I can't tell which is which anymore.

"Don't fight the wolf, Red. Become one with the wolf," the voice says.

I have no desire to become one with anything, but the voice is so compelling, so peaceful, that I find it hard to

M. H. SOARS & MICHELLE HERCULES

resist. Slowly, my heartbeat slows until I can no longer feel it jamming like mad inside the confines of my chest.

"I want you to take deep breaths and focus. Feel the wolf's power in you."

Feel the wolf's power? What is he saying? Am I a wolf? That's insane. A hazy memory comes to the forefront of my mind. A wolf in the woods turning into Samuel Wolfe. Did that really happen? Maybe there is no one holding me. Maybe the voice I'm hearing is the doctor's in the hospital where I'm a patient. I'm having some kind of psychotic reaction to my attack, and my mind can't cope. Yes. That's it. Knowing I'm not really a wolf and that I'm safe in a hospital room finally allows me to relax.

I focus on my breathing. When the voice tells me to see myself as human again, I follow along. I picture each individual part of my body, starting with my toes, then my feet, up my legs, and so on, until I actually feel whole again. When I open my eyes, the colors have returned to normal. I can see clearly now. The problem is that I'm not in a hospital room, and there isn't a doctor anywhere.

I'm still being held by someone, though. My body tenses when I feel the sleeve of his shirt brush against my nipples. I'm naked in front of three strange men. Why am I naked? My panic returns with a vengeance. I push the guy's arms away and roll off his lap, scooching backward until my back hits a wall. I bring my knees up and hug them, trying my best to cover myself.

"Who are you?" I demand more than ask. "Where are my clothes?"

"Relax. We're not going to hurt you," Samuel says.

"Relax, my ass." I glance around, searching. "Where are my damn clothes?"

"What do you remember from last night?" the taller and more muscular of the three guys asks.

I can see a resemblance between him and Samuel. They both have the same squared jaw and piercing, intense eyes.

But while Samuel has a friendly manner, this dude is watching me with suspicion, as if I committed a crime.

"A wolf attacked me," I finally say.

"What were you doing walking alone in the woods in the middle of the night? Were you looking for a hook-up?" he continues, making me see red.

"Fuck you. I don't owe you an explanation."

"Oh, she has spunk. I like her already." Samuel chuckles, but the smile vanishes from his face when I glare at him.

"Why am I here and not in a hospital? That wolf got me and—" I stop talking when I touch my shoulder, finding nothing but smooth skin.

What the fuck! That damned wolf bit me twice. I'm sure of it.

"What have you done to me?" My voice comes out shaky.

"I'd like to know the answer to that same question," someone says from behind the men.

They move to make room for the newcomer, and my jaw drops when I recognize Dr. Mervina Wolfe, Elliot's veterinarian. She moves with an imposing presence, and Mr. Asshole loses his arrogance in a heartbeat. I would have felt relief if the woman's presence here wasn't strange as hell.

"Dr. Mervina? What are you doing here?"

She glances at me briefly before turning to glare at the others. "Please don't tell me you were interrogating the poor girl while she's naked, afraid, and confused. Shame on all of you."

"We weren't, Mom," Samuel says.

Mom?

"I mean, Dante and I weren't. It was Tristan who started it."

Mr. Asshole turns to Samuel. "The sooner we get answers, the better."

"I agree. So why don't you start giving me some?" I snap.

Fear has ebbed way, making room for my anger to grow. I aim all my ire at him. Never mind that the man is attractive enough to melt my panties away in another lifetime. Thinking of which, I'm still naked.

As if reading my mind, he raises an arrogant eyebrow. "I thought you wanted your clothes first?"

I clench my jaw hard before answering. "Yes. I'm tired of you three stooges ogling my body."

Dr. Mervina takes off her light jacket, then drapes it over my shoulders. "There." She turns to her sons. "Now off with you. Ask one of the girls to fetch some clothes from the training center."

Mr. Asshole is the first to leave with stiff shoulders and heavy steps. The second man, the tall one who can only be Dante, looks at me in a peculiar manner before he follows his brother. Samuel stays behind.

"I'm sorry you got embroiled in our world, Red. But in time, you'll see that wolf life is not so bad."

And with those parting words, he leaves.

What does he mean by wolf life?

CHAPTER 6

RED

Dr. Mervina only opens the door a sliver when the knock comes, blocking the entrance with her body. I'm grateful for that since I'm not in the mood to meet anyone else while naked as a newborn baby. I had my fill with Samuel, Dante, and Mr. Asshole. Whoever brought me new clothes, though, doesn't come into the room.

I'm still trying to wrap my head around the fact I didn't know that Samuel Wolfe, the most notorious manwhore in town, has two impossibly good-looking brothers. I'm not new in Crimson Hollow—at least, I don't consider myself as a newcomer any longer after two years—and thought for sure Kenya would have mentioned them. My best friend has all the eye candy in town cataloged. Plus, their mother is my dog's vet.

Were they hiding under a rock all this time?

Oh my God. Grandma. I can't believe she hadn't entered my mind until now. She must be going crazy worrying about me. I need to let her know I'm okay.

"How long have I been here?" I ask.

"My sons brought you in last night, so around eight hours."

"I need to call my grandmother."

Dr. Mervina sets the clothes on the bed, and glances at me with a friendly smile on her lips. I haven't moved from my spot in the corner of the room, and I'm still using Dr. Mervina's jacket to cover myself.

"These clothes should fit. I can wait outside while you change to give you some privacy."

"I want to talk with my grandmother," I say louder, irritated the vet doesn't seem to care about my worries.

"I spoke with Wendy last night."

Her answer gives me pause.

"Why isn't she here?" I begin to worry. Grandma would have come if she knew…

"Wendy knows you're safe. Don't worry, child. Now get dressed so we can talk more."

I scoff. What's the point? Everyone has already seen me naked anyway, and what I want the most right now are answers.

"Are you going to tell me what the heck I'm doing here?"

Dr. Mervina takes a deep breath, then sits on the only chair in the room. "Last night you were attacked by a rogue wolf, and he infected you."

"Infected me with what? Some sort of messed-up rabies?"

She shakes her head, her lips twisting into a grimace. "No, with the virus that can change humans into shifters. Wolves."

I blink a couple of times. My brain has a hard time comprehending the words that came out of the vet's mouth. After a couple of beats, I throw my head back and laugh like a maniac. "Nice one, Doc. Why don't you spare me the bullshit and spit out the truth already? Your son must have slipped me some kind of hallucinogenic pill at the music venue last night, and then he kidnapped me. Are you guys running a cult?"

"I'm not lying to you, Amelia. You've experienced your first shift already. You felt the wolf inside of you."

I wave dismissively. "Side effects of the drug."

"You're stubborn. You'll need that here in the compound, especially around my sons."

My spine becomes taut at their mention. "What's that supposed to mean?"

Dr. Mervina smiles enigmatically. "You'll find out soon enough."

Standing, she begins to unbutton her shirt.

"What are you doing?"

"I'm going to show you that I'm not ly—" A loud knock on the door makes Dr. Mervina freeze. "Who is it?"

"It's Valentina. Terrence cut himself while chopping wood. He's bleeding pretty badly."

Dr. Mervina's lips turns into a thin flat line, and her eyebrows furrow. It's clear she isn't happy with the interruption.

"I'll be back as soon as I can, Amelia. Why don't you take a nap? The first shift is always hard."

I don't reply, but I have no intention of going to sleep. Dr. Mervina seems to read that in my expression, so it's no surprise when I hear the door lock click from the outside after the vet leaves. I'm not even alarmed she was summoned to tend to a guy's wound. It's clear they have their own set of rules here, wherever the hell here is.

I wait a few seconds before I put on the clothes they brought me. No shoes, though. *They don't want you to go anywhere, so why would they give you shoes?* It doesn't matter. Lack of shoes won't keep me from trying to escape.

The only window in the room is too high off the floor for me to reach it, so I use the chair and attempt to pull the lever. I'm still not high enough to gain leverage. Cursing under my breath, I step off the chair and eye the bed. If I put the chair on top of it, I'll be at eye level with the window. If the lever doesn't budge, I can always break the glass.

The chair sways precariously when I step on it, and it sinks into the soft mattress. But it only takes me a few seconds to regain my balance. Curling my fingers around the metal lever, I grunt as I attempt to turn it. "Come on, you stupid thing."

My knuckles turn white with the strain, and the sharp edge of the metal bar leaves indentions on my palm. I let go with a curse, opening and shutting my hand to get ready for the second round. This time, I try with both hands. Finally, the lever moves a fraction. It takes another minute before I manage to turn the damn thing all the way up.

Slowly, I push the window open. The gap is barely big enough to stick my head out, but I figure that with some maneuvering, I'll be able to slide out. First, I check to see if the coast is clear. No one in sight. The window faces a small courtyard, but I spot a trail going toward a cluster of trees. I don't know if there are fences in place or guards, but I won't find out by standing here.

For the first time ever, I'm glad I don't have a voluptuous body like my friend Kenya. If my boobs were any bigger, I might have gotten stuck. Even wearing the borrowed sweatshirt and yoga pants, I end up scratching my back and elbows. Victory courses through me when my feet land softly on the stone floor. The fall doesn't even jar my bones. I don't remember being so agile, but I'm not going to start complaining now.

I wait a second, listening carefully. Two seconds pass before I hear voices in the distance. That's it. It's now or never. I break into a run toward the dirt path. Adrenaline kicks in, and my muscles fill with energy. I've never run so fast in my life. After a couple of minutes, I leave the path and veer into the woods.

Maybe the property doesn't have a fence. Maybe I can make it home.

The sound of wind rushing past me steals my focus, as do all the forest smells that are somehow enhanced: the dirt, the pine leaves, the wildflowers. I can smell them all as if I had buried my nose in them. *Shit.* Maybe I'm suffering from the side effects of whatever drug Samuel gave me last night. It doesn't matter. I escaped. Soon, I'll be at the sheriff's office giving my statement. Wolf life, my ass. So what if my kidnappers are sin incarnate or that I'd gladly go home with any of them—or all three at the same time.

God! What am I thinking?

I slow down when I see the shape of a wire fence ahead.

Damn. So the property is surrounded. It appears to be a regular fence, but I'm not stupid to touch it before testing it first. I search the ground around me until I find a small piece of wood, then I throw it at the fence. Nothing happens. Great. It's not electrified.

I walk the perimeter for a little bit, looking for a hole I can pass through. *Nada.* Not willing to push my luck, I curl my fingers around the wire and begin to climb. I bite my lower lip when I put weight on my feet, the wire digging in my unprotected soles. By the end of this ordeal, they'll be bleeding for sure.

"Leaving without saying goodbye?" someone says from behind. "I'm offended."

With a surprised yelp, I almost lose my footing. Peering over my shoulder, I find Samuel standing right behind me. I hadn't heard a thing. How was he able to move through the forest undetected? I prepare to jump, but before I make my move, he snakes an arm around my middle and pulls me from the fence.

"Let me go!" Kicking my legs, I hit his arms to no avail.

"Calm down. I'm not going to hurt you."

Since what I'm doing is not working, I decide to stop struggling. But I have every intention of running once he drops me to the ground. The problem is Samuel doesn't let go when he puts me down. Instead, he hugs me from behind, bringing his body flush against mine. *Holy Batman.* My entire body catches fire. I'm all too aware of the way his strong frame molds perfectly with mine, and how his woodsy scent is the most intoxicating smell I've ever known.

Closing my eyes, I get lost in the moment. What I'm experiencing is completely crazy. The guy drugged and kidnapped me, but tell that to my hormones. Samuel brings his nose to my ear and murmurs, "Are you going to behave if I let you go?"

I lick my lips before I say, "No."

When he chuckles, his warm breath fans across the sensitive

skin on my neck, giving me goose bumps. *Hell and damn.* No wonder those groupies were ready to drop their panties for him. It turns out I'm not wearing any, which reminds me *why* I'm not. The thought is like a bucket of cold water over my head, sobering me in an instant. I elbow his stomach, catching him by surprise, then I use his moment of distraction to my advantage, managing to get free at last.

"Red, wait. Don't run."

I should ignore him, but there's something in his tone that compels me to turn. "What do you want from me?"

"I know everything is strange and confusing right now, but I swear we don't mean you any harm."

"Next, you're going to tell me the same wacko story your mother tried to. Come on. How gullible do you think I am? Werewolves don't exist!"

"Yes, they do. But we aren't werewolves."

Frustrated, I throw my hands in the air. "Now we're discussing semantics. Fucking great."

"I'll prove it you."

Samuel grabs the back of his T-shirt and pulls it off, messing up his hair in an adorably sexy way. I bite the inside of my cheek to stop my mind from wandering to naughty places. His jeans are shed next, and he stands completely naked in front of me. That should be my clue to get the hell out of Dodge, but my feet are planted to the ground. Instead, I take my sweet time traveling the length of his impressive body. Samuel's chest is smooth, not a single hair in sight, while his abs are the stuff of dreams. He belongs in a Calvin Klein underwear ad. Funnily enough, he covers his crotch with his hands.

"I didn't peg you as a prude," I say boldly, surprising even myself.

"I don't want to frighten you more." He smirks while amusement dances in his eyes.

"Cocky much?"

"Careful, Red. You don't want to tease the Big Bad Wolf now."

I open my mouth to rebuff him, but Samuel's body begins to shake so rapidly he flickers in and out of focus. My gasp is loud in the silence. He drops to the ground, his muscles starting to move in an unnatural way, shifting beneath his skin.

With my hands covering my mouth, I take a step back. Samuel shimmers for a brief second before he changes into a white wolf. My heart is beating so fast I'm afraid it'll jump out of my chest. I would scream if that made any difference. My mind and eyes are at war with one another. I don't know what to do.

The wolf shimmers, its form distorting until Samuel again stands in front of me just as naked as before. This time, his hands aren't covering anything. My eyes widen at the same time my throat turns unbearably dry.

I'm still staring at his impressive length when Samuel says, "So, now do you believe me?"

Dazed, I reply in a breathless whisper, "Yes."

And I'm not only referring to the wolf part.

CHAPTER 7

DANTE

Instead of following Tristan, I head in the opposite direction. The clinic's back door leads to a shortcut path to my studio, but getting there quicker isn't what prompted me to choose that specific route. Something is compelling me to check out that less-used exit.

As soon as I walk into the small and deserted courtyard, I discover the reason. Seth, Tristan's closest friend, is looming just outside of Red's room. The windows are shut, but with his superior shifter's hearing, I'm sure Seth heard everything we said.

My nostrils flare as a low growl escapes my lips. Unlike Tristan, I don't trust the guy. There's something off about him. Seth is one the strongest enforcers we have. Since everyone is dead certain Tristan will be the new alpha, it's obvious Seth thinks his close relationship with my brother will guarantee him a spot as the new beta. Sam and I are too strong to be considered for the role. Once a new alpha is picked among the three of us, the other two will be banished from the pack… or worse, killed by the new alpha.

It's a savage rule, but a pack can only have one ruling couple. Never in the history of the Crimson Hollow's wolves has there been three strong contenders for the role, much less contenders who were triplet brothers. I researched the subject extensively, but the closest I came to an out-of-norm arrangement was the legend of the Mother of Wolves, the first female alpha. She'd never had a consort, but ruled over her pack alone while taking as many lovers within the pack as she pleased. She was so powerful there had never been a male wolf strong enough to challenge her, or to be worthy of ruling by her side.

"What are you doing, Seth?" I glare at the blond man.

The enforcer straightens his back and frowns, his lips turning into a white slash. "Nothing. Just came here for a smoke."

"Right. And the best spot for a cigarette just had to be under our new guest's window. Snooping is most definitely not a quality we look for in a beta."

Seth sneers, a reaction I expected from the guy. I've never hid that I don't like him.

"I wasn't snooping, but the pack needs to know we have a newly made wolf."

"The alpha will let his wolves know when he deems appropriate. Or do I detect a challenge in your tone? I'll be happy to let my father know one of his enforcers is challenging his authority."

Seth's glare morphs into a glint of caution. No one in the pack dares to challenge our alpha, not even my brothers or me. It would lead to certain death. Anthony Wolfe is a beast, no pun intended. The largest wolf in the pack, his reputation precedes him. He was a key player in avoiding the complete destruction of our town during the Thirteen Days of Chaos, an event that took place twenty-five years ago and changed the lives of Crimson Hollow's supe community forever.

"Of course not. Do you know who attacked the girl?" Seth asks.

I pause and study the guy, knowing I have to be careful. The pack has a strict rule that attempting to change a human into a wolf must be approved by the alpha first. If one of our own were to go rogue and do it, the punishment would be severe. I most definitely don't want to disclose to Seth that Red was infected by a rogue from another pack. We're risking a lot by keeping her here since she technically belongs to the Shadow Creek wolves. If that information leaks, it will lead to unrest and distrust in my father's leadership. He might even be forced to get rid of Red, send her to those savages up north. I can't allow that to happen. She's too important to us.

Like my mother, I have the sight. For the last couple of weeks, I've been plagued by visions of Red. Only, I hadn't known it was her until I saw her for the first time in person, half dead in Sam's arms. Now, I have to figure out how she'll impact our lives.

"No," I say. "We found her in Irving Forest by a creek. We couldn't pick up her attacker's scent."

Seth flattens his lips. "It could have been a loner. You know they tend to go crazy without a pack."

"Yes, it's possible."

A lone wolf would be the most logical explanation, but I can't help the sense of apprehension that drips down my spine. Becoming a loner could very well be in my destiny. If Tristan becomes the new alpha, Sam and I will have to leave the pack forever. It's highly unlikely that any other pack will accept us unless we challenge their alpha and win.

"The order right now is to keep this quiet until my father makes the announcement himself. Is that clear, Seth?"

He turns to me, a look of disdain in his eyes. "Crystal clear, *Beta*."

He stalks off, and I wait until he's no longer in sight. Seth will be a problem, and I don't need any special gift to see that. A light tingle concentrates at the base of my spine. That's the signal I get when I'm about to be hit by another vision. I take the track toward my studio, a chalet buried deep in the woods right on the outskirts of the compound's property. It's on top of a hill, and it provides breathtaking views of the forest. From its vantage point, I can also see the town.

As soon I enter my sanctuary, I feel the itch, the urge to

paint something. It isn't a regular bout of inspiration like normal artists have. It feels more like a compulsion. With a jerky movement, I pull my shirt off, throwing it in a corner in the room, then grab a massive white canvas, setting it on the easel.

Then I allow the craze to take over, losing myself to the gift until the message is imprinted in some type of art. It's usually abstract paintings for me.

I'm conscious of my fingers dipping into the paint containers, the feel of them gliding over the canvas. But I don't know what I'm painting or how long it will take for me to finish. All I know is I won't be able to stop until it's done.

Hours must have passed before I collapse on the floor in exhaustion. My arms ache, and I can't feel my fingers any longer. I'm covered in paint from head to toe, but I don't care about any of that. My eyelids are too heavy, and fighting sleep is pointless. My last thought before I shut my eyes is of Red and how I crave her like I've never craved anything else in my entire life.

∞⦿∞

I curse at whoever is banging at my door. It feels as if I just shut my eyes. It's a Herculean effort to peel my eyelids open. My brain is foggy as hell. When I look out the window, I discover I didn't just fall asleep. The sky is tinted bloody orange. It's near sunset already. I slept the entire day away. Damn it.

My back muscles protest when I roll over on the floor. The paint covering my body is dry, and it's making me itch like crazy.

"For fuck's sake, Dante. Open up. I know you're in there," Sam yells from outside.

With a groan, I spring to my feet and rub my face, hoping the movement will kickstart my brain. Sam knocks on the door again, much louder this time. If I don't answer him, he'll knock it down.

"I'm coming!"

I barely have the door open before Sam pushes me out of the way, striding in followed by Tristan.

"What the hell, Dante? Now is not the time to play the hermit artist. We have a sticky situation on our hands, and we need to—"

"What the hell is that?" Tristan cuts Sam off, staring dazedly at the painting I just finished.

I turn without knowing what to expect, since I passed out before I could really examine what I did. My jaw drops as I stare at my newest artwork—Red sitting in a throne-like chair, surrounded by three white wolves.

'Dante?" Sam probes again.

Swallowing hard, it takes me a moment to reply. "I have no fucking idea."

CHAPTER 8

RED

I'm so angry at myself, I could scream in frustration. I was so close to running away from this madness, but I had to go and get all hot and bothered by Samuel Wolfe. It doesn't escape my notice that I'm focusing way too much on the rock star's sexy good looks and how he managed to coax me to come back, rather than on the fact he turned into a wolf. *A wolf!*

Crimson Hollow was a quirk town filled with mysticism and legends, but I had no idea they were true. Did Grandma know? I need to go home and tell her everything, but I can't until Anthony Wolfe, Samuel's father—the alpha—authorizes it. Such bullshit.

After Samuel did his little demonstration, he brought me back to the clinic and left. I was too stunned to fight him. That's what I get for letting my hormones take control of my brain.

I'm going out of my mind when he finally returns by sundown to escort me to a different place. I try to get more information from him, but he isn't keen to talk now. Fucker.

We don't venture outside. Instead, he takes me to a different section of the building. The décor changes from simple and clean to lavishly decorated rooms. The furniture is all classic dark wood, and the furnishings and rugs are in deep jewel colors. The paintings on the walls are modern, though, very abstract and colorful. When I examine them closely, it seems they were painted by the same artist.

"What's this place?" I ask as I take everything in, trying to absorb as much as I can of my new surroundings.

"This is the alpha's manor."

"And the place I was before?"

"The clinic. It's connected to the main house, so Mom can get to it quickly."

"Why is that? Is she the resident doctor?"

Samuel chuckles. "Something like that."

"I guess it makes sense that she's a vet and not a human doctor."

Samuel doesn't reply. He seems tenser than before. I wonder what the heck happened between my failed escape attempt and now. He stops in front of a door down the hallway and knocks. A rough voice tells us to come in. It gives me the chills. Mr. Asshole is on the other side.

Samuel pushes the door open, and we enter an office furnished with sturdy dark wood furniture. The smell of cigar and whiskey reaches my nose. I would have wrinkled it in disgust if Tristan's scent wasn't in the mix as well. A tendril of desire curls around my spine, and I have to fight the feeling with all my strength. It's bad enough to lust after one brother, but the tall and imposing man standing behind the desk glaring in my direction makes everything so damn complicated.

Tristan and Samuel share the same dark brown hair, but whereas Samuel's style is edgy, Mr. Asshole sports a boring and predictable haircut. Since I'm already ogling the man, I might as well give him an elevator glance when he walks around the desk. He's in business casual clothes—dark slacks paired with a button-down shirt.

His stare blazes through me, piercing me in a way that leaves me breathless. I gasp when I feel a shift in the air surrounding us. I'm not going crazy—something strange is going on here. First my reaction to Samuel, and now this. Is it a wolf thing?

"You tried to escape. That was foolish," Mr. Asshole finally says.

His comment breaks whatever spell I'm under. I cross my arms, bringing forth the anger from before.

"I'd be foolish if I didn't try."

"Well, I hope you got that notion out of your head because you're not going anywhere any time soon."

"What?" My voice rises shrilly.

I turn to Samuel, feeling betrayed. True, he didn't say I could go home, but he never said I'd be a prisoner either.

"I'm sorry, Red. You're a new wolf. You can't go back to your normal life. At least not until you learn how to master your new reality."

"You're out of your mind if you think I'm going to stay here for an undetermined period. I have a life, and my grandmother is sick. Who is going to take care of her?"

"Your grandmother will be fine," a newcomer says from behind me.

I glance over my shoulder, knowing very well Dante is the one who spoke. As if by magic, my rage ebbs away, just like it did when I was in wolf form and he calmed me down. It's like he's the wolf whisperer or something.

I hadn't had the chance to really look at him the last time we were in the same room, but I can't keep my eyes off him now. He's so darn cute with his dark blond hair sticking out in all directions. Now I know why it's hard for me to feel animosity toward the guy. He oozes wholesomeness, a stark contrast to his brothers. Samuel has that mischievous glint in his eyes, and Mr. Asshole is... well, he's an asshole.

"You can't possibly know that. Are you a psychic, too?"

Dante raises both eyebrows, his cheeks turning a deep shade of red. He glances away, rubbing the back of his neck. "Something like that."

I was not expecting that answer. "Do you all have special gifts besides turning into wolves?" I eye the others.

"No. Dante is the only one with the extra gift." Mr. Asshole taps his knuckles on the desk once before folding his arms.

"Hold on. I think my gift in bed can be considered an extra. It's definitely a *gift* to the ladies." Samuel winks at me.

Heat rushes to my cheeks, but I roll my eyes, trying to downplay my reaction. I will not picture myself in bed with the rocker. *Ah, fuck. Too late.* I already had, my body reacting accordingly. My nipples are now hard, and there's a light throbbing between my legs. Never in my life had I gotten turned on by a man like that so fast. And now I'm having all sorts of inappropriate feelings for three strangers, one of whom I dislike immensely. I pinch the bridge of my nose, wanting this nightmare to be over already. I want to go home where life is normal, where I don't get hot and bothered by a simple glance from a hot dude.

A noise that sounds a lot like a growl comes from Tristan's direction. Not wanting to miss the opportunity to antagonize the man, I turn to him with an eyebrow raised. "What's the matter with you? Got a stick up your butt?"

"He sure does." Samuel laughs.

"As I was saying," Dante continues. "Your grandma is fine, and she knows where you are."

"Does she know what happened to me, too?" I ask, afraid to know the answer.

Dante stares at me for a couple of beats. I feel the pull, a force that reels me in like a fish caught by the hook. His deep emerald-green eyes seem to hypnotize me. Crap. What if he is hypnotizing me? I take a couple of steps back until I hit a bookshelf.

He frowns. "What's the matter?"

"Stop looking at me like that." I hug myself like that action can protect me from a wolf spell, if that's even a thing.

Samuel hits his brother on the shoulder. "Yeah, Dante. Quit being a creep."

"Bite me," he snarls back.

"Enough, you two." Mr. Asshole steps in between them, then turns his attention to me. "I don't know if your grandmother knows, but it doesn't matter. You can't leave the compound until the al—"

"Until your damn father says so," I say through clenched teeth. "Yeah, Samuel already gave me that spiel. I don't care about your father. I'm an adult, and this is a free country. You can't keep me here against my will."

Tristan takes a couple of steps forward, stopping only when he's invading my personal space. I swallow hard as my body becomes tense, but I won't cower in front of this infuriating man.

"I can and will. Don't cross me, Amelia."

Very few people call me by my given name. I hate admitting it, but hearing Mr. Asshole say it gives me goose bumps. *No, no, no. You don't like him, remember?*

"Or what?" I ask, lifting my chin in defiance.

He curls his lips, revealing sharp canines that are most definitely not human. His irises churn, turning molten gold instead of gray. My gums ache as I start to shake a little.

Dante and Samuel pull Tristan away, and I can finally breathe out. What the hell was that? I touch my teeth, relieved they are still human. I'm almost certain I was beginning to shift. I still remember how much it hurt the first time. No way do I want to go through that again.

"If speaking with your father is so important, why haven't you brought me to meet him yet?" I ask.

"He's out of town," Samuel answers. "But we can make a quick run by your house to get your stuff."

Mr. Asshole whips his face toward his brother, his expression twisted into a scowl.

"When you say 'we,' do you mean you and your brothers or you and me?" I ask before Tristan can put the kibosh on Samuel's idea.

A wicked smile blossoms on Samuel's lips, his eyes twinkling with mischief. It gives me shivers. "You and me," he replies in a voice that's equal measures whiskey and honey, and totally meant to seduce.

"What? That's out of the quest—" Mr. Asshole begins to say, but Dante interrupts.

"It will be fine, Tristan. I'll join as well. Or do you have so little faith in us that you don't think we can handle a brand-new pup?"

"Hey! I'm not a pup. I'm a woman!"

Tristan ignores my outburst, addressing Dante as if I'm not even there. "Fine. But I'm coming as well."

Fuck me gently with a chainsaw. My gums begin to ache again. This time, I taste blood on my tongue. A foreign sound emanates from my throat as I take a step forward. Something savage woke up inside me, and I'm on the verge of unleashing it.

The brothers fall silent, staring at me like they're seeing a ghost.

"What the hell?" Samuel says, his eyebrows almost reaching his hairline.

"What?" I ask, my voice a little garbled and rough.

"She can do a partial shift already? Impossible," Mr. Asshole mumbles.

I growl. They'd better stop with this bullshit of talking about me as if I'm not in the room, or I'm going to lose it. Maybe I already am losing it.

Dante offers me his phone. "Look at the camera."

Reluctantly, I do as he asks. In the screen, the most atrocious sight ever greets me. My face had morphed into something out of nightmares. Jaw elongated, eyes glowing yellow, and canines the size of my pinkie. I do the only thing any sane person in my place would. I leap back, drop the phone, and scream at the top of my lungs.

CHAPTER 9
TRISTAN

"What's going on here?" Mom asks from the door.

I'm not even surprised. She always knows when we're doing something she doesn't approve of. I'm twenty-five, and I still have to put up with being scolded like a child.

She glances over my shoulder, and her glare morphs into something else when she sees Amelia's face. Her jaw drops. "Blessed Mother, how did that happen?"

"Red got mad at Tristan and, well, that's the result," Sam replies.

"Stop staring at me like I'm a freak!" Amelia turns her back to us, curling her shoulders forward and hugging her middle.

Guilt twists my guts. It's the only reason I don't offer a retort to my brother's comment.

"You have to relax," Dante suggests.

The woman goes to my desk and sweeps her arm over it, throwing everything to the floor.

"Don't tell me to relax!"

I glance at my brothers. In that action, a silent communication is exchanged between us. I make a motion toward Amelia, ready to restrain her, but Mom is faster. Before we can do anything, she sticks a syringe in the woman's neck. Amelia has no chance—her body turns limp in seconds. Mom catches her without effort. Slowly, the pretty blonde's features return to normal.

"What did you do?" Sam takes a step forward, his body tense as if he's ready to pry Amelia's limp form from our mother's arms.

"I gave her a special sedative. You should know better than to antagonize her." Mom doesn't look in my direction, but I know that comment was for me.

Dante gets to Amelia first, and Mom surrenders the woman to him without a fight. She's never made it a secret that Dante is the only one she trusts completely. He's always been her favorite, maybe because they possess the same gift. Their special connection used to bother me greatly when I was younger, but I've learned to accept it over the years.

Dante makes a motion to exit my office, but Mom raises her hand, stopping him.

"Just one second. I would like to know exactly what happened while I was busy tending to Terrence."

Clenching my jaw, I glance at my brothers. When neither offer Mom anything, I answer, "The girl managed to escape, but Sam was able to catch her before she could jump the fence. He brought her back to the clinic, then he came looking for me."

"Go on," Mom says.

Crossing my arms, I stare pointedly at Dante.

"I had an episode," he says.

"A vision?" Mom takes an eager step toward him.

"Yes, but I don't know what it means." He rubs his face as his gaze turn inward. "The painting is in my studio."

Mom nods, but instead of going out the door to see Dante's new artwork, she leans against my desk and folds her arms.

"Now explain to me what happened to trigger a partial shift in a wolf barely a day old."

"We don't know." Sam shrugs. "She got mad when Tristan told her she couldn't go home and, well, he got in her face. That's when she shifted. I thought only alphas and betas were capable of that."

"Do you think Amelia could potentially be an alpha?" I ask cautiously. First, Dante's painting shows the woman surrounded by three wolves, and now this? As much as I'd like to dismiss Dante's episodes as inconsequential, I'm not foolish. Amelia is not an ordinary wolf.

"Well, Lyria would *love* that." Sam juts his chin at me, making me bristle. The last thing I want to worry about is the pack's female beta.

Mom pinches the bridge of her nose, closing her eyes for a brief second. "Did you at least explain the rules of the pack to Amelia?"

"We didn't get the chance before Tristan went all caveman on her," Sam said, once again opening his big mouth.

"Are you trying to get me to punch you?" I say, but once I catch Mom's death glare aimed at me, I lower my gaze, dropping the aggressive stance.

I'm a grown man, and she's still able to stir fear in me. Mervina Wolfe is the female alpha for good reason.

"I spoke with your father. He's stuck in Vancouver for three more days, so we've decided to introduce Amelia to the pack before his return."

My spine goes taut. "Do you think that's wise? What if she loses control and partially shifts again in front of everyone?"

"We'll have to make sure no one aggravates her enough for that to happen, which means you must control your temper." Mom shifts her focus to Dante and Sam. "All of you."

"My temper is fine," I reply through clenched teeth.

"Clearly," Sam mutters.

"How long until the sedative wears off?" Dante asks.

"She won't be up until tomorrow morning. Let's bring her to the guest room. Dante, please stay with her. I don't want her to be alone when she wakes up. The poor girl needs answers."

"Why Dante? I can do it." Sam takes a step forward, making Dante hold Amelia tighter against his chest. Ah, shit. I hope they don't start fighting over her. She's not even a Crimson Hollow wolf for crying out loud.

Mom cuts Sam a glacial stare. "Because I said so."

Dante clears his throat, commanding everyone's attention. "I caught Seth snooping right under Red's window this morning. He knows we have a new wolf in the pack. I'm not sure how long he'll keep his mouth shut."

The accusation in Dante's tone is clear. Never mind that Seth is one my closest friends and I'd trust him with my life. It seems everyone is dead set on pissing me off this week.

"Seth won't say a word." I watch Dante through slitted eyes.

"Your trust in him is misplaced, brother. He's a sneaky bastard."

"Is that your opinion or is your statement based on facts?" I don't even attempt to hide my irritation.

"Didn't I just give you a fact? Why was Seth listening to a conversation not meant for his ears?" Dante raises an eyebrow.

"Yeah, I'm not a fan of the guy either," Sam adds. "No facts to back it up, though. It's just a feeling."

Clenching my jaw, I try to not let my temper get the better of me. Seth has been my best friend since we were young. He was the only shifter in the pack who hadn't treated me differently because I was the alpha's son. I know Seth is ambitious and hopes to one day become the pack's beta, but I don't see any problem with that.

"Get the wolves ready for an assembly in two hours. I'll make the announcement about Amelia. It'll hopefully give the pack enough time to digest the news before we present her to them," Mom says.

As usual, she doesn't make any comment about Seth. Dante never hid the fact he disliked my friend, but Mom has always chosen to remain neutral. If Seth was up to no good, she would be the first to point it out. One more reason for me to ignore Dante's opinion.

"I'm going to spread the word about the assembly," I say.

Not waiting for a reply, I stride out of my old office. I've barely used the room since I moved to the city. The studio apartment above the company's office is where I spend most of my nights. It allows me the privacy I'll no longer have if I become the new alpha.

Groaning, I shake my head. I don't want to think about a future that most likely won't come to pass for another decade. My father is still in his prime, and I don't foresee him stepping down any time soon.

As soon as I step out of the alpha's manor, Lyria finds me. I know immediately that seduction is not part of her game today. On the contrary, she's pissed.

"Where the hell have you been? You were supposed to train the new enforcers this morning."

Ah, fuck. I forgot about that. "I was dealing with an emergency."

"What kind of emergency? I wasn't told anything."

"You'll find out soon enough. Mother has called an assembly in two hours. Call everyone."

I try to sidestep her, but the woman grabs my arm. "I'm the beta, Tristan. I should know before everyone else."

Narrowing my eyes, I look down at her hand. "Watch yourself, Lyria. You're only the beta because all the other females in the pack are too afraid to challenge you. I'm still the stronger wolf here."

She winces as if I'd slapped her. Implying she's not as good as she thinks she is was a low blow on my part. But I won't take it back.

Letting go of my arm, she steps back. "Are you threatening me?"

"No. I'm reminding you of a fact. Now do as I say."

Lyria watches me through narrowed eyes. "Fine. But you're wrong about me, Tristan. I'm the beta because I deserve to be."

She strides away with tense shoulders, head held high. I shouldn't have mentioned anything about her status. I've never once contested she was the beta by merit and not by default. But once Amelia is presented to the pack, Lyria will no doubt make the connection. She'll know Amelia is a threat to her position.

Way to go, Tristan. You just put a target on Amelia's back.

CHAPTER 10
SAMUEL

For the first time in months, Tristan slept in his old room. It doesn't take a genius to figure out he doesn't want to be too far from Red no matter how much he acts like a total douche-canoe around the woman. He's ensnared by her just like Dante and I are, but he's fighting the pull like crazy. *Idiot*.

Deep in my bones, I feel there's something different about her. She's a pretty sexy thing—I would have totally banged her before if given the chance—but now that she's a wolf, it's more than mere lust, which makes things complicated.

Curse the wolves and their hierarchy. No wonder Mom asked Dante to keep an eye on Red; he's the one she trusts the most to keep his dick in his pants.

Stopping in front of Red's door, I press my ear against it. It's dead silent on the other side. She must still be sleeping. It's an effort to walk away, but I have things to do, so I continue down the corridor until I'm banging on Tristan's door.

"Yo, Tristan! Open up."

There's a grumble, then the sound of sheets rubbing together. After a few moments, Tristan opens the door in a brusque movement and glowers. "What do you want, Sam?"

Pushing him out of the way, I go straight for the curtains in his room, yanking them apart so the morning sunlight can come through.

"Rise up bright and sunny, sunshine."

"Fuck off." In jerky motions, Tristan heads to the chair in the corner on the room and grabs the T-shirt he left there.

"Since when do you wake up before noon?"

"I didn't sleep at all last night, and we have shit to do."

When Tristan's head pops through the neck hole of his shirt, his eyes are narrowed to slits.

"How many cups of coffee have you had already?"

"Five, but who's counting?"

"Is our guest up yet?" I don't miss Tristan's contemptuous tone. He won't be winning the Mr. Congeniality title any time soon.

"I don't think so." Moving to his dresser, I randomly grab one of Tristan's cologne bottles. After I remove the cap, I take a whiff, grimacing when the scent hits my nose.

"Then what do you want?" Tristan grabs the bottle from my hand, placing it back on the dresser.

"You mentioned the kid from the hardware store might be able to help identify the tracking device."

Tristan freezes, his jaw locking tight. "Let me guess. You want to go there now."

I nod, bouncing on the balls of my feet. Maybe I did have one too many cups of coffee. Sex would have been able to take care of the jitters, but I'd have to go into town for that. I hadn't wanted to—nor had I been able to, if I were being honest—leave the compound last night.

Tristan stares out the window, rubbing his jaw. "I suppose we should take care of this sooner rather than later. Carpe diem and all."

"Yeah, yeah. Let's seize the day."

I swing around, ready to leave his room, but stop in my tracks when I don't sense Tristan following me. He's gazing at the wall to his right, the one separating his room from Red's. Ah, fuck. I knew he wasn't immune to the woman.

"Are you coming or what?" I ask.

"Yes, give me a minute, will you? I'll meet you outside."

"Hell to the fucking no. I'm not waiting an hour for you to finish your beauty rituals. Let's go."

"I don't have beauty rituals," Tristan replies through clenched teeth.

"Really? Shall I go into your bathroom and count how many creams and hair products you have?"

Tristan glares with jaw locked tight. I maintain eye contact despite his stupid expression. It's like when we used to play games as children to see who could go longer without blinking.

"Fine. Let's get this over with. Being in your presence this early is already giving me a headache."

It's been ages since I drove into town this early in the morning. I'm a nocturnal person, preferring to stay up all night and not wake up until the middle of the afternoon. It's a preference that suits my lifestyle as the lead singer of a rock band, or maybe I picked that career *because* I enjoy the nightlife so much. Who cares? The truth is nothing really exciting happens in this town during the day. Most shenanigans—caused by human or supes—happen at night ninety-nine percent of the time.

The hardware store sits in the corner of the main street facing the square. It used to be a hole-in-the-wall store when it first opened more than thirty years ago. It has now expanded to take up three large retail spaces, but that's not surprising. What are people to do in such a small town besides fix things in their houses?

It's not even nine, yet it's already open while most other businesses don't start welcoming customers until ten. I follow Tristan in, the bell chiming as he swings the door open. I do a quick once over, feeling bad for the people who work here. I'm already bored by all the merchandise and the neutral color scheme of the place.

Tristan continues toward the back of the store, so I increase my pace to keep up. There's a guy wearing thick-rimmed glasses behind the customer service counter. His head is down as he stares at his phone. He glances up when we approach, then he straightens his spine and hastily puts his phone away. I drop my eyes to his name tag. *Peter.*

"Mr. Wolfe, how can I help you?" he asks.

"Hi, Peter. I was wondering if you could help with some technical stuff." Tristan rests his hands casually on the counter. He's trying his best to turn the menacing-wolf vibe down a notch. It's something we all have to do when dealing with non-supes, because even in human form, the otherness energy surrounds us. Tristan has always had trouble keeping his beast in check.

Peter quickly spares me a glance, and I catch a hint of surprise in his eyes. He turns his attention back to Tristan almost immediately and asks, "Computer related?"

"Not exactly." Tristan reaches inside his jacket pocket, then pulls out the tracking device we found on the rogue. "I was wondering if you could tell me what this is."

The guy takes the device from Tristan, and begins to inspect it. After a moment, he says. "This is high-tech stuff. I believe Australian ranchers were working on something similar."

"Please explain," Tristan replies.

"With consumers more and more focused on the quality of the food they eat, free-range livestock is the way of the future. But letting a two-ton animal go wandering can cause a lot of stress to ranchers. So they came up with something similar to this. It's basically a combination of GPS technology and biometric sensors."

"Biometric sensors? Like what? A Fitbit for cows?" I raise an eyebrow.

"Something like that." Peter examines the device more closely, frowning. "Except this apparatus looks a little different than the stuff I've read about. Actually, holy shit!"

Peter's eyebrow shoots up to the heavens, and his mouth hangs open.

"What?" Tristan almost growls.

"Give me a second." Peter reaches down to a drawer, then pulls out a pair of small pliers. With care, he eases free a couple of thin wires that were hidden under a plastic round circle. "I've seen something like this on a TV show once. Scientists were trying to find a way to control certain behavior on animals. They'd attach a small device like this on the back of their heads, and electrical conduits would send pulses of energy to the animal's brain. Depending on the frequency, it could tell a lab rat to eat, run, and even attack."

"What the fuck! How is that legal?" I ask.

Peter shrugs. "I don't know."

"Are you sure we're looking at the same thing?" Tristan chimes in.

The guy turns the device again, scrutinizing it carefully. "Well, not one-hundred percent sure. But it sure looks like it. Do you see these two round bumps?" He points at the small protuberance on the back of the device, and Tristan and I lean forward to see it. "Well, this is what made me think of the stuff I saw on that show, plus the little wires."

"I see." Tristan's eyebrows are furrowed as he stares hard at the mysterious gadget. His mind is probably going a hundred miles an hour thinking of all the ramifications if Peter is correct on his assessment.

"Where did you get this, if you don't mind me asking?" Peter pushes his glasses back up his nose, trying to look and sound innocent.

Yeah, I'm not buying it. No geeky guy would just answer questions without wanting to know more.

"It was a gift from a fan." I make a motion for Peter to hand over the device.

"Strange gift," he says, still eyeing the object too intently as he hands it over.

I curl my fingers around the little box, then shove it in my pocket and away from the guy's curious eyes. "Well, maybe she saw the same show you did and was hoping to control me."

Jesus, that was lame. I don't think I could have sold that story to a five-year-old. But what was I supposed to say? If I told Peter we found the device in the forest, he could get ideas. We definitely don't need a curious human poking around pack business.

CHAPTER 11

RED

My mouth tastes like ashes, and my head feels like it's going to explode. When I open my eyes, the little illumination in the room only makes my headache ten times worse. My forehead is clammy, and I'm unbearably hot. With a groan, I push the covers off my body, but that does little to cool me down. I get rid of the sweatshirt next, breathing a sigh of relief when the cool air from the AC hits my naked skin.

"Good morning," someone says from the corner of the room.

I scream, pulling the sheet over my body to cover myself. Dante is sitting on a chair in the darkness.

"What the hell are you doing in my room?"

"Mom asked me to keep an eye on you."

My jaw slackens, and it takes me a moment to find my voice. "You spent the night here?"

"Yup." He nods, resting his elbows on his knees and leaning forward.

"That's an invasion of my privacy."

"I'm sorry. She didn't want you waking up alone."

"Because she thought I would try to escape again." I don't make any attempt to hide the bitterness in my tone.

I'm in a different room. The walls are covered by a paisley-print wallpaper. Heavy curtains block the light coming from outside, and only a few rays manage to pass through the barrier.

"What happened to me last night?" I ask.

"You got mad at Tristan. Somehow managed a partial shift. Then you freaked out. Mom had to give you a sedative."

Closing my eyes for a moment, I pinch the bridge of my nose. Now I know why I feel hungover.

"You could have warned me of your presence before I took my clothes off."

"I'm sorry. I guess I dozed off. When I woke up, you were already naked."

I study Dante's face. I don't think he's lying. If that statement had come from Samuel, it would have been another story.

"Right. Well, it's not like you haven't seen me without my clothes anyway."

Dante eases back on the chair, rubbing his jaw. His hair is still as messy as I remember from last night, but he's sporting a five o'clock shadow now, too.

"You need to get over your issues with nakedness. Since our clothes don't magically appear and disappear when we shift, we often have to take them off in front of others. Trust me, nobody cares. It's a natural thing."

"Well, I haven't embraced the wolf life yet. It's only been a day. And I don't believe you guys don't stare."

"We don't. Believe me. We're used to it by now."

A crazy impulse takes over me. Deliberately dropping the sheet covering my upper body, I reveal my breasts to Dante. My nipples turn hard in an instant, but I'm not sure if it's just because of the cold air. "So, this does nothing for you?" I ask, voice low and sultry.

Dante's gaze drops to my chest, lingering there for a couple of beats. His Adam's apple bobs up and down, and I'm sure he's clenching his jaw. He's staring at my boobs all right. I made my point, so I should probably cover myself up again, but I'm loving that Dante is admiring my body. If only he would move from his chair and sit next to me, maybe even touch me a little, that would be great.

Wait? What? That random thought is what brings me back to reality. I pull the sheet up, berating myself for such stupidity. There's a low throbbing between my legs, and I'm afraid Dante can sense my desire from where he sits.

He clears his throat, dragging heat-filled eyes to my face. "Touché. I'm not immune, but it's because you're new. It'll wear off."

I can't help the feeling of disappointment. It's crazy, but I don't want Dante to stop admiring me. I don't know him, and I'm not even sure if I like him yet.

"Okay, besides not feeling embarrassed about taking my clothes off in front of strangers, what else do I need to know?"

"For starters, you need to respect the pack's hierarchy. Here, the alpha's word is law. Disobedience means you're challenging his authority, and that can lead to death."

"That's medieval. What about your mother?"

"She's the female alpha."

"What does that mean? Is it only a glorified title because she's married to the alpha? Does she actually have any authority?"

"No, it is not glorified. She's the female alpha by merit, by being the strongest female wolf in the pack and all. That's why she's the alpha's consort."

Dante's explanation gives me pause. It sounds like the way relationships work among wolves is a bit different than for humans. Or maybe not.

"So that means the alpha can only marry the strongest female wolf? What if he falls in love with someone else?"

"Love doesn't enter the equation."

I flatten my lips. Why does the lack of choice bother me so much?

"That sucks. Does the rule apply to all wolves or only the alpha? And can a wolf marry a human?"

Dante narrows his eyes. "No, the rule doesn't apply to all wolves, but I have never seen a beta hook up with an omega, for instance. The relationship wouldn't be balanced. But why do you ask about humans? Are you in lo—I mean, do you have a boyfriend or something?"

I almost laugh at Dante's question. I've only fallen in love once—or so I thought at the time.

"No." I don't elaborate, but my answer seems to mollify Dante. The frown on his forehead disappears, and he appears to be less tense.

"Good. Less complications."

"Does that mean it's not allowed?"

"I didn't say that, but relationships are usually complicated with someone from your own species. I've never heard of a relationship between a wolf and a human that worked out."

Now it's my turn to watch Dante through slits. "Don't lie to me. Your mother was human once. She told me."

Tilting his head to the side, he studies me. What is he looking for? Maybe he's trying to read my mind. *Shit, can he do that?*

"Did she also tell you that the percentage of humans who survive the shift is less than one percent?" he asks.

Dread drips down my spine. "No, she didn't. So, am I lucky to be alive?"

"Yes."

I'm speechless. With the whole wolf business, I ended up pushing aside the knowledge that I almost died in the woods. That rabid wolf would have killed me if Dante and his brothers hadn't showed up. The thought is sobering, and it puts my new reality into perspective. Heaviness sets on my chest, almost caving it in.

"Do you know who attacked me?" My voice is low, almost a whisper.

Dante stands up, then crosses the room to sit next to me. I wanted him to be closer, but I'm afraid now—not of him, but of how my body immediately reacts to his proximity. He grabs my hands, squeezes them together.

"I do, but what I tell you cannot leave this room."

Swallowing the sudden lump in my throat, I nod.

"I mean it, Red. You need to swear it out loud."

"I swear. I won't tell a soul."

Dante stares at me for a moment, and I forget how to breathe. I also study him—no, not study—openly admire him. Even under the scruff, I can see the perfection of his square jaw, but I mostly focus on his lips. What would it be like to kiss him? Shit. Why am I having all these lustful thoughts?

"You were attacked by a rogue wolf from another pack."

I blink a couple of times, not understanding why Dante is staring at me like the world is going to end.

"What happened to him?"

"He's dead. But that's not the issue. According to the law, a shifted human belongs to the pack of the wolf who turned them. That means you don't belong here, and we shouldn't even have helped you."

Suddenly, my blood turns ice cold. It's bad enough I'm something other than human, now Dante is saying I have to leave Crimson Hollow?

"What's going to happen to me then? Are you going to send me to this other pack?"

Dante touches my face with the tips of his fingers. "No, of course not."

"But you just said—"

"I know what I said, but just because the rules say one thing doesn't mean we have to follow them. There's a reason my mother sent us to the Irving Forest two nights ago. She knew you would be there. She also knew you would survive the attack. Red, you belong here with us."

The tenderness in Dante's voice makes me melt like butter under the sun. I cover his hand with mine, and lean against his palm. The air suddenly shifts around us. It becomes heavy, intoxicating. My breathing changes as my heart begins to gallop at full speed. I lean forward automatically, my body acting of its own accord.

Dante's posture also changes. He caresses my cheek with his

thumb while his gaze drops to my lips. He's going to kiss me, and I'm more than ready for it. I lick my lips in anticipation, but a loud knock on the door breaks our moment. Dante jumps off the bed as if he was electrocuted, then turns to the door.

"Who is it?"

"Is Sleeping Beauty up yet?"

Dante glances at me, whispering, "It's Sam. You might want to put your top back on."

My face feels as hot as lava. I get dressed in the blink of an eye. Only when I'm presentable does Dante open the door for his brother.

"What were you two whispering about?" Samuel looks from me to Dante.

"Nothing," we answer at the same time, sounding guilty as hell.

Samuel narrows his eyes. Yeah, he totally didn't buy our lie. "Whatever. Keep your secrets. I came to get Red."

"Get me for what?" I sense that whatever is coming, I'm not ready for it.

"To meet the rest of the pack, of course."

Yup. I'm definitely not ready for that.

CHAPTER 12

RED

"Don't look at me like that. I didn't say right this instant. We're going by your house first," Samuel says with a cheeky smile on his lips.

Relief rushes through my body. Maybe I won't have to meet the pack after all. Maybe I can convince Dante and Samuel to let me stay home with Grandma.

"Good. Let's go then."

"Is Tristan joining us?" Dante turns to Samuel.

"Nope."

Samuel walks out. When Dante and I don't follow him right away, he pivots toward us, waving impatiently as he says, "What are you waiting for?"

With hurried steps, I follow him, leaving Dante behind. He catches up quickly, and matches his steps to my own. The sexual tension between us still lingers, but now I'm mortified I let things go as far as they had. I flashed the guy for crying out loud. This is so not me.

Samuel takes the stairs two steps at a time. It's like he's running away from something. When we exit, the warm summer air greets my skin, promising another scorching day. It's the perfect time to go swimming at Lake Placid, and do absolutely nothing. But I'm afraid my worry-free days are over.

Samuel's car is parked in front of the house, the engine running. Boy, he's really in a hurry.

"Wait up," Dante says. "Why isn't Tristan joining us?"

"He's with Mom. We had a productive morning."

There's an extra meaning behind his words, but Samuel doesn't glance at Dante. I'm not sure if he's being obtuse on my account or if he's keeping things from Dante as well. But since I don't want to say anything to make him change his mind, I bite my tongue.

"He doesn't know we're going to Red's house right now, does he?" Dante asks.

"Nope. Now come on. I'd like to hit the road before he comes looking for us."

Grumbling, Dante opens the back door for me. I slide in quickly, not one bit disappointed that Mr. Asshole won't join us.

Dante takes the passenger seat, and Samuel peels off the curb before his brother has the chance to buckle his seat belt up. He really doesn't want Tristan to come, and that makes me curious. Now that we're already on our way, I risk a question.

"Is your brother always an asshole or is that honor only reserved for me?"

"Tristan? Yeah, he's an ass." Samuel chuckles.

"Is that why you don't want him to tag along?"

"One of the reasons, yeah." Samuel watches me through the rearview mirror, a smirk still in place on his lips.

"*One?* What's the other reason?"

He doesn't answer my question. Instead, he asks, "You go to the community college, right?"

I pinch my lips, not amused by his evasion tactic. However, the mention of college gives me something else to worry about.

"Yeah. Will I still be able to attend?"

"It depends," Dante says.

"On what?" My voice rises, coming out a little shrilly.

"On how fast you can master the wolf inside of you. We

can't risk exposure. Not everyone in Crimson Hollow knows about us."

"When you say us, are you referring only to shifters or are there other supernatural beings—such as vampires, for example?"

"Vampires are real, but we haven't seen one in Crimson Hollow since the Thirteen Days of Chaos," Samuel replies.

"What's that?"

"Uh, some shit that went down here twenty-five years ago. Let's not worry about that now," Dante replies. By his tone of voice, I can tell he really doesn't want to talk about it.

"Fine. What else is real?"

"It will be easier to tell you what is not real." Samuel laughs.

"Stop being obtuse. If I'm part of the community now, I need to know everything about it. The pack has rules, but are there other rules I should know about?"

"Only one rule—don't piss off the witches," Dante says.

"The witches?"

"Oh yeah, that's very important." Samuel nods. "Stay far away from Mayor Montgomery and her cronies. Nasty lady. She really doesn't like the pack."

"Wait, what? Crimson Hollow's mayor is a witch?"

"Yup. She's the head of the Midnight Lily Coven."

Biting my lower lip, I half turn to stare out the window. It seems there's an entire world that I know nothing about. "Are demons real?"

"You betcha," Samuel says.

"What about angels?"

When neither speak, I continue. "What? No angels? That's fucked up. Who's going to fight the bad guys?"

"We didn't say angels don't exist," Dante replies. "But we learned a long time ago not to count on them for anything."

"Yes, fuck angels. A bunch of selfish bastards," Samuel adds, sounding almost bitter.

I hold my head in my hands, groaning. This is too much.

"Hey, girlie. Are you all right back there?" Samuel looks at me through the rearview mirror again, his eyebrows furrowed in concern.

"No, I'm not okay. How would you feel if you found out all the monsters from your nightmares are real and worse, that you became one of them?"

"We aren't monsters. We're the good guys. Tell her, Dante."

"It's true. We're the good guys."

"Maybe you and Samuel are, but Mr. Asshole is most definitely not."

"Mr. Asshole? You mean Tristan?" Samuel asks.

"Yes, who else?"

Samuel throws his head back and laughs, a loud and infectious sound that makes me feel a little better. "I can't wait to start calling him that."

It turns out the wolves' compound is not too far from my grandmother's house, and we get there in less than fifteen minutes. I'm out of the car in a flash, calling her name before I even make it through the door.

Elliot barks in response, and I'm torn between hugging the furry ball or yelling at him for running away. The gold retriever jumps on me, licking my face. I laugh. As much as I'm mad at him, I'm glad he's okay.

"Ah, there you are," Grandma says.

Pushing the dog down, I stare at her. She's smiling at me, but there's also sadness in her eyes. I run into her arms, burying my face in the crook of her neck. "Grandma, I'm so glad to be home."

"I'm glad to see you, honey."

"I have so much to tell you." I ease back, fighting the tears that are forming in my eyes. I don't want to go back to the compound with Dante and Samuel. I don't want to be a wolf.

As if reading my mind, Grandma pats my hair. "It will be okay, honey. You can do this."

Her comment gives me pause. At the same time, a sliver of dread drips down my spine.

"Do you know?"

She nods, then looks over my shoulder. I turn, finding Samuel and Dante waiting by the door. Dante seems uncomfortable with his arms crossed behind his back, but Samuel's gaze takes in everything as if Grandma's house is an attraction or museum.

"Come on in, boys. I baked muffins, and there's fresh coffee in kitchen."

"Thank you, Mrs. Redford," Dante says.

I watch the two men disappear through the door that leads to the kitchen, and a strange feeling centers in my heart. It's like they belong here, which is insane. Grandma grabs my hand, then pulls me to the couch in front of the fireplace.

"I'm so sorry for worrying you, Grandma."

"Don't be silly, Red. I wasn't worried."

My back goes taut. Again, the feeling of unease takes hold. "What do you mean you weren't worried? I went out to search for Elliot, and I never came back."

"I knew you were okay."

"How?"

She takes a deep breath, her gaze going out of focus. "Dear child, I know I should have told you the truth a long time ago, but I wanted to give you at least a few years of normalcy."

I pull my hand from hers, feeling suddenly cold. "What truth?" I ask through clenched teeth.

"I'm a witch."

I have a moment of stunned silence, staring at Grandma without blinking. When I finally find my voice, it's to say, "What?"

"Don't be frightened, Red. It's not a bad thing."

Samuel and Dante's words come back to haunt me. "Are you part of the Midnight Lily Coven?"

Grandma narrows her eyes. "Who told you that?"

I cross my arms, watching her intently. "The Wolfe brothers did. Are you?"

"I was, yes. And so was their mother."

Unable to sit still any longer, I jump off the couch and start to pace. I grip my hair, twisting and pulling it, while my heart pounds at an increased pace inside my chest. "Am I a witch, too?"

"I sensed the power in you, but your destiny lies elsewhere."

A crazy suspicion sprouts in my mind. I stop mid-step, swinging around to face Grandma. "Did Elliot really run away?"

My heart sinks when I catch guilt in Grandma's eyes. She shakes her head, dropping her gaze to her lap. "No, he did not."

"You set me up!"

My outburst alerts Samuel and Dante, who hurry back into the living room. I ignore them.

"It was time. Your destiny was calling." Grandma lifts her chin again, determination etched on her face.

"Fuck destiny. I don't want to be a wolf!" Hot tears stream down my face. The sting of betrayal feels like a sharp knife twisting in my chest.

"You're more than a wolf, honey. You'll see that with time."

"I don't want to hear anything else." I open the front door in a brusque movement, coming face to face with the last person I want to see right now—Mr. Asshole. "What the hell are you doing here?"

He takes a good look at my red face and the tears, and I swear I catch worry in his stormy eyes.

"What happened?" he asks.

"None of your business." I try to sidestep him, but he blocks my way and holds my arm.

"I'm the beta. It is my business. Now spill."

I don't know if it's his arrogant tone or the fact he's in my face again, but his presence unleashes the beast in me... literally. My body aches as my muscles change, and the wild feeling takes control. Before the shift is even complete, I launch at Tristan, ready to tear him to pieces. He moves out of the way at the last second, and I land awkwardly on the ground. Spinning, I see that Dante and Samuel are outside, too.

"Red, calm down." Dante takes a step in my direction.

I don't want to calm down. Everything in my life seems to be a sham, a lie. I was betrayed by my own grandmother, for God's sake.

Dante takes another step forward with an outstretched arm. This time, his special soothing gift doesn't work on me. The anger is still swirling inside. I snarl at him, a warning. His eyes turn as round as saucers. He wasn't expecting that.

Then Tristan's voice gets in my head, but it's different somehow. *"Listen to what Dante says."*

When I turn to my right, I find a magnificent white wolf staring at me. It's the same wolf who saved me two nights ago. I know it in my bones. Tristan shifted.

"Get out of my head." I send the mental command, hoping the communication is both ways.

"Make me," he fires back.

My wolf growls at him.

"Now you see why you can't be trusted outside the compound on your own. You're a menace to this pack."

"Fuck you!"

Wrong thing to shout telepathically to Mr. Asshole in wolf form. He jumps on me, pushing me to the ground as if I were a stuffed puppy. His jaw locks around my throat, and his sharp teeth sink in the soft skin of my neck hard enough to deliver the message.

"Don't push me, Red. I'm the beta, and you're only a Shadow Creek mutt."

I may not be familiar with the history of the pack yet, but I know Mr. Asshole just insulted me.

"Get off me."

"Only if you ask nicely." His wolf growls.

"No."

Tristan applies more pressure to my throat, making a whimper escape my mouth.

"Tristan, come on. Let her go," Samuel says.

I should say *please*, but it seems my survival instincts are on the fritz. Instead, I do the last thing I should do in this situation—I change back into human. Tristan's weight is on top of me, his teeth on my throat. It feels ten thousand times worse in this fragile form. I read the surprise in Tristan's gaze right before he jumps off me.

"Red, are you okay?" Samuel is by my side in an instant, checking my throat.

Pushing him off, I sit up. "I'm fine."

A jacket materializes out of nowhere. When I look up, Grandma is there. Without a word, I take it from her, draping it over my shoulders. Movement on my peripheral catches my attention. Tristan is shifting back to human form as well. The transformation is fast, lasting no more than a few seconds. He glances at me, fury sparkling in his grey eyes. He doesn't seem to care he's standing completely naked in front of my grandmother.

"Don't ever pull a stunt like that again," he growls. "Do you hear me, Amelia?" He points a finger in my direction. If I were closer, I would break it off.

"If you think I'm going to take orders from you, you're sorely mistaken." Bold words for someone who had her ass handed to her, and is still shaking nonstop. I clearly have a death wish.

With a snarl, he takes a step forward, but Dante gets in his way, keeping him from me.

"Let it go, Tristan. Can't you see she's distressed?"

Samuel helps me up. "Come on, Red. Let's get your stuff, then head back to the compound."

I let him lead me back to the house, even though I want to go someplace far away from here. I don't even know if Grandma is truly sick or if that was a ploy to get me to move to Crimson Hollow. My parents were against the idea. At the time, I never understood why. Didn't Dad care about his mother? But maybe he knew the truth. No matter the angle I look at things, it's still a fucked-up situation.

Lost in my turmoil, I pack without thought, randomly throwing things in my duffel bag. Samuel follows all my movements like a hawk, as if he's afraid I'm going to do something stupid.

"Stop staring. It's creepy," I say.

"I'm sorry about everything, Red. I truly am."

"Right."

He touches my arm, freezing me on the spot. Heat spreads from where his hand rests, making me forget for a moment what just happened. I'm still naked, I realize, the jacket over my shoulders barely covering my breasts. Funnily enough, I don't care. I guess I'm already getting used to prancing around in my birthday suit.

"I meant it," he says. "And don't mind Tristan. He doesn't deal with change well. He'll come around."

"I really don't care about what Tristan thinks about me. But he'd better quit bossing me around."

"I never met any wolf able to stand their ground with Tristan like that. I mean, besides Dante and me. But we're betas, too. I think that's what's ticking Tristan off the most. You're a brand-new wolf, and you're not afraid of him."

I avert my gaze to hide the truth. To say I'm not afraid of Tristan is a lie. I was terrified—still am—but my anger spoke louder.

"One more reason for him to stop picking on me. I didn't ask to be changed into a wolf."

I stuff the last piece of clothing in my duffel bag, and zip it shut. Samuel grabs the strap, then hoists it up his shoulder. "That's all?"

I do a final glance over my room. I purposely left behind a few personal belongings—such as a framed picture of Grandma and me. "Yes, that's all."

On the way out, my eyes fall on the schoolbook under a pile of clothes. "Samuel, wait."

"What is it?"

Grabbing the book, I hold it against my chest. "Will I be

able to return to college?"

He grimaces before running a hand through his hair. "Shit, Red. I don't know. After what happened here, it will be hard to convince Dad to let you back into the human world so soon."

Taking a deep breath, I drop my head. I could argue, but I have no fight left in me. It seems I've spent it all on Mr. Asshole.

"Hey, don't look so sad. I'll think of something."

Samuel gives me a smile, but I can't reciprocate, not when I feel dead inside.

CHAPTER 13

RED

$\mathcal{O}$nce we return to the compound, I'm allowed time to myself. Mr. Asshole disappears as soon as Samuel parks the car. Dante and Samuel escort me to my room, which is the same one I spent the night in. Dante says I can change the decorations if I don't like it, but I don't want to get too comfortable. I don't plan on sticking around for long.

They don't linger, and I'm grateful for that. They must have sensed I'm not in the mood for small talk. Feeling lost, I sit on the edge of the bed and turn my phone on. There are several messages from Kenya asking where I am, along with a few missed calls from Peter. He left a voice mail, which I delete without listening to. Damn it. I'll probably need to quit my job.

I let out a heavy sigh, my shoulders sagging forward. So many changes, so many things I have to learn. But the worst part is not having anyone I can talk to about it all. Kenya is out of the question. I doubt I'll be allowed to breathe a word about shapeshifters and all the other inexplicable things happening in Crimson Hollow. Witches, vampires... what else is there?

I don't want Kenya to worry and demand her mother, the town's sheriff, to start a search party for me, so I text her and say I'm okay. She doesn't reply or call right away, which means she must not be up yet. Throwing my phone on the bed, I begin to unpack. When I catch my reflection in the mirror, I wince. I haven't showered in two days, and it shows. My hair is matted, stuck flat against my skull. My skin has a sickly hue to it, and the only color on my ashen face comes from the smears of dirt on my cheeks.

The guest room has a bathroom; Samuel showed me. After I grab a few items from my bag, I head for the shower. I'm glad I remembered to pack my favorite shampoo and conditioner, even through my haze. I wait until the water is scalding hot, my sore muscles needing the soothing relief. My body rejoices as I wash away all the grime with glee, but there's no hope for the hole in my chest. With a sob, I finally allow myself to drown in the sorrow. My crying jag is ugly and loud. It shakes my entire body, and I'm glad no one can hear me. The tears won't stop—not when I wash my hair twice, nor when I rub my arms and legs until they're raw. I only get out of the shower when the water turns cold. By then, my tears are finally dry.

Wrapped in towel, I return to my room. My phone is ringing, but it stops before I can get to it. Glancing at the screen, I see Kenya's name flashing on it. With a deep breath, I call her back. I might as well get this charade over with.

She answers on the first ring, "Red, finally! I've been trying to reach you for days."

"I'm sorry, Kenya. I've been busy."

"I can't believe you bailed Thursday night without saying goodbye. You suck."

"I texted you. Elliot had run away, and Grandma was worried." The lie feels bitter in my mouth, even if it's not mine.

"I know, I know. Did you find him?"

"Yup. He's good. It's all good."

"I'm glad, girlie. Too bad you had to leave the concert early, but it's not like you missed anything. Thirty minutes after you left, The Howlers stopped playing and Samuel took off. I was so disappointed."

Of course Samuel had to bail. He was busy saving me. I press the heel of my hand against my forehead, trying to suppress a headache that's beginning to brew again.

"I'm sure they'll reschedule," I say.

"They'd better. I paid to watch a two full hours of Mr. Delicious singing. I feel short-changed."

"You never told me Samuel Wolfe had two older brothers," I say, not meaning to sound accusatory, but managing to just the same.

"Hold up. You didn't know? The Wolfe triplets are legends. Granted, I rarely see Dante and Tristan in town. Dante is this enigmatic artist who almost never ventures out of his cave, and Tristan, well, he's too busy building his empire. I only see him when my mother forces me to attend town meetings."

"He's an asshole."

"Wait. When did you meet him?"

Shit. I said too much. "Uh, he came into the hardware store once."

"Tell me more." There's a new tone of interest in Kenya's voice. "He's so handsome, but I still prefer Samuel. That's who I'd pick to bang."

Jealousy hits me like a cannonball, and I suck in a startled breath. I don't want to picture Samuel hooking up with any girl, especially my best friend.

A knock on my door interrupts what I was going to say. "Red, are you ready to make new friends?"

It's Samuel. God, it's like he knew I was talking about him.

"Who's that?" Kenya asks.

"The TV. Sorry, Kenya, I have to go."

"Okay, then. I'll see you on Monday."

I end the call right before Samuel opens the door a tad and sticks his head in.

"Hey! Who told you to come in?" I hold the towel around me tighter.

"Oops. Sorry. When you didn't answer, I thought, well,

never mind. Get dressed. We don't want to leave the others waiting. Wolves are not patient by nature."

"Fine. Give me five minutes." Turning to my bag, I start to dig clothes out. "What should I wear?"

"Whatever you like. Jeans and a top is fine. This isn't a fancy occasion."

"Okay." I separate my favorite outfit from the pile—a pair of skinny jeans and a faded Ramones T-shirt. This was my laid-back Sunday style when I lived in Chicago.

Tossing a glance over my shoulder, I see that Samuel is still there. He's leaning casually against the dresser with his hands in his pockets. His low-rider jeans are pushed even lower thanks to that, showing a little bit of skin. Clenching my jaw, I force myself to look away. Why does the man have to be so irresistible?

"Aren't you going to wait outside?"

"Do you want me to? It's not like I haven't see you naked before." He chuckles.

With jerky movements, I pick up my clothes before striding into the bathroom. The snick of the lock is oddly satisfying.

"Aw, come on, Red. I was just teasing."

"Whatever. I'll be right out."

I get dressed as quickly as I can because even with the door separating us, I don't want to be naked for too long with Samuel nearby. It's stupid. He's seen me naked a bunch of times already in the last forty-eight hours, but he doesn't need to see how my traitorous body reacts to him. I want to ask someone if extra horniness is something all wolves experience, but the idea of breaching the subject to any of the brothers or worse, their mother, is embarrassing as hell. I guess I'll just have to ride it out.

Samuel stands straighter when I return to the room, his electric-blue eyes dropping to my bare feet and slowly traveling up the length of my body. Heat spreads across my cheeks as I try not squirm under his scrutiny. Glaring, I cross my arms in front of my chest.

"What?"

"You look good in anything, don't you?"

I snort. "Please. You don't need to keep throwing your rock-star charm my way. I'm not going to try to run away again."

He raises an eyebrow, the corners of his lips twitching upward. "I can't help it. It comes with the package."

Rolling my eyes, I put on my slippers. "I'm ready."

Samuel opens the door, then motions with his arm. "Ladies first."

I barely set foot in the hallway before Dante comes running up the stairs. "There you are. Everyone is already waiting for you."

I nod as I try to control the crazy butterflies that are suddenly creating havoc in my belly. My hands are sweaty by the time we end up outside the alpha's manor. The Wolfe brothers remain silent as we make our way to the square between the main house and another large building. A lump forms in my throat when I see the gathering waiting for me. There must be around thirty people, and they all turn in my direction when I approach the assembly.

Suddenly feeling like an intruder, I don't make eye contact with any of them. Instead, I keep my eyes trained on the gazebo where Dr. Mervina stands with Tristan by her side. My gaze lingers on him despite everything he has put me through. He changed into casual clothes—a pair of dark jeans and a polo shirt—but even so, he seems more polished than his brothers. It must be his arrogant expression. He senses my stare and turns to me, not breaking the connection until I go up the steps to stand next to his mother.

The silence is so absolute I could hear a pin drop.

"Thanks for coming on such short notice. I appreciate it," Dr. Mervina says. Her voice is clear and full of authority. "As I mentioned in the previous assembly, our pack acquired a new member. Please meet Amelia Redford."

Murmurs carry through the crowd, and Dr. Mervina waits until it dies down.

"How is that possible?" someone asks, a man with a bushy beard and salt-and-pepper hair.

"A lone wolf attacked Amelia two nights ago, as I explained earlier. She was lucky the betas were near the area and prevented the worst."

"She doesn't belong here." It's a beautiful brunette who spoke, her sharp gaze cutting straight through me. My spine goes taut as I take in the full blast of her animosity.

"Lyria, shut your mouth," a blond man says, earning a glare from her.

"Bite me, Seth. You know the rules. She belongs to whoever infected her."

I bristle immediately, opening my mouth to rebuff that statement. Dante places a hand on my arm, giving a minute shake of his head.

"There are no rules when the wolf is a loner. Since she was rescued by this pack, she'll stay with us," Dr. Mervina says, her face devoid of any emotion.

"You said she was attacked two nights ago," another man speaks. "Shouldn't she still be in bed recovering?"

"Amelia's transformation is complete," Dr. Mervina replies evenly.

"What? That's impossible," someone far back in the crowd says. "It takes weeks for the human body to assimilate to the virus."

"Yes, that's usually the case. Amelia is an exception."

With a snarl, the woman named Lyria takes a step forward. "If that's the case, then I think she should shift for us."

Stomach dropping, I glance at Dante, panicked. Nobody said anything about shifting in front of all these people.

"It's up to Amelia." Dr. Mervina raises an eyebrow in my direction.

I shift my weight from foot to foot, wriggling my fingers. The two times I shifted, I was angry. I don't know if I can do it on demand like that. What if I can't?

Samuel places a hand on my lower back, leaning in close.

"Don't stress about it. You can do it."

"I'm not so sure about that. What will happen if I refuse?" I whisper.

"Don't refuse."

Great. I get the message loud and clear. If I say no, bad things will happen.

"What's the matter, blondie? Are you afraid?" Lyria sneers, a glint of arrogance in her eyes. Swinging her gaze to Tristan, she licks her lips.

Ah, now I understand where her nastiness is coming from. She must have the hots for Mr. Asshole and thinks I'm a threat.

I don't reply to her comment. Closing my eyes, I try to remember what I felt the times I shifted. I wish I had asked more questions about the process. I'm going blind here. Dante's voice speaks in my head, making me gasp.

"You can do this, Red. Focus on the wolf's essence."

"How are you doing this?" I ask.

"What?"

"Speaking to my mind. I thought it only worked in wolf form."

"To most, yes. But I'm different. Now focus."

I do as he says, turning my awareness inward. At first, I feel nothing different. Nervous sweat breaks on my forehead. I'm too conscious of the crowd watching me, waiting for me to fail. Someone snickers, and I know it's that odious woman. Anger builds, and that's when I feel the wolf inside me stir. It's only a slow unfurling of warmth in my chest until it suddenly becomes a ball of swirling energy in my core. I can't believe I didn't sense it before. It's suddenly all I can feel.

I imagine my muscles changing, taking the shape of the animal, and then it happens. The pain comes first, sharp and fast. But this time, I'm prepared for it, so I'm able to ride it out without whimpering like a fool. My gums ache as my canines elongate, blood pooling in my mouth. I wonder if I'll bleed every time. When I hear fabric ripping, I drop to my knees. Shit, I forgot to take off my clothes. I can't believe I ruined my favorite outfit. Sadness overwhelms me for a split second, but then a shiver runs down my spine. The wolf's wild emotions erupt like a geyser, taking me over.

When I open my eyes again, the assembly stares at me in bewilderment. Well, everyone except Lyria. She sheds her clothes and shifts as well, changing into a beautiful black wolf. If she was savage as human, I bet she's ten times worse as a wolf.

She enters my mind with ease, but her presence there feels more like an invasion.

"Not bad for a noob. Let's see how you handle a run with the pack."

Lifting her snout, she howls, her call followed by several others. Half the pack members have shifted already, including Tristan, Dante, and Samuel.

I guess I'm running with the wolves. I never thought I'd say that.

Tristan takes the lead, followed by Samuel. Dante stops next to me, then nudges me with his nose. *"Come on, let's go. It'll be fun."*

Without waiting for me, he takes off. I sprint after them, but they're faster. Soon, I fall behind. It feels strange to be running on four legs. The group veers toward the forest surrounding the compound, but I get distracted by everything. With enhanced sensorial skills, little noises and faint smells are amplified. I don't know the way, so I have to be careful where I step.

From my peripheral, I catch a glimpse of a small grey wolf. He slows down just a fraction to let me catch up with him. He barks like I'm supposed to understand what he's saying. Maybe I will eventually learn to speak wolf. He shakes his head as other wolves join us.

A dark brown one hits my companion on his side, making him fall with a whine. Slowing, I look over my shoulder. If that's wolf's play, it's a little rough. The grey wolf gets up, shaking his head. He doesn't seem hurt.

Movement to my right catches my attention. I have a new companion next to me—Lyria. Before I have time to understand what's happening, she jumps on me. She tries to bite my shoulder, but I manage to avoid her attack as I fall.

Adrenaline kicks in. I spring to my feet before she can get to me again. She snarls as she approaches, her unfriendly intentions clear. Other wolves join her, and instinct tells me to flee. I back away as they advance. When my rear paws begin to slide, I realize I'm on the edge of a precipice. There's nowhere to go. *Where are Dante and Samuel?* I'm all alone, facing a jealous, mean wolf and her posse. This is clearly an ambush.

I jump to my left as Lyria pounces again. She misses me by a hair, but one of her friends gets me. Claws scratch my side. I try to defend myself, but I'm outnumbered. Fear like I've never known freezes me. Even when I see an opening, I don't run away. I drop to the ground instead, covering my face with my paws. I should be fighting back. Heck, I was able to go against Tristan for crying out loud. Why can't I stand up to Lyria and her friends?

"Red, what are you doing? Get up," Samuel says inside my head.

Lifting my head, I spot him farther away, outside the circle of wolves taunting me. Tristan and Dante are next to him.

"I can't."

"She's pathetic. What a poor excuse for a wolf." It's a woman's voice in my head now, and my guess is it's the odious Lyria.

"Get out of my head!"

Her laughter fills my head, then she shoves me back to the ground when I try to get up. Snarling, she snaps at my throat, clamping her jaw against the sensitive skin. *"What are you going to do now, Amelia?"*

I don't move. Don't answer.

My head begins to throb right before all my muscles cramp up. A loud whine escapes me as the wave of pain renders me useless. Without meaning to, I begin the shift back. It's only then that she lets go. My fingers curl around the rough ground, dirt getting under my nails as I fight to get air in. Tentatively lifting my eyes, I realize I'm the only one who has shifted back. At least the wolves are no longer attacking me. Lyria turns to Tristan, and I'm sure they're communicating telepathically. Tears of shame form in my eyes, but I manage to keep them from spilling. Crying in front of this crowd would be the cherry on the top of this humiliation cake.

Tristan's wolf howls, and the other wolves answer him. He glances my way for a split second before turning and taking off. All the other wolves do the same, including Dante and Samuel. *What the hell!* Did they just leave me behind?

I don't notice I'm not completely alone until the small grey wolf from before nudges my shoulder with his nose. I shrink back, not knowing what he wants from me. His frame begins to shake until he changes into a young man.

"Why didn't you leave?" I ask.

He shrugs. "I know what it feels like to be picked on by the others. I tried to warn you by the way, but I couldn't get into your head."

"So not everyone can do that?"

"If you keep the barrier to your channel up, only the alpha can."

I open my mouth to say the triplets are also able to invade my thoughts, but I don't know if I had my barrier up with them or not. Better not to say anything.

"I'm Billy." He extends his hand, and I shake it. Never mind that we're both naked.

"My name is Amelia, but you can call me Red."

He raises an eyebrow, the corners of lips twitching upward. "Red?"

"It's short for Redford, my last name."

"Gotcha. Well, we'd better head back. I'm in enough trouble as it is for not going with the others."

"Doesn't anyone have free will in this pack?"

"Of course, but there are certain rules we must follow. You'll learn soon enough now that your place in the pack has been established."

"My place in the pack? What do you mean?"

"That was what this run was all about—to test you."

"So you mean Lyria didn't really want to kill me?"

Billy laughs. "I don't know. Maybe she did think you were a threat to her spot as the beta. But now she won't bother you as much anymore."

"Why is that?"

"Well, now there's no way in hell you can compete to be Tristan's mate."

Crossing my arms, I frown at the kid. "I have zero interest in that jerk."

"The point is moot anyway. You can't hook up with him or the other betas; not being an omega and all."

A shiver runs down my spine as I intuitively realize being an omega is not something I'm going to like.

"Isn't the omega at the bottom of the wolf's hierarchy?"

"Yep."

"What does that entail exactly?"

"Let's see. You have to put up with taunts from everyone. You get assigned the worst jobs. You're pretty much a glorified punching bag. It's peachy." He gives me sardonic smile.

"Fuck that. I don't want to be the omega."

"Not *the* omega, *an* omega. I'm your counterpart. Anyway, you don't have a choice. You were tested, and you folded like a house of cards. You're an omega whether you like it or not."

Shaking with anger, I stand. Billy's eyes drop to my chest, but I don't care if he's checking me out or not.

"We'll see about that," I say through clenched teeth.

Swinging around, I veer in the opposite direction of the compound. As angry as I am at Grandma, there's no way in hell I'm going back to the pack to be bullied daily. I didn't sign up for that.

My decision flashes in my head as clear as day. I'm going

home.

Back to Chicago.

CHAPTER 14
DANTE

"This is all your fault, Tristan!" I glare at my brother.

"How is this my fault? I couldn't stop Amelia from going on the run."

"You know very well the only reason Lyria challenged Red to it is because of you. You should have never encouraged her advances if you didn't want to mate with her."

"That's not your damn business, Dante!"

"It is my business. You're not the only beta in the pack."

Tristan folds his arms, glaring at me. "Oh, now we're getting to the bottom of this. You're jealous Lyria picked me over you."

I roll my eyes, something I rarely do, but this warrants it. "I wouldn't touch that woman with a ten-foot pole. She's mean and conniving, not exactly qualities I look for in a mate."

"So you prefer them blonde and foolish?"

Sam gets in between us with arms raised. "For fuck's sake, will you two stop fighting over this? The run is over; Red survived. End of story."

"End of story? She probably hates our guts right now. Never mind that Tristan decided to abandon her in the forest."

"What did you want me to do? Shift back and carry her in my arms? *That* would send the right message to the pack."

I don't miss Tristan's sarcastic tone. Pinching the bridge

of my nose, I walk to the window of his office and let my thoughts wander. We came here after the wolves were dismissed. Mom was nowhere to be found, but I'm sure by now she knows about Red. As much as I'd like to give Tristan more grief for his decision, he really didn't have a choice. If any of us had protected Red, it would have messed with the balance of the pack. Our hierarchy is what binds us together; any disturbance in its harmony can be fatal.

A knock on the door has my attention. Sam answers it. In comes Billy, seeming a little paler than usual. He's Seth's younger brother. In spite of him being the pack's male omega, I like him way more than I do Tristan's best friend.

"You stayed behind." It's the first thing out of Tristan's mouth.

"Yes, I felt like I had to."

I expect my brother to give the young kid a tongue lashing. Instead, he just nods. Billy's actions today earned him more points in my book than he'll ever know. He disobeyed Tristan's command to comfort a fellow wolf. That takes character and courage.

"How is she?" Sam and I ask at the same time.

"Uh, well, I don't know." He drops his gaze, scratching the back of his neck.

"What do you mean?" Tristan takes a step forward, and the kid seems to shrink.

"I told her she was an omega."

"And?" Sam makes a motion with his hand.

"And I explained to her what that was like. She wasn't happy with the news."

"Where is she now? Back in her room?" I make a motion for the door.

"No. That's why I'm here. She took off."

I trade a glance with Sam, knowing exactly what's going through his mind. Red ran away again. My hands curl into fists by my side, but not because I'm angry at her. I'm angry at myself for not explaining things to her better. Maybe I should have asked Mom to postpone Red's introduction to the pack, get her used to the wolf life first. But I was too eager to discover what Red meant to us. I hadn't foreseen Lyria's challenge.

"She must have gone back to her grandma's place," Sam says.

"Can I help?" Billy asks as we start to leave

I tap him on the shoulder. "No, Billy. We got it from here, but let's keep this between us."

"Yeah, of course. I won't tell a soul."

No one argues when Tristan jumps into his truck. It's parked closest to the manor, and time is of the essence. It won't bode well for Red if the pack discovers she bailed. They'll see it as another weakness, and make her life even more difficult than it's already going to be. Wolf life is savage.

It doesn't take us long to arrive at Mrs. Redford's old chalet in the middle of the woods. At first, I thought it was a peculiar location for a sickly woman to live, but now that I know who she really is, it's not so strange. She defied the Midnight Lily Coven by leaving their midst. It makes sense she doesn't want to bump into Mayor Montgomery or the other members of the coven too often. We wolves have our hard rules, and we're considered wild and unpredictable by the rest of the supe community, but at least we have honor. I'm not sure the same can be said about the witches.

"Let me speak with Red first," Sam says as he opens the door.

"Why you?" I ask.

"Because she's knows me from before. Besides, my power of persuasion is better than yours."

Tristan lets out a growl. "You mean your power to make women drop their panties for you?"

Sam places a hand over his heart, faking a shocked expression. "Take your mind out of the gutter, will you? Not everything is about sex."

"With you, everything is about sex." I look out the window

toward the house.

The door opens, and Red comes out carrying a large suitcase. Her hair is pulled up in a ponytail, and she's dressed in jeans, a simple top, and sneakers. She's leaving town. I'm out of the car before Sam, breaching the distance between Red and me.

Her eyebrows shoot to the heavens before furrowing into a scowl. "Don't even try to stop me."

"Where are you going?"

"Back home. There's nothing keeping me here anymore."

"And where is home?" I ask.

"You're going back to Chicago," Sam says from beside me, his stance way more relaxed than mine. He does think he can convince Red to stay without breaking a sweat.

"How did you know—never mind. I'm leaving."

"No, you're not." Tristan jumps into the discussion with his usual Neanderthal finesse.

"Try to stop me. I have the sheriff's number on speed dial. I'd love to give her a call."

Tristan a takes a step forward. "Go ahead. Do it. She'll be the first person to hand you over to the pack if you try to cross the border."

"What?" Red's face goes even paler.

"She knows about us, Red," Sam explains.

Red curls her hand tighter around her purse's strap, her eyes widening. "Why? Is she also supernatural?"

"Her family was one of the first settlers here. The knowledge has been passed down through the generations," I chime in.

"Does Kenya know, too?"

"I'm not sure. If she doesn't, my guess is her mother's waiting for the right time to tell her."

Red covers her face with her hand. "I'm not going back to the compound."

Her tone is no longer defiant; it's weak.

"You have to, Red. Maybe once you learn to master the wolf, you can move back here."

She cocks her head at me, blue eyes blazing. "Billy told me

what it means to be an omega. I didn't sign up for a lifetime of bullying."

"Did he also explain to you the vital role omegas play?" I ask.

"I don't care!"

Tristan moves again. From his body language, I can tell he's on the verge of throwing Red over his shoulder and carrying her away. But the sound of an approaching vehicle stops him in his tracks. Red peers into the distance. When the car finally comes into view, she lets out a curse.

"Who is that?" Sam asks, moving closer to her.

"My coworker."

A young man steps out of the car. He's wearing some type of uniform—khaki pants and a navy-blue polo shirt. He quickly glances at the three of us before staring at Red. "Is everything okay here?" His gaze drops to her suitcase. "Where are you going?"

"Uh, I'm going to—"

"She's moving in with us," Sam answers, earning a glare from Red.

Her friend's spine goes taut. He glances at Tristan, and I'm not sure what he sees in my brother's expression, but the guy is suspicious for sure now. Goddamn it. We really don't need a stupid, curious human poking around.

I turn to Red, taking note of the flush on her cheeks and the hard set of her jaw. I don't need my abilities to guess what's on the tip of her tongue. But by some miracle—or maybe it's the wolf's self-preservation instincts in her—she doesn't call Sam on what she perceives as a lie. To be certain she won't say anything compromising, I reach out to her mind, prying open the natural barrier she has there. It's much easier to speak to her in wolf form, but I need to communicate with her fast.

"Think carefully about what you're going to say, Red. Your friend doesn't know supernatural beings exist. There's more at stake here than your wishes."

"Are you going to hurt Pete if I tell him I don't want to go

with you?"

"I'm not. But I can't answer for Tristan."

"You're all vile people." Switching her attention to her friend, she replies out loud. "Dr. Mervina hired me to help at the ranch. I'm just going to stay there for a few weeks."

"Wait. You took another job? What about the hardware store?"

The guy appears genuinely upset, but I sense there's more to it than merely losing a coworker. He's in love with Red. It's obvious in the way he looks at her, and I can also smell it in his scent.

"I only work there twice a week. I can do both," she replies.

"Oh, okay. Well, I came by to ask if you wanted to go to the movies with me since you weren't answering your phone."

Red shifts from foot to foot, the muscles on her face becoming a little tense. She doesn't care for the guy, not like a lover would. The knowledge gives me pleasure… way too much pleasure.

"Ah, yeah, sorry about that. It's been a crazy couple of days. But as you can see, I'm busy today. We'll talk later, okay?"

Red's friend can't hide his disappointment, and I kind of feel bad for him. Not that I know anything about unrequited love, but I suppose it must suck. He gets in his car with hunched shoulders, then drives off.

"Boy, that was brutal. You shouldn't lead that guy on, Red," Sam says with a laugh.

"I'm not leading Peter on. And that's none of your business anyway."

"All right, let's get moving." Tristan motions with his hand, pointing at his car.

"I never said I was coming with you. I don't want to be an omega."

Tristan surveys her, an arrogant glint in his eyes. "If you don't want the title, you'd better step up your game."

He enters the car without a second glance back.

"Has he always been this much of an insufferable ass?" Red

asks.

"Oh, yeah, always," I say.

"And what does he mean about stepping up my game? Can I cease being an omega?" She turns to me with such hopeful eyes that I don't have the heart to tell her it will be almost impossible to accomplish that.

"It's complicated, but it can be done."

CHAPTER 15

RED

I still haven't wrapped my head around Kenya's mother knowing about the shifters, the witches, and everything else in between this effing weirdo village as I head to the compound's mess hall, flanked by Dante, Samuel, and Tristan, aka my captors. The open space, a rustic barn-like building with a domed ceiling and exposed wooden beams, is packed to the max. Long picnic tables are occupied by a loud group of shifters, but once our presence is acknowledged, the conversations cease abruptly. Everyone turns to stare at us, or more precisely at me. The newest omega. No, bitterness doesn't pool in my mouth when I think about what that term means.

I spot that bitch Lyria right away, and the humiliation she put me through tinges my gaze crimson. She smirks at me, basking in my faster-than-lightning descent in the pack's rank. A low growl rumbles, and I belatedly realize it's coming from me. A touch on my lower back catches my attention. Cutting my eyes to my right, I see Dante. His hand doesn't linger, though, but his voice echoes in my mind.

"You don't want to challenge Lyria, at least not until you have a chance of winning the fight. If you do, she has grounds to kill you... and we won't be able to stop it."

I swallow the huge lump that has formed in my throat, but

I'm not sure if it's fear or anger that's squeezing my chest tight and giving me this bout of apprehension. Tristan and Samuel walk ahead of me, making a beeline for the table where Lyria sits. Dr. Mervina is there as well. So, that's where the cool kids in the pack sit. *Fuck them.* Dante throws me an apologetic glance before he follows his brothers. What—does he think I want to sit over there with the bitch who tried to kill me? He's out of his mind.

Conversations resume. Now that the betas have deserted me, the rest of the pack is no longer interested in me. I'm nothing more than a lowly omega after all. I search the perimeter, looking for my counterpart. I find Billy sitting at a table in a far corner of the room. Alone, he's hunched forward as he eats his meal quietly.

After I grab a tray, I put random food on it. My mind is racing, and I honestly don't think I'll be able to eat anything. But right now, I'm more interested in blending in and learning from observation. Dante's comment that I can change my status in the hierarchy of the pack is forefront in my mind. He never really gave me details on how I can do that, but by the little I've seen, I can guess it will be bloody and maybe even deadly.

Billy looks up when I sit next to him. He smiles before whispering, "I'm glad you're back."

"Not by choice," I reply through clenched teeth.

"It's gonna get better. I promise you."

"You can't make that promise. You've been a wolf your entire life. You have no idea what's like to go from a regular human to this."

"You make it sound like a curse." He puts his fork and knife down, appraising me. "The fact you were able to survive the shift and go through the process so quickly tells me you weren't a regular human at all."

I narrow my eyes, suspicious now. Does he know my grandmother is a witch? "What do you know?"

With a shrug, he resumes eating. "I'm an omega, but I'm

not stupid. Plus, I love to read. I probably know more about the pack's history than the alpha himself."

My spine goes taut as my interest is piqued. "Really? I'd love to get familiar with it as well."

"That's a smart move. As an outsider, you're at a serious disadvantage."

I open my mouth to ask Billy more questions, but feel a presence looming in front of our table. There are two teens smirking at us, and dread drips down my back. I know by their mean looks that they're up to no good.

"Hey, Billy. Give me that pie," the tallest says.

"Why? You hate chocolate." Billy leans back, his expression one of boredom.

"Give me the fucking pie, Billy."

With a sigh, Billy begins to push the plate across the table. I snap out my arm to hold his wrist, stopping him.

"Don't talk to him like that. You want pie? Get your own." My voice is cold and tight.

The kid turns to me with mouth slightly open, but the surprise only lasts a split second before a sneer twists his face into an ugly mask.

"Who the hell do you think you are talking to me like that, mutt?"

I was never one to take shit from anybody—the fact I let Lyria make me cower is still an event I'm trying to understand—but right now, I'm not getting lip-serviced by a pimple-covered punk. Placing both hands on the table, I stand slowly.

"I'm not a mutt, and I won't tolerate that kind of bullshit in front of me."

"You are an omega. You can't talk to him like that," the younger teen says.

"I'm not a fucking omega. I'm Amelia Redford."

"She has no respect for the pack," a man sitting at the table next to us says. Murmurs of agreement follow his statement.

"Then it's time we teach her a lesson." A redheaded chick stands up, then marches toward me.

I saunter around the table while curling my hands into fists. I've never once took martial arts or self-defense lessons, but I'm hoping the action movies I've watched will help. My wolf is churning inside my chest, its savagery pumping into my veins. I'm braced for the fight that's sure to come when a booming voice echoes in the mess hall, freezing me to the spot.

"Enough!"

The redhead stops in her track as well, lowering the arm that was poised to strike me.

A tall man with massive shoulders and a neck as thick as a tree trunk strides into the room. His hair is silvery, but his face is too similar to Tristan's to not clue me in that the alpha has just arrived. Even if there wasn't any resemblance, it would be impossible not to guess his status. The man oozes power. As he walks in my direction, I have to lock my knees tight to avoid my legs from giving out under me. His scrutinizing gaze makes my entire body shake. The redhead moves out of the way, all aggression gone from her stance as she lowers her gaze to the floor.

The alpha stops in front of me. Every instinct I have is shouting I should look down. But I can't... and it's not because I'm defying him. I'm paralyzed.

"So, you're the reason I was called home."

I don't know what to say, so I just remain quiet.

Dr. Mervina joins her husband, but her presence is neither comforting or antagonizing. I'm sure what I did was completely unacceptable by their standards, but I couldn't help myself.

"This Amelia Redford, Wendy's granddaughter."

"That explains the rebellious nature," the alpha says, his voice still very much cold.

I frown, not knowing where he's going with this. It doesn't sound like he's angry at me, though.

"So, you're not happy with your lot as the newest omega, is that right?" he asks.

My tongue is dry and stuck to my mouth, but I somehow find a way to reply. "No, sir."

He nods. "I accept your challenge. You and Rochelle will fight tomorrow at dawn."

"What?" The redheaded chick lifts her head.

The alpha turns to her, his jaw clenched hard. "You heard me. The omega didn't yield to you. You know the rules."

The woman drops her gaze and mumbles, "Yes, Alpha."

The man swings around with Dr. Mervina by his side. It's only when he leaves the mess hall that I turn to Billy.

"What just happened?"

"You fool. You challenged another wolf, someone who is much stronger than you."

Folding my arms, I watch Billy through a narrowed gaze. "What was I supposed to do? Sit meekly in my corner and let her do whatever she pleased with me?"

"Yes, that's exactly what you were supposed to do."

"I'm not a doormat!"

Billy shakes his head, laughing without humor. "Doormat… you don't know what you're talking about."

"Oh, really? In my world, it makes you a doormat when you let bullies do as they please with you."

"You're not in your world anymore. You know what? I don't care what you do. Just stay out of my business."

Billy shoves the chocolate pie plate into his tormentor's hand, then strides out of the hall.

Fuck, what the hell did I do wrong?

CHAPTER 16
DANTE

"Dad, you can't let Red fight Rochelle. She's not ready," I say.

From behind his mahogany desk, our father leans back on his leather chair, folding his hands together. "She should have thought about it before she openly challenged the enforcer."

"She didn't know any better."

"It doesn't matter."

I turn to Sam and Tristan. "Help me out here?"

Sam shrugs. "I think you're making a big deal out of this. Red can handle Rochelle."

"She's one of our best enforcers!" I throw my hands in the air.

"It will serve the woman well to lose the challenge to Rochelle. If she weren't so busy fighting the inevitable and trying to run away, maybe she would have learned a thing or two about what it means to be a wolf." Tristan crosses his legs, leaning against the wall with his hands in his pockets. He's not fooling anyone with the casual stance. I can see the tension emanating from his frame in waves.

"Your concern for the omega is troubling, Dante. You know very well we can't bend the rules to benefit one individual. Amelia will fight Rochelle, and you will not interfere." Dad pierces me with his alpha stare, and any retort dies on my lips.

"Now, we have more pressing matters to discuss. Tell me everything you know about the Shadow Creek rogue and the device you found on him."

Tristan stands straighter, while Sam switches his weight from foot to foot.

"It seems the device was used to control the rogue," Tristan replies.

Dad leans back, his eyes narrowing to slits. "Is that the opinion of an expert?"

Samuel and Tristan exchange a glance before Sam answers, "The guy who works at the hardware store."

I see the change in my father immediately. His shoulders tense as he rests his elbows on the desk, linking his hands together. "I need more than the word of an amateur to look further into this matter. I don't need to remind you how tense our relationship with the Shadow Creek pack is. One wrong move on either part, and we'll have enough bloodshed to mirror the Thirteen Days of Chaos."

A shiver runs down my spine. We were born right after the event that almost tore Crimson Hollow apart. A portal to a hellish dimension was opened, and what came through it was worse than any nightmarish creature residing in our peculiar town.

"And now that Montgomery has gotten involved..." Dad continues.

"Wait. What does that witch have to do with anything?" Tristan takes a step forward, his face twisting into an angry scowl.

"She's backing the claim that the new Wolfe Construction's development land belongs to the Shadow Creek pack."

"What? That fucking bitch!" Tristan balls his hands into fists, starting to pace. "I knew she was planning something foul. I knew it!"

"Their claim is without merit, but she's going with it because I refused to endorse her run for re-election."

"You've never endorsed her before. Why is she pissed that

you refused now?" I ask.

"Because she's lost support from a number of factions in the community, and she needs me." Dad's gaze turns inward as he stares at point on the wall. "I can't support her. We need fresh blood in the office. Montgomery hasn't had the best interest of the supe community in years."

A dark cloud descends upon us. I can't speak for my brothers or my father, but my biggest concern right now is Red. I understand the need to discover if the Shadow Creek wolves are up to no good, as well as put a stop to Mayor Montgomery's nefarious plans, but to me, Red's imminent fight with Rochelle trumps all other problems.

"I'd like to train Red for her challenge," I say after a minute of impenetrable silence.

My father cuts me a glance so glacial it's almost impossible to maintain eye contact with him. All my wolf instincts are screaming for me to lower my gaze, but if I do, I can forget getting permission to help Red. So for her sake, I'll openly challenge the alpha.

"That will disrupt the balance in the pack. Betas have no business showing preference to omegas."

"I don't think Red is a true omega. Her actions today and the fact she was able to challenge Tristan without fear proves that." I catch Tristan shifting where he stands from the corner of my eye, but he doesn't contradict me. Maybe his ego is sore that he couldn't scare the shit out of a newly turned wolf.

Dad keeps scrutinizing me, but at least he dialed the alpha stare down a notch. I open my mouth to continue my argument, but Sam beats me to the punch.

"We failed Red. She was a regular human only three days ago. We never really let her accept her new reality before we introduced her to the pack. Did you throw Mom to the wolves as soon as she shifted, or did you prepare her?"

Dad's eyebrows soften at the mere mention of his mate. "Your mother was a different case. She already knew about us before she chose this life."

The realization hits Dad all at once. He loses the tightness around his mouth and his shoulders sag a little. He just made my case, and I'm sure it wasn't his intention. He's silent for a couple of beats, shifting his gaze from each one of us before contemplating the wall behind me. My guess is that he's weighting the pros and cons in his head before giving his final decision.

"You may explain things to Red in the privacy of her room. No practical lessons out in the forest. I don't want word to get out that you're assisting her in any capacity."

Fuck. How am I supposed to train Red to fight Rochelle if we're constrained to her room?

"Can I train her in my studio? It's bigger and secluded enough. No one ever goes up the mountain."

"You're pushing it, Dante. Be prepared to face the consequences if anyone finds out."

"I'll be careful. May I be excused? I'd like to start now. We don't have much time."

Dad nods once before asking to see the device we found on the rogue wolf. I make my leave as quickly as I can, catching the look of incredulity in both my brothers' gazes as I do so. I'm glad I wasn't present when Sam and Tristan paid a visit to the hardware store. My father would for sure request that I stay if I had.

I stride toward Red's room with a sense of urgency. I'm not sure in what state of mind I'm going to find her. Before I knock on her door, I hesitate, focusing on my enhanced hearing. It's not as powerful as it would be in wolf form, but it's more acute than human senses.

Dead silence. Is she even in her room?

I knock on the door. "Red? Are you there?"

"Go away, Dante."

"Please, can come in?"

"I don't want to talk to anyone."

I rub my face, feeling frustrated. It seems I've lost the little trust I gained with her. "I want to talk about your challenge."

She doesn't reply this time, but then soft footsteps pad on the carpeted floor before the door swings open. Red's face is flushed, her eyes puffy and red. She's been crying, and my guilt expands until it's all I can feel in my chest.

"What about the challenge?" she asks.

I don't want to talk about it here in the hallway. Even though this is the alpha's private home, we never know who is around.

"Fancy going for a walk? I'd like to show you my studio."

Narrowing her eyes, she crosses her arms in front of her chest. "I have zero interest in seeing your studio. Why don't you just spill what you have to say already and go?"

There she goes again, defying another wolf without fear. Her attitude makes my blood pump faster, and the desire to touch her, mark her in a way only an imprinted wolf can, is almost overwhelming. I take a step closer, invading her space, then lean down until my lips are inches from hers. Red's breathing hitches as her mouth parts with a gasp.

"I'm here to help you, Red. You have to believe me," I whisper, then ease back. Being this close to her is giving me way too many ideas, the wrong kind, and I'm not here to start anything with her, no matter how badly my body wants to.

She's still looking at me with distrust in her eyes, so I continue. "You're unprepared for your fight with Rochelle. You say you don't want to be an omega, but you have to earn the pack's respect. Losing terribly to one of our best enforcers will not accomplish that."

"You say it like losing is inevitable."

"Would you prefer if I lied to you? You've only been a wolf for three days, and you haven't managed a shift without the use of anger to push you through. The chances you'll be victorious tomorrow are almost nonexistent."

"Then why is your father forcing me to fight that woman?"

"Because you challenged her!" I raise my voice a little, and Red winces. Running my hand through my hair, I look away. "Listen, we could spend hours here debating how the pack's rules are unfair, but we don't have much time. Contrary to what you may think, I don't wish to see you get hurt." I pause, then look at Red once more. "Actually, it's going to kill me watching you fight a wolf more skilled and stronger than you."

I catch Red's hard swallow right before she rests a fisted hand on the center of her chest. We engage in a silent staring contest that seems to last an eternity. I can't read anything in her gaze that gives me any clue as to what's going on in her head.

"Okay, let's go then." She walks out, closing the door behind her.

CHAPTER 17

RED

I follow Dante in silence, too busy with all the troubling thoughts running through my head to make idle conversation. He knows I've been crying—there was no way to hide the redness in my eyes—but better him see that than the other two brothers. My chest is heavy, but not only because I'm worried about my approaching doom. My heart feels bruised, as if the brothers' lack of support back at the mess hall was a betrayal of epic proportions. If I think rationally about it, their behavior is consistent with the little I've learned about the pack's interactions. Dante, Samuel, and Mr. Asshole are too high in the food chain to bother with troubles from little fish. But my heart has not gotten the memo about that.

Dante takes me up the mountain through a narrow trek, thick vegetation on both sides making it almost impossible to see. Once or twice, I have to duck or move out of the way or risk getting my arm or face scratched by spindly branches. The path widens as we approach the top. Looming over the rise is a rustic house that could easily fit an entire family. It's at least four times bigger than my grandmother's chalet. The walls on the ground level are stone tiled, whereas the second floor is mostly glass panels. It makes sense for a studio to have as much natural light as possible.

Ignoring the door on the ground level, Dante takes the stairs that leads to the wraparound balcony on the second floor. He unlocks a simple wood door that I imagine is the main entrance to his studio. The smell of oil paint and solvents reaches my nose immediately. Without thinking, I cover my face, trying to prevent inhaling those fumes too much. It's completely futile.

"I never realized how strong the smell of paint is," I say.

"Welcome to enhanced wolf's senses." He smiles softly, but I don't reciprocate. I don't have it in me right now.

"I don't know how you can stand it." I look around, curious about Dante's refuge. There are canvases of all different sizes lying around, but they're all blank. Strange.

"I never knew any different, but you'll get used to it," he replies.

"How come you don't have any finished paintings here?"

Dante heads to the middle of the room. Without looking in my direction, he replies, "They're stored downstairs."

He then grabs the back of his shirt, pulling it over his head and chunking it in a corner. A back corded with sinuous muscles greets me, and my mouth begins to water. What's with these brothers getting naked in front of me?

"What are you doing?"

He turns, his hands already on the fly of his low-rise jeans. Oh my God, that V... I want to know where it leads. Dante is ripped just like Samuel is. Even though he's on the leaner side, he still oozes a raw sexual power that's wrapping around me in an invisible hold, pulling me toward him.

"We have to shift. How did you think you'd fight Rochelle tomorrow?"

Suddenly, I become very nervous. It's easy for me to defy the others in my natural human form, even though I'm no longer the later. But when I'm a wolf, I lose all my confidence, all my willpower.

"I don't know if I can shift just like that, especially with you staring at me."

"I can always call Tristan if you need someone to make you

angry." Dante's lips pull up in some semblance of a smile, but I don't read humor in his eyes.

"That won't be neces—"

Dante peels his jeans off, letting them fall where they may, and begins to shift. He does it fast, maybe because he doesn't want to intimidate me with his nakedness—unlike Samuel who was more than happy to show off his hot body and everything else. A few seconds later, a white wolf is staring at me.

Knowing I don't have a choice but to attempt a shift, I take my clothes off. It's easier to get naked in front of wolf Dante than the man, never mind that I already flashed the guy on purpose. For some ridiculous reason, I wonder if I should forgo wearing underwear altogether. I'd die of mortification if I had to shift on laundry day—meaning on the day I'd be wearing granny panties.

Dante throws his head back and howls, a short signal I think means encouragement.

"Easy for you to do. You were born a wolf," I grumble right before I close my eyes. *Concentrate, I must concentrate.*

I reach for that spark of wildness that now lives inside of me, the essence of the wolf, and will it to expand, to take over my human senses. To my surprise, I'm able to grab on to it much easier than the last times. Soon, I lose control of my body as it shifts. I drop to my knees, clenching my jaw hard as I ride the pain.

"It will get better with time," Dante's voice echoes in my head.

"What will?"

"The pain."

"Gosh, I hope so, because this sucks." I open my eyes, knowing immediately I've successfully completed the shift.

I don't have time to take in my surroundings using my wolf senses before Dante begins to circle me, growling.

"What are you doing?" A spike of adrenaline shoots up my veins. On instinct, I back away from the bigger wolf.

"What does it look like? I'm teaching you," he says in my head. At the same time, he advances with his jaw open and sharp teeth ready to take a bite of me. I jump back, bumping into something solid. A can of paint falls to my right, startling me even more.

"Really? It looks like you're ready to make a meal out of me."

Dante doesn't speak before he jumps, knocking me down effortlessly. I let out a yelp of surprise, but that's all the sound I can make before Dante's powerful jaw is locked tight around my neck.

"This isn't funny, Dante. Get off me."

Instead of doing so, he bites harder. My wolf whimpers.

"Cut it out," I say again, but it has no substance. It's almost vapor.

He finally jumps off, going back to his side of the room. Slowly, I stand, still shaking. Man, who knew wolves could do that?

"If that's how you intend to fight, you might as well forfeit and accept your destiny as the female omega."

"That's not fair! You didn't give me time to prepare."

"Prepare?" Dante's wolf makes a noise that almost sounds like a human scoff. *"As a wolf, your normal state should be high-alert mode."*

I growl right before I try to inflict some kind of pain, but I'm too slow, too predictable for Dante. He moves out of the way, then slams into my side head-first, sending me careening across the floor. I hit a shelf, causing painting supplies to fall. One heavy metal object hits my head, and I see stars. If I thought that would give Dante pause, I was mistaken. He clamps his jaw around one of my hind legs and pulls me from the crap I was buried under, but he doesn't do it to help. Once again, he gets on top me of me, keeping me in place by locking his jaw tight around my neck.

Freezing, I wait for him to let go. He doesn't; instead, he bites harder. *"Fight me."*

"I can't."

He waits—one, two, three seconds—before he lets go, shaking his head as he trots away. Shame takes over me. He seems to be disappointed. How the heck I know that is a mystery.

"Yes, I am very disappointed, Amelia."

"What the fuck? You can read my thoughts?"

"I'm in your head, aren't I?" He stares at me with his intense yellow eyes, and the hairs on my back stand on end.

"I'm in yours, too. How come I can't hear your thoughts?"

"Because I know how to shield them from you."

"I don't want you to hear what I'm thinking. You're supposed to be teaching me stuff."

"Try picturing your brain as a house. Your communication channel would be the living room, so once you open the door, guests can talk to you. But maybe you don't want them to see that your bedroom is a mess, so you don't invite them for a tour of the rest of the house."

That makes sense. Concentrating, I bring my parents' apartment in Chicago to the forefront of my mind. I can't bear to think of Grandma's house as home anymore. Her betrayal still hurts. I imagine Dante in my parents' living room, checking out their modern art collection. He would fit perfectly there. He begins to explore, heading for the hallway that leads to the bedrooms. I jump in front of him, blocking his passage. That's where I locked away my inner thoughts. I'm not sure if that's what Dante had in mind, but I hone in on that image of me denying him access, hoping it will keep him from reading my mind.

When I finally bring my attention back to the present, I notice that Dante has already begun circling me again, the muscles on his back tense. He's preparing to attack.

The wolf in me wants to retreat, but that didn't serve me well before. I have to override the animal's natural instincts. Yes, Dante is a much bigger and stronger wolf than me, but cowering is what made me an easy target to the rest of the pack. Even if I'm weaker, I have to stand my ground or I'll always get run over.

Since Dante is not giving me any pointers—his teaching methods are horrible—I copy his stance. His muzzle is lowered a bit as he stalks me, and I realize his head is angled in a way that allows him to see through his peripheral if an attack comes from his vulnerable side.

If I turn to run away, he's going to chase me. But what if I only pretend to do so, then change course in the last second? Would he be surprised? Well, if he's still reading my mind, the answer is no. There's only one way to find out.

I spin around, heading in the direction of the front door. Dante seems to have taken the bait. Judging by how fast he is, it will only take him a few seconds to overtake me. I'm focusing so hard on the sound of his paws hitting the floor behind me that I yelp in surprise when my view suddenly changes. I'm no longer seeing the front door ahead, but myself running away from Dante. Oh my God, am I seeing what he's seeing? How is that possible? I forget my diversion plan, my legs faltering. When Dante pounces on me, I see it all through his eyes and it's terrifying.

I land hard on the concrete floor, Dante's weight on top of me blocking my airway. His gaze zeroes in on my neck; he's going to pin me down again. But instead of freezing up and becoming completely useless, a fire ignites in my core. I don't know if it's the pitiful glint I see in my eyes or if maybe I'm finally learning how to be a wolf, but I manage to free one of my front legs. Swinging my clawed paw hard across his face, I draw blood. The movement seems to stun Dante, and I'm back in my own head again. He slides off, shaking his head from side to side, then he stares at me.

He keeps staring and staring without saying a word telepathically. Unnerved, I ask, "What?" But I still have no answer.

Then Dante shifts back into human form, so I follow suit. The gashes on his face look much worse without the fur covering them. Three angry slashes mark his cheek, and blood drips from the wound.

"Dante, I'm so sorry."

He touches his bloody face, smearing it with his fingertips before looking at them as if in a daze. That's gotta hurt like crazy.

"I didn't mean to hurt you like that. I swear." I bite my lower lip, guilt making me forget that he asked for it.

When he glances up, I see fire churning in his eyes right before he breaches the gap between us, captures my face between his hands, and crushes his lips with mine.

CHAPTER 18

RED

Holy Mary, Mother of God. Dante is kissing me, and it's the best damn kiss ever. My legs turn to mush, and I'm glad he's holding my face or I'd be down on the floor already. The smell of earth after it rains, the feel of a soft cool breeze after a scorching day under the sun, the high from jumping off a cliff—those are the feelings kissing Dante evokes. Gripping his forearms, I step closer. My breasts rub against his warm skin, reminding me that we're both naked, but I don't care. I want to feel every inch of him without any barriers.

There's no hesitation on his part as his tongue probes and teases, which surprises me since he's a beta and I'm still a lowly omega. He doesn't seem to care about pack rules, and neither do I. He tastes too delicious—a mix of honey, whiskey, and mint—a combination so intoxicating I'm running the risk of becoming irreversibly addicted to it, to *him*. I've been taken over by an ice-cold fever, a head rush, something I never experienced from a kiss before. It's only when I taste the hint of copper on my tongue that I ease back.

"We should take care of your wound," I say breathlessly as I stare at his lips.

"I'm fine."

I touch his cheek, dabbing the tips of my fingers with blood. "You don't look fine. Maybe you need stiches."

A chuckle bubbles up Dante's throat as amusement dances in his eyes. He grabs my hand, then kisses my palm. "I'm a wolf. We heal quicker than most."

Narrowing my eyes, I examine the gashes more closely. They do seem a little smaller, as if the wound is already healing.

Dante brings his head down, kissing the curve of my neck, and goose bumps spread all over my body. Desire curls at the base of my spine, and the throbbing between my legs is incessant and impossible to ignore. I arch my back, bringing my body flush with his. His erection presses against my belly, hard and smooth at the same time.

Letting go of his arms, I run my nails down his back until I'm resting my hands over his butt. I give it a little squeeze, making Dante snicker against my skin. He runs his tongue down my collarbone, going lower and lower until he finds one of my nipples and runs lazy circles over it.

"Dante," I breathe out, the only word I'm able to speak.

He squeezes my hips right before he lifts me. My legs wrap around his waist. In this new position, my core rubs against his shaft. Holy Batman, talk about an explosion of the most wonderful, earth-shattering sensation. Need spreads like wildfire through my entire body, an uncontrollable force that shifts my world to something raw and primal. The wolf's energy swirls inside of me, and I yield a little bit of control to it, wanting the animal instinct to override my human emotions.

Dante takes control of my mouth again, and I rock against him, trying to increase the friction. His response is a growl that's most definitely not human.

"I'm about to cross all the lines, Red," he whispers against my lips.

"I know." I kiss his jaw, then lick up his chin until I reach his lips again, pressing a soft kiss there. "If you're asking me tell you to stop, forget it."

He leans back, gazing into my eyes as if he's searching for the truth.

"You're not trying to read my mind, are you?" I ask.

"No, I'd never invade your privacy like that. Before, it was part of your training. You had to learn to shield your thoughts." He touches my face with the softest caress. "You're so beautiful. I could stare at you all day."

"Please don't." I rotate my hips again, reminding him that we're way past platonic gestures, and a hiss escapes his lips. His eyes flash ember for a split second before returning to their normal emerald green.

He strides across the room with purpose, stepping over boxes and anything else that's in his way, before coming to a stop. I glance over my shoulder, finding a bed with crumpled satin sheets behind me. Everything is in a warm brown color, reminding me of melted chocolate, silky and decadent. Much like its owner.

Dante kisses my neck while lowering me to the bed, but the coolness of the soft fabric does nothing to soothe my burning skin. There's no hope besides letting the fire consume me whole. He cages me in by placing his forearms on each side of my head, keeping his body hovering above mine. I don't like this sudden gap between us, so I lock my hands behind his neck and pull him to me. He resists.

"What?" I ask.

He gets this strange, faraway expression in his eyes that makes me think I did something wrong... or worse, that I'm boring him. Insecurity rears its ugly head, even if his erection is still very much evident.

"I never imagined it would feel like this," he finally replies.

"You're not making any sense."

"You're new. It will with time."

What kind of answer is that? I open my mouth to demand a proper explanation, but the words never make it out. Dante lowers his body to mine, fitting nicely between my legs. His erection is positioned in just the right spot to bring the final act home, and I forget what I was about to say. My curiosity veers into a completely different direction. I want to explore every inch of Dante's body—feel every sensation our joined bodies will bring.

A lurch in my chest has me gasping, and then my entire body begins to tingle. Oh, no. I can't possibly be shifting now.

"It's okay, Red."

"What's happening? Am I changing?" Panic is laced throughout my tone.

"Only a little. Partial shifts are common during sex, even among wolves who generally can't manage it any other time."

He nudges my entrance with his cock, sliding in an inch, making me arch my back as a high-voltage current seems to be running through my veins. My gums begin to ache, then I feel the tips of sharp canines with my tongue. I touch my face, afraid it has morphed into a monster like it had before—half human, half wolf. Dante pulls my hand away, then kisses the line of my jaw at the same time he plunges a little deeper. Fuck, it feels so, so good.

"God, she feels amazing." The thought pops into my head so suddenly that I first think Dante spoke the words out loud. But his mouth is busy suckling my neck, so I must have heard what he's thinking.

"Dante?"

"Hmm?" He rotates his hips, sheathing himself completely in me this time, making my toes curl.

"Did you mean to let me hear your thoughts just now?"

He stops abruptly, leaning on his forearms to stare at my face. The furrowed eyebrows and eyes that are full of surprise clue me in that he didn't.

"What did you hear?"

Heat rushes to my face as shyness takes over. I was never one to feel comfortable with talking dirty during sex.

"Uh, you said I felt amazing."

Dante keeps looking at me without blinking for a few seconds before his lips crack into a smile. "You do feel amazing." He runs a hand down the side of my leg, then lifts it and drapes it over his shoulder. "So fucking amazing."

Pulling his cock almost all the way out, he then slams into me hard, making me scream out his name. My eyes roll back into their sockets, and my toes start to tingle. This new angle… holy shit, I'm going to come in the next second. Keeping the rhythm steady, Dante lowers his body again, covering my mouth with his and swallowing all my moans. I brush his elongated sharp teeth with my tongue, and that shoots another zing of pleasure down my body, straight to my core. As much as I'd like to prolong this torture, I can't fight the surge. My body shatters, my mind losing grip on reality as the wave of pleasure takes over. I hear a wolf howling in the background. After a moment, I realize I'm the one making that noise. The notion doesn't scare or bother me. Instead, it gives me power. It makes me want to really let go. Surrender to my new wild side.

In a swift motion—one I hadn't known I was capable of—I switch positions with Dante, forcing him to his back so I can ride him. He doesn't seem surprised by my action, nor does he stop pumping into me from this new angle. Gripping my hips, he continues moving, completely lost in the moment. I begin to move in sync with him, feeling the tension building up again. I've never had multiple orgasms before, but there's no doubt this is happening. I could honestly come just by watching Dante's sexy expression as he fucks me. His face is flushed, his ember eyes are glowing, and the tips of his canines are showing through his partially opened lips.

Getting swept away by a crazy impulse, I offer the underside of my forearm to him. "Bite me."

He doesn't stop—doesn't ask questions—just clamps his jaw around my arm, sinking his teeth into my skin hard enough to fill me with indescribable pleasure, not pain. I throw my head back, howling again as I'm hit with another orgasm, more intense than the one before. Dante pumps his hips faster, his cock becoming even larger inside of me, before he releases my arm to let out a string of curses. His entire body trembles as he rides his orgasm, and it might be my imagination, but it seems to last longer than with most guys.

Once the grip on my hips eases and Dante's body stops moving, I rest my hands on his sweat-covered chest, dropping my head. My leg muscles are mush and my sex is throbbing from all the pounding, but despite that, I'd be game if he asked me to do it all over again right this second. I'm not sure if that's wolf stamina or if it's the Dante effect. Maybe both.

He wraps his arms around my back, then rolls me off him, pulling me closer to his body. When he drops a kiss on the top of my head, I snuggle deeper to rest my head on his chest, making lazy circles over it with the tip of my fingers as I wait for my heartbeat to return to normal. His is pounding at warp speed, just like mine.

"Is it always like this among wolves?" I ask.

"What is?"

"Earth-shattering, world-tilted-off-its-axis kind of sex?"

Dante laughs, hugging me tighter. "I'm sure it feels a little more intense than what you're used to, but the answer is no. That was a new experience for me, too."

I lean on my elbow, peering into his face. "Really?"

His stares intently at me, his eyes still infused with lust. "Yeah," he answers with a voice so loaded with need that it makes me all hot and bothered again.

My eyes switch to his cheek. The blood on it is already dry, with no sign of any scar. "You're healed." I touch his skin to make sure.

"Yes, I am."

His serious tone makes me look into his eyes once more, and I immediately know he's referring to more than just the scratches on his face. I feel a clench in my chest, followed by an overflow of emotions that are intense and a little scary. Leaning against his chest again, I hide my face from his view. I don't want Dante to read the fear in my eyes. What we did here will have repercussions, and I can't show weakness when the time to face those consequences comes.

I couldn't have imagined I'd have to do it so soon, though.

A loud knock on Dante's door, followed by Tristan's voice calling out for his brother, has me sitting up on the bed faster than lightning, pulling the sheet with me to cover my body. Why did the consequences have to be delivered by Mr. Asshole?

CHAPTER 19

RED

"Fuck." Dante rubs his face before he swings his legs to the side of the bed and gets up.

"Why is your brother here?" I follow him, still wrapped in the satin sheet, which is stupid since I just slept with the guy.

Ignoring my questions, Dante asks, "What do you want, Tristan?"

"To piss all over your party, naturally," Samuel answers this time. Fuck me. Both brothers are out there? Why?

"You guys are a pain in my ass." Dante picks up his jeans from the floor, getting dressed in brusque movements, not bothering to put his boxer shorts on. Partially dressed, he takes a step toward the door, freezing suddenly to look over his shoulder, as if he just remembered I'm there.

"You'd better get dressed, too," he whispers, then he mouths the words, "I'm sorry."

He is sorry. I can see the sincere apology shining in his eyes, but it doesn't change the way I'm feeling, which is a little, I don't know, dejected.

I put my clothes back on as fast as I can. Once I'm dressed, I finger comb my hair, trying to get rid of the tangles. I'm still busy with the task when Dante opens the door for his brothers. Tristan stalks in first, his senses on high alert as if he's smelling an ambush. His nostrils flare, his spine going taut a moment later. He whips his face to me, his gaze sharp and menacing before he turns on Dante.

"What have you done?"

Samuel whistles as he enters the studio. His eyes linger on me for a second as he gives me a half smile, but there's no joy in his gaze.

"Do you really have to ask?" he says. "You could smell what was going on here from miles away." He smirks at Dante, but it feels more cold than amused. "Boy, you really didn't waste any time."

"Piss off, Sam." Dante crosses his arms, glaring at his brothers.

"Was that your plan when you volunteered to prepare Amelia for the fight tomorrow? To fuck her?" Tristan barks, making me wince.

That wasn't what happened here, and the fact Mr. Asshole is throwing accusations without any information is making me see red.

"Why do you care about what happened between Dante and me?" I take a step in his direction, practically blowing steam from my nose. Tristan opens his stupid mouth, but I cut him off. "Spare me the spiel that Dante is a beta, and I'm only a worthless omega."

"Omegas aren't worthle—" Samuel begins to say, but I whip around to him, glaring so hard he pipes down.

"Red is not a true omega," Dante replies. "And even if she were, it wouldn't matter at all. It's not like I'm set to be an alpha. It's pretty much a given that the honor will go to you; isn't it, brother?"

I don't miss the bitterness in Dante's tone, nor the way Tristan reacts to his brother's statement. His scowl morphs into an expression I can only describe as regretful, and I'm totally unprepared for it. It's almost like he either doesn't want the role, or feels guilty that the pack will choose him. The fact he does care about Dante's feelings shows me he's not a complete asshole like I pegged him to be. But I still don't like him.

"Hey, slow down for a second." Samuel raises both hands, edging in between his brothers. "Tristan becoming the new alpha is not a sure thing. But I'm going to side with him that you sleeping with Red right before she has to fight Rochelle was not a smart move, Dante."

"Hey!" I yell, forcing the three men to look at me. "Quit talking about me as if I'm not in the room. I chose to sleep with Dante. It wasn't his decision alone. If you're all going to butt into my business, let me assure you that I fucking loved it. If he wants to do it again, I'm game."

My confession drops like a bomb in the tense room. Dante's eyebrows shoot to the heavens while the corners of his lips twitch upward. Samuel's jaw drops right before he crosses his arms and frowns. Tristan's expression is the most predictable one. He looks like he's sucking a sour grape while having an aneurism at the same time.

"Your disregard for pack rules is appalling," Tristan replies with unveiled contempt.

"Is there really a rule set in stone? Did your father know that your mother would become a female alpha before she turned? Do you think he would have discarded her if she weren't up to snuff?"

My question seems to penetrate his thick skull. He breaks the staring contest first, glancing at the floor and rubbing his face.

Samuel comes closer, and I eye him with suspicion. His eyes are widely innocent, but the grin curling his lips tells me he's up to something.

"Man, I never stopped to think about that. You just made an excellent point, Red." He throws an arm around my shoulder, then squeezes it a little. "It makes it easy to forgive you for jumping into bed with Dante first."

"First?" I step out of his embrace.

He shoves his hands into his pockets, then shrugs. "Well, it's only a matter of time before you succumb to my charms."

"Oh my God." Dante rolls his eyes, then looks up at the ceiling.

"Did you just proposition me in front of your brother? What do you think this is? A gang-bang?" I try to sound appalled, but the idea of sleeping with Samuel—or even sharing a bed with him and Dante at the same time—doesn't sound horrible at all. I wonder if this lack of restraint when it comes to sex is a wolf thing or I'm just now realizing I've always been a nympho.

Samuel places a hand over his chest, faking distress. "I'd never suggest that."

"So, sharing the same woman is something wolves do? I always thought they were loyal animals."

Dante and Samuel exchange a glance, and Tristan makes a disgruntled sound in the back of his throat. "What? Am I missing something here?"

"Actually, wolves are not into sharing, but…" Dante stops, clamping his mouth shut as if he's debating whether to continue.

"But what?" I place my hands on my hips, frowning as I wait for him to spill the beans.

"You should show her the painting, Dante," Samuel replies.

"Oh, please. That painting means nothing." Tristan shows us his back, morphing into his antagonistic armor.

"What painting?" I swing my gaze between the brothers, frustrated no one seem inclined to give me any answers.

"Dante has inherited our mother's gift of foresight. But his visions manifest in art form," Samuel finally replies.

"I want to see that painting. Where is it?"

Dante lets out a heavy sigh before he replies, "Downstairs, in the garage. But Red, I swear that what happened here had nothing to do with it."

"You're making me nervous. Why don't you just show me the damn painting already?"

After a brusque nod, he veers to the front door. I follow Dante out and down the stairs, knowing Samuel and Tristan are close behind me. Dante stops in front one of the garage doors, then punches a code into the security panel mounted on the wall. A soft beep sounds before the metal door begins to lift. The light switches on automatically when he walks in, revealing a myriad of colorful canvases in all sizes and shapes. My jaw slackens as I take in Dante's brilliant artwork. They're mesmerizing. So vivid, raw, and full energy. So him. Some of the images seem like they're going to leap off the canvases at any moment. I recognize his signature style, realizing the paintings at the alpha's manor are his.

Dante keeps heading toward the back of the room, where a canvas as tall as him and twice as wide is propped against the wall. A white sheet covers the art beneath, and anticipation gnaws at my insides. My heartbeat has increased tenfold. Whatever vision is painted on the canvas will change my perspective on this new life for good—I know it in my bones. Maybe I've been blessed with the sight, too. Just great.

Dante spares me one final glance before pulling the sheet down. My stomach bottoms out, my legs becoming so weak I'm afraid I'm going to fall to the floor in a heap. I'm staring at a surrealistic, messy, colorful painting of me dressed in a red gown, surrounded by three white wolves. A crown made from wildflowers adorns my head. I don't need the sight to guess those three wolves are Dante, Samuel, and Tristan.

"What does that mean?" I ask in a whisper.

"I don't know," Dante replies, staring at his painting as well.

"No one knows. It could be anything." Tristan throws a meaningful glance in Samuel's direction, and I immediately want to know what he's thinking.

"You're hiding stuff from me, and that's terribly unfair. I'm in the middle of that painting for crying out loud. My grandmother knew I would be attacked by a rogue wolf that night. She sent me to the forest for that reason. I don't understand why I had to become a wolf, and now this?" I point at the painting. "Does that mean I'm supposed to mate with all three of you?"

Dante swallows hard, eyes on the painting again. Tristan just clenches his jaw tight, grinding his teeth in the process, and stares at the floor. Samuel is the only one who holds my gaze.

"It's a possibility."

"A very small possibility," Tristan grunts, arms now folded almost defensively in front of his chest.

"Well, I don't want to be your mate!" I snap at him, hating how he always seem to think I'm the scum of the earth, unworthy of his attention. Fucker.

"It would explain why I didn't feel like ripping Sam's head off for even suggesting you hook up with him." Dante still carries an undecipherable glint in his eyes as he takes me in. "Wolves never share."

"Well, you're forgetting the legend of the Mother of Wolves," Samuel chimes in.

"What's that?"

"There's a story that talks about the first female alpha." Tristan moves closer to the painting, but keeps his distance from me. "She never took a consort. Ruled the pack alone. Mind you, there's never been any proof that she actually existed."

"Legend says she had many lovers, and despite a wolf's territorial nature, none of her wolves minded sharing." Samuel bumps his elbow against my arm. "Not a bad deal, huh?" He flashes me a sinfully sexy grin.

"I don't think I could ever have more than one lover at a time."

As I watch Samuel's smile wilt to nothing, I feel bad for lying to him. I *do* think I'm capable having more than one guy in my life. If he really tried, I wouldn't resist him. Does that make me a whore? I hate how my mixed feelings toward the Wolfe brothers have me questioning my own morals. Or is it modern society morals? Way back when men were nomads and the society was matriarchal, a woman having multiple consorts was the norm. Actually, it was encouraged.

Samuel recovers his humor fast, though. Glancing at Dante, he says, "That's too bad, bro. Once Red has a taste of the Sam machine, she won't go back to you."

I roll my eyes, but manage to stop the smile that was blossoming on my lips when I catch Tristan's furious gaze aimed at me. My humor changes violently, anger taking control. "Why are you glowering? Do you think I planned this? What—you think I *made* Dante dream up that painting?" I scoff.

"No, I don't think you're that powerful, but you seem too eager to embrace what that image represents. So, you think you can rule the pack alone?"

"What? What kind of logic is that?" I ask, genuinely perplexed by Tristan's insinuations.

"You're not throwing a hissy fit, demanding to return to your old life. We pretty much told you that you might have to mate with all three of us, but you don't seem too repulsed by the idea despite the fact you seem to despise me."

Balling my hands into fists, I stride toward him. The wolf's essence churns inside me, but I have a better handle on it now. I'm not going to shift unless I want to. I stop in front of him, not letting the sheer size difference between us intimidate me.

"Have you ever stopped to consider that if I'm actually the female alpha, I can simply kill you if I wish?"

Tristan bares his elongated canines while a terrifying growl emanates from deep within his throat. "Is that a threat?"

"You bet your ass it is."

He leans down, his nose now almost touching mine. Tingles run down my spine, and they're not related to my anger or the adrenaline kicking. My fucking body is betraying me, Goddamn it.

"Survive your challenge with Rochelle, and I'll let you have a go at me. Bear in mind that if we fight, I won't be merciful."

"Wasn't counting on it," I reply through clenched teeth, while in the back of my head, my sanity is screaming at me to shut up.

Tristan eases away, then swings around to march out of the garage. My breathing is completely out of sync, as if I've just ran a marathon.

"Fuck. You're crazy, Red." Samuel stares in bemusement at the door Tristan just vanished through.

Dante grabs my arm, spinning me around. A panicked glint shines in his eyes. "Do you realize what you just did?" He shakes me a little. "Do you?"

"Let go of me." I pull my arm from his grasp, rubbing away the sore spot. Dante begins to pace like a maniac, gripping his hair and pulling at it. "Why are you freaking out?"

Samuel glances at me like I've asked the most idiotic thing in the world. "Hmm, let's see. You threatened to kill the second strongest wolf in the entire pack, then you accepted his challenge to fight to the death. I think that pretty much sums everything up."

I open my mouth, but no sound comes forth. Now that I replay that scene, I realize Samuel summarized my fuck up perfectly. Unless I have some secret weapon I don't know about, I'm completely screwed... and not in a good way.

CHAPTER 20

RED

It's no surprise that I couldn't sleep for shit last night. I kept tossing and turning in the king-sized bed. Despite being extremely comfortable, it still felt like a stranger's bed. But that wasn't the reason sleep eluded me. I kept replaying all the events from the day, which were many. The altercation with Rochelle that resulted in a fight with the woman today. Then me sleeping with Dante and everything else that followed: the painting's revelation, Tristan's animosity, and ultimately, me challenging him. I really ought to learn how to keep my mouth shut around these wolves, or I won't survive to see the end of the summer.

Speaking of which, summer term starts in a few weeks. At this rate, I might have to withdrawal from college. Unless I win the fight against Rochelle today, and prove to the alpha I can be trusted outside the confines of the pack's compound.

With a brusque movement, I throw my legs to the side of the bed and sit up, leaning my elbows on my knees and holding my head between my hands. This is hopeless. I'm really good at fighting with words, but I have no game when it comes to brawling. The wound I inflicted on Dante was a fluke. I'm sure if he hadn't stopped the training, he would have won the fight.

I look at my phone; it's only four in the morning. I still have a couple of hours until my next humiliation. Not knowing what else to do, I open my laptop and Google videos of wolves fighting. Maybe I can learn something from the internet. I'm immediately enraptured by what I see. It's different to watch those animals knowing I can change into one now. I bring out the nerd inside me, starting to take notes as if I'm preparing for an exam. After an hour of watching wolves hunting, playing, and even mating, I have piles of papers surrounding me.

"I'm so fucking ridiculous it's not even funny. This is useless." I stare at the sheets of paper in dismay.

A knock sounds and I absentmindedly tell whoever it is to come in. My gaze is still on my notes when a throat clearing brings my attention to my visitor. My face heats up, and I'm unable to contain my surprise. Tristan is in my room, looking too attractive this early in the morning in his button-down shirt and slacks. His expression, though, is cold and neutral.

"What are you doing here?" I ask.

"I came on my father's request. Your fight with Rochelle will be happening at dawn, or have you forgotten about that already?"

I glance at the time on my computer, noting it's only five-thirty. I still have some time left, but I know Tristan will drag me out by my hair if I don't get moving. Hastily closing my laptop, I then start to put my notes away, all too aware of Tristan watching my every movement. I slept in nothing more than panties and a long T-shirt that barely covers my ass, but shit, he's probably not fazed by my lack of clothes, so I why should I care? I pick up my pile of notes and laptop in one big swoop, but I lose a few sheets in the process. Tristan bends to pick them up, frowning as he reads my handwriting.

"What's this?"

I pull the notes from his hand, then put them away with the rest. "Nothing."

"Were you studying wolf behavior?"

"Maybe."

He doesn't speak for a couple of beats, making me curious.

I find him staring at me too intensely for my taste.

"Are you going to leave so I can get changed?"

In silence, he breaks the distance between us, stopping so close he's now invading my personal space. He picks up a strand of my hair, then brings it to his nose. "What is it about you that has my brothers so entangled?"

"I don't know. Why don't you ask them?" I force the words out, trying to keep them as steady as possible. Something hard to do when my heart is fluttering like mad inside my rib cage. I should push Tristan away. He's nothing but a mean bully, so why can't I force my body to move?

He pinches my chin between this thumb and forefinger, bringing my face up so he can stare into my eyes. "I couldn't sleep last night, thinking about what happened in Dante's studio. By all rights, I should have ripped you to shreds right when you threatened to kill me; yet, I didn't. Why is that?"

Fear drips down my spine because I can tell he's not kidding. He so easily could have killed me before his brothers could stop him from doing so.

"I-I don't know."

He leans closer, brushing his lips against mine. Electricity crackles between us, and my entire body begins to shake. Like a fool, I do nothing but wait for him to finish the job and kiss me. Why am I not pushing him away? I despise him, right?

He doesn't kiss me, only brings his nose to the crook of my neck, inhaling deeply. Goose bumps break out all over my body, and I have to close my eyes because the room has started to spin out of control. This is insane. Why am I reacting like this?

He pulls away suddenly, and my eyes fly open. Tristan is breathing hard, desire and anger flashing in his eyes. Whatever just happened has given me a whiplash, and I have to hold on to the desk behind me to keep myself on the vertical.

"Take a shower. You have Dante's scent all over you. I'll wait outside. You have ten minutes."

He spins around and leaves, closing the door behind him

with a loud bang.

It's safe to say I didn't do anything to piss him off this time, which means Tristan is a fucking crazy bastard.

⚬☾☽⚬

ᏟRISTAN

Being out of her room is not enough; I have to walk down the hallway, put as much distance as I can between us, or I'll be back there to finish what I started in no time. Fuck. I almost kissed her. Every fiber of my being demanded that I kiss her, but if I succumbed, I'd have to admit that Dante's painting is not a fluke and Red does have a hold on us. She thinks I have grudge against her. Maybe in the beginning I had, but only because she made me feel things I hadn't expected or wanted. I have no desire to yield to anyone. That's the truth. It's the reason I've never wanted to take a mate, and probably why I never fell for Lyria's seduction traps.

But my body and worse, my heart, yearns for Red, a stranger who probably wouldn't have even registered on my radar if I had met her before. Fuck. What the hell do I do now? If she survives the fight against Rochelle—which she probably will—I'll have to hold her accountable for the challenge she issued. I'll have to fight her. It's what the law demands, but I know I won't be able to kill her, even though I said I wouldn't show any mercy.

The door bursts open in the opposite direction, making me spin around. Red is ready, her hair damp and her clothing sensible: yoga pants, flip-flops, and a tank top. Not that it matters; she's getting out of those anyway.

Her face is all pinched eyebrows and lips that are nothing but a thin, flat line. The physical distance has not diminished the pull, though. It's still there, relentless, unyielding. I'm

136

tethered to her whether I want it or not. Clenching my jaw and shoving all those pesky feelings to the side, I cross the distance between us with large steps.

"Ready?" I ask, stopping a safe distance away from her.

She regards me through slitted eyes, before nodding and motioning to the stairs. "After you."

I take the lead; it's better if I don't have to follow her from behind. I don't need to be reminded of what I'm denying myself. Not that I would ever take what I wanted without the woman being on board with it, but I've read the signs. She's also affected by whatever crazy link that binds us.

Outside, the air is still cool and crisp. I take a deep breath, enjoying the fresh scent of moist earth and green leaves that comes with it. But my peaceful moment only lasts a split second. When Red stops next to me, it's like my entire essence zeroes in on her. It's a struggle not to shift my body in her direction. I rub my face, then roll my shoulders back to release the tension there.

"Where to?" she asks.

"The woods." I start in that direction, fighting the urge to glance back at Red. I know she's following me.

I was never one to need to fill uncomfortable silences, but I find myself speaking nonetheless. "Rochelle is a tough enforcer, but she has weaknesses."

"Oh? And they are…"

"She always forgets to protect her left side, and she's not fast enough to react when an opponent changes course abruptly."

"Aim for the left side, make false plays. Got it."

Unable to stop myself, I cut my eyes in her direction. She's staring at the ground with her hands linked behind her back, biting her lower lip.

"Don't be nervous."

She lifts her face, frowning. "I'm not nervous. I'm thinking about my strategy."

"Good." I force myself to look away.

"Why are you giving me tips, anyway?"

"I know you think I'd love for you to lose, but this is not a fair fight. Unfortunately, you're not used to the way we do things here. You keep confronting wolves, threatening them without thinking about the consequences."

"I know." She sighs. "I have a big mouth and an even bigger temper. And do you want to know the worst of it?"

"There's something worse?" I watch her from the corners of my eyes.

"Surprisingly, yes. I was never like this before. I avoided confrontations as much as I could. I always preferred the most peaceful approach. But since I changed into a shifter, it seems I can't open my mouth without issuing death threats and whatnot."

"I can't say I understand. I was born a shifter, so I don't know what it's like for humans."

"So, if I don't die today, are you still going to make me fight you?"

There's no challenge in her voice. It's actually a little subdued. I want to answer no, that I'd never make her fight me, but I can't do that. She challenged me, and I accepted it. "Yes."

She doesn't speak for a few seconds, and I let her digest my reply.

"I'd better discover my special powers then, because I sure as hell don't want to be shredded to pieces by you."

We reach the edge of the forest, and I stop. Red does, too. At the same time, we angle toward each other. "Listen, I don't want you to worry about fighting me. Focus on besting Rochelle. She has experience and she was born a shifter, but she's not the best fighter in the world."

"Is she going to kill me if I lose?" There's real fear in Red's eyes. For the first time, I catch a glimpse of the woman behind all the bravado. A great sense of guilt settles on my chest, making me wish I hadn't been so stubborn, so horrible to her, since she arrived at the compound.

"No. I won't let that happen."

"Okay." She bites her lip, fidgeting slightly, before she continues. "During the run, something strange happened. When the wolves turned against me, I panicked. My body wouldn't move. I couldn't do anything but cower. I couldn't pull out of it, even though I knew I was stronger than they were, that I could fight them."

"It's not so strange. It was your first run with the wolves."

"Maybe."

I realize she's stalling, and I'm letting her. Or maybe I'm the one who doesn't want to take her to the challenge. Either way, we have to get moving or my father will have my ass. Side by side, we take the path that leads deeper into the forest, trudging in silence until we reach a clearing. The entire pack is already assembled there, waiting for the newest member to make an appearance. Half have already shifted, including Lyria, who is standing next to Rochelle. The enforcer is still in her human form, but already naked and ready to shift.

"I was beginning to think you had run away," she says snidely.

"I wouldn't dream of it." Red stops on the other side of the circle that has formed. Without hesitation or a trace of embarrassment, she pulls off her tank top and pants.

Sucking in a breath, I avert my gaze right away. I shouldn't be affected by the woman's nakedness. Shifters don't usually get aroused like that, but I'd better not risk it. She's not a regular wolf, that's for sure.

Dad moves to the center of the clearing, commanding everyone's attention without the need for words. All conversations cease. Only then does the alpha speak.

"Amelia Redford, the newest member of our pack, has openly challenged Rochelle Stinson. I, Anthony Wolfe, Alpha of the Crimson Hollow pack, have accepted the challenge as valid." He glances at Rochelle, and then at Red.

"Since you're new and don't know our ways, I'll call the challenge as over whenever one of you gets seriously injured. Not abiding to my command is punishable by death, and it will be enforced. Is that understood?"

"Yes, sir," Red replies loud and clear.

Dad walks back to his original spot. On the other side of the clearing, Rochelle is already mid-shift. I glance at Red, worrying she going to choke and not be able to shift with everyone's eyes on her, but she seems to have found her ground as a wolf and changes without effort. She glances at me when the shift is complete, then at her opponent, who is a brown wolf a little bigger and muscular than she is. Rochelle throws her head back and howls, a call that's answered by all the pack members who have shifted.

Red doesn't join the call. Instead she begins to circle Rochelle, eyeing her opponent with care. Rochelle growls right before she leaps, teeth bared and all, but Red moves out of the enforcer's range, just to turn and sink her sharp teeth into the brown wolf's shoulder. Rochelle lets out a whine, but recovers quickly, getting Red good on her ear. The scent of Red's blood fills my nostrils, and I have to fight the urge to shift so I can protect her. The compulsion is something only mated wolves feel, so why the fuck am I having to battle that now?

The sounds of wolves snarling keeps getting louder and louder. I hadn't had a clue it would be this hard to watch the challenge, but at least Red is holding her own. I sense someone staring at me. Breaking my concentration on the fight for a brief second, I discover Dante watching me through hooded eyes. Opening my channel, I ask, *"What?"*

"We could have stopped this."

"She's fine."

"But you aren't."

I shut him off, then break our staring war to pay attention to the fight once more. I'm just in time to watch Rochelle slam into Red, who loses her balance, granting the enforcer the upper hand. Rochelle is now on top of Red, trying to immobilize her by locking her jaw around Red's neck. But the smaller wolf is having none of that. She rolls on the ground, then pushes Rochelle off with her hind legs. Bouncing to her paws, she jumps on the enforcer's back, biting the soft spot between her shoulder blades. Rochelle lets out a mix between a snarl and a whine while shaking from side to side, trying to dislodge Red. Both are now covered in blood.

I glance at my father, willing him to call off the fight. But he doesn't seem remotely inclined to do so yet. Damn it. What is he waiting for? For one of them to get seriously maimed?

A loud howl catches my attention. I whip my face back to the fight, but before I even have time to process the scene, my powers are already manifesting. My entire frame begins to shake. I'm on the verge of a spontaneous shift, something that hasn't happened to me since I was a young pup.

Red is on the ground, unmoving, but her eyes are wide open and focused on a point in the distance—not on Rochelle, who is about to attack.

"Get up, you fool!" I send the message telepathically, finding nothing but a void. I don't possess Dante's ability to communicate mind to mind while in human form.

Right before Rochelle is about to end the fight, Red lifts her muzzle and howls, a deep and sorrowful sound that has me grinding my teeth hard. The enforcer stops in her tracks, dazed eyes staring at Red for a couple of beats before she drops to the ground with a whine of pain. Red stands with a leap, glances at Rochelle, then takes off.

CHAPTER 21

RED

Shit. Shit. Shit. Why does weird stuff keep happening to me? I was so winning that fight until my skull felt like it was splitting in two, and then I was lying on the ground, unable to move. Even Rochelle was surprised; she didn't take advantage of the situation and attack right way.

Then the images came, messy and confusing at first. It took me a moment to make sense of them, and then I recognized the place where I was attacked. A lonely black wolf was hurt badly, running away from someone. Then I saw their guns and dark clothes. The hunters. Three men were blazing through the forest, holding state-of-the-art hunting rifles. Their faces were blurry, but one detail I was able to see clearly was the tattoo of a raven on each of their necks.

Rochelle connected telepathically with me. She warned she would attack and end the fight if I didn't get up. I wasn't sure how I did it, but I was somehow able to show her what I was seeing. What I didn't expect was her to double over in pain.

I couldn't stay behind to find out what was happening to her. A great sense of urgency took hold of me, then I was leaping in the air, propelled by an invisible force that told me I had to get to that wolf. I had to try to save him.

The forest goes by in a blur as my paws hit the ground hard. It's like there are wings attached to them. I've never ran so fast in my short wolf life. The cuts and scratches from the fight with Rochelle are long forgotten; I barely even feel their sting anymore.

There's no sound of pursuit, nor any communication from Dante telling me to get the hell back. I know my reckless act will cost me. Hell, maybe the alpha will decide to off me, but those are all problems I'll have to worry about later. I have a wolf to save now.

I reach the clearing where not even a week ago, I was attacked by that rogue, my life changed forever. I smell the hurt wolf right away, along with his pursuers. After I veer in his scent's direction, I find his form near the creek a second later. He's barely moving. As I approach, it's evident he's hurt in several spots. He also left a trail of thick and dark blood in his wake. I howl, trying to get his attention. He lifts his head and peers over his shoulder, right before he speaks to me.

"You shouldn't be here; they'll catch you as well."

"I'm not going to leave you behind."

"I'm not worthy of your help. I broke away from my pack."

I want to ask him the name of his former pack, but shouts in the distance catch my attention. Swinging around, I position my body protectively in front of him. When the first two hunters appear up the rise, my entire body tenses, the hairs on my back standing on end. I peel my lips back, showing off my sharp teeth as I snarl at them.

"Looks like we'll take two for the price of one," one man says with snickers.

His companion points his gun's muzzle in my direction, but oddly I'm not afraid of his weapon. Instead, I take a step forward, making my aggressive intentions clear.

He fires, missing me by a hair when I leap to the side. I hit the ground running. Like a speeding train, I'm on him before he has the chance to take aim again. My teeth sink into his arm, and the momentum of the jump pushes him to the ground. Crimson rage tinges my vision as the taste of his foul blood hits my tongue. I shake my head from side to side, thrashing his body like he's a rag doll, shredding skin and muscles in the process. His screams of agony don't faze me one bit. The wolf doesn't give a fuck about his pain. Honestly, my human form doesn't either. I want this man dead.

Sharp pain explodes on my temple when I'm hit on the head by the butt of a shotgun. I let go of the man, rolling on the ground to get away from another hit. The second hunter lets out a string of curses as he aims at me, and I know I won't be fast enough to avoid the bullet this time. In my rage, I forgot there was a second threat.

Suddenly, fiery energy surges within my body, something powerful and foreign. It is most definitely *not* the wolf's essence. If feels different, not as primal as the wolf's, but equally as overwhelming. It expands from my core down to my limbs until it explodes out of me. Tendrils of blue crackling light spread in a spider web-like manner, covering the ground around me. The hunter with the gun pointed at me widens his eyes, then takes a couple of steps back.

"Motherfucker, what the hell is that?"

Reluctant to break eye contact with the man, but also wanting to know if there's a new threat coming, I break my gaze away from him for a second, looking in the direction he is. In bewilderment, I watch the tendrils of energy wrap around twigs, rocks, and leaves, then lift them in the air and assemble them together. Piece by piece, they take the shape of an enormous wolf. I blink my eyes to make sure I'm not hallucinating, but if I am, so is the hunter. He switches his aim to the beast with shaking arms. A growl that sounds nothing like the sound a real animal would make erupts in the forest, and I feel it down to my bones. For some reason, I'm not afraid. I know the wolf monster is not a threat to me. Actually, it almost feels like we're connected somehow.

I look at the tendrils of energy that still surrounds the beast's paws, and the pattern those links made on the ground, leading to me. Somehow, I *am* bound to the monster. But how?

"Kill the wolf. Kill the fucking wolf!" somebody shouts out

in the distance, the third hunter.

"Which one?" The terrified man begins to switch his aim from me and the new threat in a jittery motion.

A gunshot echoes. A split second later, pain explodes on my shoulder. I let out a whine, and my front legs fold under me. My entire left side is burning, and I know I was just hit by a bullet. The mysterious wolf jumps, taking the man in front of him down. In a vicious frenzy, the apparition sinks his teeth into the man's flesh, tearing him to pieces. At first, his desperate screams are loud, mixing with the sounds of his bones cracking under the weight of the monster on top of him. But soon enough, once his blood has soaked the earth, he falls silent. He's dead.

A sharp smell of urine hits my nose, and I turn in the direction the stench came. The third hunter is frozen to the spot, hand slack on his gun, staring wide eyed at the gruesome scene in front of him. Horror is etched on his face, and he doesn't seem to have noticed he's soiled himself.

The monster wolf raises its grotesque head, blood and torn flesh dripping from his large teeth, and growls at the paralyzed man. Finally managing to snap out of his terror, the guy runs away, tripping over nothing as he makes his way back up the hill. The monster wants to give chase; I'm as aware of it as if its will is my own, but I notice the energy that links us is beginning to fade, just like my strength is diminishing with every breath I take.

The monster wolf turns to me as if it he's waiting for my command. His eyes are nothing but two blue spheres of swirling energy, and they seem to carry secrets that transcend time and space. A great sense of familiarity takes hold of me, as if the beast and I are old friends.

What are you?

The sound of howling in the distance distracts me from my musings. The pack—they're finally coming for me. I feel the three brothers before they even appear up the rise. Tristan, Dante, and Samuel break through the forest shrubbery in all their wolf glory. They pause when their eyes take notice of the monster in the clearing. The last tendrils of strength desert me, and the power that links me to the apparition begins to recede. I turn just in time to see the pieces that make the supernatural wolf fall to the ground until the monster is gone.

There's a nudge on my flank, then a warm furry body pressing against my side. The black wolf has crawled all the way to me from the stream's bank.

"Thank you," he whispers to my mind before closing his eyes. His chest stops moving, and his presence in my head is gone. The wolf is dead.

Overwhelming sadness takes over me. I throw my head back, howling long and hard because it's the only thing I can do in wolf form to express the crushing grief in my chest. I didn't know this wolf, but I'm feeling his loss as if I lost a member of my own family. With tears in my eyes, I lay next to him and wait for a fate that might not be too different from his. I ran away from the pack again, broke the rules, and I know the punishment will be severe.

Did the Wolfe brothers come at the order of the alpha? Or did they defy him? I don't know which outcome would be worse.

CHAPTER 22

SAMUEL

There's a collective gasp when Red up and runs toward the forest while Rochelle remains immobile on the ground, whining in pain. I glance at Dante first, finding him staring in shock in the direction Red went.

Lyria howls and leaps forward, ready to chase Red, when the alpha commands her to stop.

"Nobody follows that wolf. I'll deal with her."

Mom leans closer to whisper something in his ear. He shakes his head, then kisses her cheek, but the sadness I find in her gaze is enough to clue me in. Dad thinks Red ran away, and he's going to make her pay. I can't let that happen.

Before my father can stop me, I break into a run. Jumping aside when Seth moves to block my way, I shift in midair. When my paws hit the ground, Dante's voice is loud and clear in my head. *"Right behind you, brother."*

He soon joins me, being the fastest in the pack and all, then he takes the lead. Another wolf is close behind me, and I know without looking that Tristan is with us as well.

"So, what do you think Dad will do to us for disobeying his orders?" I ask.

"Flay us alive, no doubt," Tristan replies.

"I'm surprised you're here," I say.

"I'm not," Dante chimes in. *"Tristan has finally pulled his*

head out of his ass, and realized fighting the connection to Red is futile."

"It might be all moot. I'm not sure Father will let Red live after this," he replies, his tone now somber.

Dante doesn't have a reply to that, and I wish now more than ever that he would say something reassuring. We do have a strange and yet powerful connection to Red. It's almost like we all imprinted on her, which is crazy because if that were the case, we would be fighting amongst ourselves for the right to be her mate. And yet, I don't feel the urge to rip out Dante or Tristan's throats.

I don't see any sign of Red, but her scent is fresh in the air, which means we're going in the right direction. But how in the world had she managed to run so fast? She had less than a minute of a head start.

I hear angry shouts right before a gunshot is fired. Adrenaline kicks in, spurring my legs to run faster. We all seem to have pressed the turbo-speed button, zooming through the forest like a speeding bullet. I smell Red's blood before I get a visual of her. She's down the hill, close to the stream with her face down. A black wolf is slowly crawling his way to her. He's hurt, badly so. But it's the creature not too far from her that makes my heart leap into my throat and get lodged there. A dark creature made from twigs, leaves, and rocks is staring at Red. It has the shape of a wolf, but it's twice as tall as one. His eyes shine with an unearthly blue light, and I can safely say I've never seen anything like that before. The creature glances in our direction for a second before it loses its shape, crumbling to pieces on the ground.

"What the fuck was that?" I ask no one in particular.

"Witch-fucking-craft," Tristan replies, not hiding the disgust in his tone.

"Red!" Dante takes off down the hill in her direction. The mental shout wasn't meant for us. He's trying to reach her mind, but in this situation, I don't blame him for messing up the mental channels.

Tristan and I follow him. By the time we reach Red, Dante has already shifted into human form. Red raises her head, whining a little when Dante touches the area on her shoulder that's drenched in blood.

"I know it hurts, sweetheart, but you need to shift back so I can have a better look. Can you do that for me?"

Red howls before lowering her head to the ground. Nothing happens. She's not attempting to shift, her gaze trained on a spot behind us. I turn to the carnage a couple of feet away from us. Next to a pile of rocks and twigs—what's left of the wolf creature—there's a body that's so mangled it's barely recognizable. Limbs are torn, and where the torso should be, there's nothing left but a bloody pulp. If I weren't in wolf form, I might throw up.

The sound of leaves shuffling puts me on a high alert. Flaring my nostrils, I pick up another blood scent. A second man is slinking away, trying to hide behind a boulder. I can't believe I hadn't seen him before. Shit! Dante just shifted in front of him. Dad is definitely going to flay us alive.

Tristan leaps in the guy's direction. The human curls into a ball, begging for his life. My brother ignores the pleas, snagging his teeth in the man's shirt and forcing him to look up.

"He saw Dante," I say.

"I know." Tristan's reply is pissed, even in my head.

"We need to get Red back to the compound." Dante has Red in his arms, and I wince when I see she's already shifted back. Blood drips down her arm from the torn skin on her shoulder. "She got shot, and she needs medical attention ASAP."

The fur on my back stands on end as a warning shiver ripples through my spine. The alpha is here. I turn, seeing the magnificent white wolf at the top of the rise, flanked by Mom, Seth, and Lyria. Damn it. The presence of the top wolves in the pack doesn't bode well for my brothers and me.

"What happened here?" my father asks.

"We don't have time to explain." Dante makes the trek

toward him. "Red is hurt. She needs assistance."

Dad takes a step forward, baring his teeth and growling at Dante. Right now, he's not our father. He's the pack's alpha. Dante realizes he crossed a line, but he doesn't show fear or submit to our father's warning.

"You can punish me all you like later. But please let me get Red some help."

Mom howls, then turns to Dad. They're communicating mind to mind, a private channel that doesn't include us. Meanwhile, Tristan doesn't waver his hold on the only witness to what happened here. I have a feeling Dad won't take Red's word for it, and the black wolf she was protecting can't speak on her behalf since he's dead. That reminds me... who the hell was he?

Returning to his carcass, I take a good whiff of his fur. I don't recognize the scent, which means he's not from the area. That's good and bad at the same time. If he'd been a Shadow Creek wolf, it wouldn't be good for Red. Most likely, Dad would ship her off to those assholes up north without blinking an eye if he thought she had any strong connection to them. So the biggest mystery remains. Why had she bolted like that? How had she known this wolf was in danger? Is it possible she has the sight just like Mom and Dante? The wolf was killed by professional hunters, which poses an even bigger problem. Hunting is forbidden in Crimson Hollow. We need to know who these men are. Were they working alone, or can we expect more of those assholes to come?

Mom's voice brings me back to the here and now. She has shifted, and is now examining Red's wound. "Let's get the girl mended, then we'll talk about what happened here."

I decide to shift back because somebody has to carry the dead wolf back to the compound. Maybe Mom or Dad will be able to tell where he came from.

"What about that vermin there?" I point at the man Tristan has trapped under his jaw.

Dad howls, then answers into my mind. *I'll handle him.*

Then I'm coming for you and your brothers."
Of course he is. We're so fucked.

CHAPTER 23
TRISTAN

I was the only one who didn't shift back. Dante and Sam had their reasons. Dante carried Red, and Sam brought the fallen wolf back to the compound. I also had a load, but the scumbag who tried to gun Red down didn't deserve to be carried. So I dragged him through the forest, careful enough not to inflict any fatal injuries, but if he got more banged up than he already was in the journey, it was fitting.

Hunters in our fucking forest. We hadn't had those since I was a young kid. Montgomery wasn't the mayor then, and I can't help but blame her for their presence now. Maybe not directly, but through negligence. She needs to be voted out of office.

Seth tried to talk to me telepathically—even when our channels aren't open, we can feel someone's presence outside, like a knock on the door. I shut him out, which I'm sure he didn't appreciate. But he has questions I'm not ready to answer.

Once back in the compound, Dad orders me to leave the hunter with Seth. Despite the fact I want to start interrogating the motherfucker right away, I can't defy the alpha again. I'm in enough trouble with him as it is.

In silence, I follow him into the alpha's manor, shifting as I go since he has already done so. Sam joins us a second later, the stench of the dead wolf all over him. I don't recognize the scent, but at least he's not a Shadow Creek mutt.

"What did you do with that black wolf?"

"I left him at the infirmary. Mom wants to perform the autopsy."

"Did she—"

"No, she doesn't know where he's from," Sam answers, knowing exactly what I was going to ask.

I glance to my right. More precisely, to the door that leads to the infirmary.

"Where the hell is Dante?" I ask Sam.

"Where do you think? He went with Mom. He won't leave Red's side."

"Stupid Dante. Dad will kick him out of the pack."

"I know, but I think Dante has imprinted. I'm mean, we probably all have, but since he and Red hooked up, I think it might have sealed the deal."

I clench my jaw hard because I can't deny there's a strong possibility my brothers and I imprinted on the same woman. The biggest question is why? What makes her so special? Sam's idea she might be like the legendary Mother of Wolves is hard for me to swallow. I never believed in that story. It's not in a wolf's nature to share.

Dad disappears inside his office down the hallway. Even though I'd prefer to put some clothes on before facing his wrath, I don't want to keep him waiting. We find him already dressed in jeans and a muscle T-shirt when we enter his office. Even in human form, there's no doubt the man is the alpha. Corded with powerful muscles, he could easily win a fight against me or my brothers without putting forth a lot of effort. His eyes are crackling with fury, the irises glowing an intense ember color.

"Shut the door," he commands, standing by the side of his desk. He's too wired to sit.

Sam clicks the door closed, but remains near the exit. Without being conscience of doing so, I position myself in front of my younger brother, protecting him from Dad. If the alpha decides to strike, I'll take the first blow. As the oldest, I've always seen it as my duty to protect my brothers. I know they think I'm an asshole, and maybe I'm harder on them than I need to be, but I don't know any other way to prepare them for a future where I'm not around.

"You don't know how much it costs me not to punish you like the pack's law dictates. How dare you challenge my authority like that!"

"You were going to kill Amelia," I say.

"You're damn right I would. That girl has caused nothing but trouble since she arrived here. She's a Shadow Creek wolf through and through. It was a mistake to allow her to stay."

"She belongs with us." Sam takes a step forward, his hands balled into fists at his side.

Dad cuts a glare in my brother's direction. It's meant to instill terror, but Sam doesn't cower. "Why? Because you think you've imprinted on her?" Dad laughs without humor. "That girl comes from a powerful witch bloodline. I'm not convinced there isn't a ploy here to destroy our pack from within."

"What are you saying?" I ask, a mix of worry and adrenaline swirling in my chest.

Dad lets out a heavy sigh, his shoulders slouching forward as he crosses his arms in front of his chest. The aggressive stance seems to evaporate out of thin air, a change so out of character for him that it does my head in. What the hell is going on here?

"Dad, what happened at the meeting in Vancouver?" I ask.

"Nothing out of the ordinary there." He raises his head, the ember color gone from his eyes.

"Your mother has seen my death."

"What?" Sam and I say at the same time.

Dad's gaze seems to go inward as he stares at a point over my shoulder. "Right before I left, Mervina told me. She was afraid something bad would happen during my trip, so she warned me to be careful. I knew she didn't part with that information lightly. Certain visions should never be discussed. As it was, I didn't think much about it. Your mother has had visions in the past that never came to pass. But when I returned to the compound and met Amelia for the first time, I saw the shadow of death surrounding her."

"Do you think she's going to be the cause of your ruin?" I ask, and my mind goes back to Dante's painting. She's portrayed as a queen in that picture; it wouldn't be too farfetched to assume she was an alpha there.

"I saw through your eyes what she did in the forest today. She summoned that beast, Tristan."

"You don't know that," Sam starts, but Dad interrupts.

"Yes, I do. Your mother confirmed it."

"So if Mom also saw that, why did she agree to tend to Amelia? Why didn't she let you get rid of the perceived threat you're so afraid of?" My question seems to bring even more grief to our father's gaze.

"Because Mom doesn't agree with Dad," Dante announces, coming into the room as silently as a ghost.

Dad stares at him, grinding his teeth so hard I can hear it from where I stand.

"How is Red?" Sam asks, ignoring the murderous glint Dad is throwing at Dante.

"She's fine. The bullet only grazed her shoulder. Mom gave her a sedative, so she's sleeping now."

"Your mother's opinion of that girl is clouded because of Dante's vision. She thinks she'll be this pack's salvation." Dad sneers, his face morphing into something vile, something not like my father at all. The sudden changes in his mood are giving me a whiplash.

"When you die, only one of us will be able to stay and become the new alpha," Sam says. "But if Red is like the Mother of—"

"That woman is not the Mother of Wolves!" Dad hits the wooden desk so hard it cracks the surface. "She's a Shadow

Creek mutt who can't follow simple rules. And today, she just proved she will be this pack's damnation."

An urge to defend Red comes out of nowhere, overriding the will to submit to the alpha. I peel my lips back and growl, taking a step forward. "You'll not kill her. I won't allow it."

"Are you challenging me, boy? Do you really want to go that route?" Dad meets me halfway, baring his teeth as well.

"You're not making sound decisions. You have no proof that Red is the enemy," I counter.

My words seem to penetrate my father's brain. The rage seeps from his expression, replaced by a troubled glint in his eyes. It only lasts a split second before he narrows them in a cold manner.

"I do not wish to kill you, Tristan, so I'll forget you ever spoke those words to me." He turns to Sam and Dante, who are standing still with muscles tense, ready for battle. "That goes for you two as well. Whether you like it or not, I'm still the alpha, so my word is final. If I want that woman gone, she will be gone, one way or another."

Dante moves closer, his green eyes flashing ember now, and his canines elongated. I move to block him. There's something going on with our father. He's not acting like he used to. His emotions are all over the place, and he's letting them control him. I need to speak to Mom about it.

A loud knock echoes in the room, and we all turn to look at the closed door.

"Who is it?" Dad growls.

"It's Seth."

Dad spares me one more glance of disdain, before telling the enforcer to come in. I don't need to read my best friend's thoughts to know he came to deliver bad news.

"What happened?" I ask.

"The hunter we brought back is dead."

"How is he dead? Did you kill him?" My tone is accusatory, and Seth winces in turn.

"Of course not. I put him in a cell, didn't touch the guy.

I peeled my eyes away for one second, and then I heard gurgling. I turned to find the scumbag convulsing on the floor, frothing white foam from his mouth. He must have had poison on him. He'd rather die than be interrogated."

"Son of a bitch." Sam runs his hand through his hair, and I share the sentiment.

I regret trying to be the good and obedient beta now. I should have followed my instincts to interrogate the guy right away. My father should have made the exact same call, not ordered my brothers and me into his office to yell at us. Maybe Mom's revelation about his death did affect him after all. It would explain his erratic behavior.

"There's more... he had this with him." Seth drops a small electronic device that looks almost the same as the one we found on the rogue wolf from Shadow Creek.

Dad picks it up, turning it around in his fingers and examining it intensely. "Do you know what this is?"

"I don't have the faintest idea." Seth cocks a brow at me, a question in his gaze. I shift from foot to foot, breaking eye contact. I can't tell him we've seen something like that before. That would mean revealing that Red was attacked by a Shadow Creek wolf, and the pack cannot know that.

"I'll take this to Zeke." Dad puts the device away.

"The imp?" Seth's eyebrows arch until they almost meet his hairline. He's not alone in his surprise. Zeke Rogers is an imp who came to Crimson Hollow around fifty years ago, and he's as shady as a lower demon can get.

The leaders of the supe community didn't consider Zeke a threat, and they valued his connections to the underworld, so they let him stay to set up shop. He chose to open a bakery of all the businesses he could have chosen. It was a peculiar choice, but only to us supernaturals who know about his true nature.

"You can't trust that guy." Sam makes an exasperated gesture with his hand, but he shuts his mouth quickly when Dad cuts him a glare. Smart move. We don't want to reawaken the beast, especially in front of Seth.

"I want to know if there's something supernatural about it. You can't be too careful these days." Dad gives each of us a meaningful glance, and it's obvious he's referring to Red. He won't let go of the idea that she's dangerous to us, which means she's not safe here.

CHAPTER 24
RED

There's a terrible cry in the forest, followed by the howl of a dying wolf. In the next second, I understand that the dying wolf is me. Lying on the ground, I feel the moisture that's slowly drenching the earth. It's thick and sticky—my blood. I glance down at my body, trying to find the puncture wound, but it's impossible to tell. My entire gown is stained red.

Overwhelmingly sadness takes over me, and I call out their names. *Dante... Samuel... Tristan...* The wind carries the sound, and I can almost imagine the letters that compose their names dancing in the air. I know they won't be able to hear me. I'm far away from home, that much is certain, and I can't feel their presence within me. Are they aware that my strength is waning with every beat of my heart, with every breath I take? Would they mourn my death just as fiercely as I'm regretting not having had the chance to spend more time with them?

Red. A whisper reaches me, so softly I almost don't hear it. I think it's Samuel, and my heart beats faster. I focus on my hearing, hoping he'll call me again, but nothing reaches my ears besides the natural noises of the strange forest. Then, a blue light seeps through the trees, slowly creeping toward me. I hold my breath, terrified of what is producing that mysterious glow.

The blue light finally reaches me, wrapping around my limbs and torso. Gradually, the red staining my dress begins to disappear, as if the light is draining it somehow. The pain vanishes along with it.

The sounds of dried leaves getting crunched under a heavy weight makes me turn my face back to the forest. A great wolf made from pieces of wood, leaves, and pebbles is staring at me with glowing blue orbs instead of eyes. He's standing there at the edge of the clearing, as if waiting for something—maybe a sign—from me. He's a beast, taller and wider than any real wolf, with long, sharp canines that would go through my skin as if I were made of butter, yet the terror from before has ebbed away. The reason is simple; I know that wolf. I've summoned him. I don't know how the knowledge is now in my head. Maybe through the energy linking us.

"Why are you here?" I ask.

"You know the reason. Through time and space, even after death, we'll always protect you." The beast speaks to my mind, sounding like several people are speaking to me all at once.

"Who is we?"

"The wolves bound to you."

"I don't have any wolves bound to me. I just became one not too long ago."

"You'll remember with time, Mother of Wolves."

Mother of Wolves? What the hell is he talking about?

The wolf retreats, taking with him the ebbs of blue energy. He vanishes into the forest, then a blinding light assaults my sight.

I throw my arm over my eyes to protect them, groaning in the process.

"Amelia, you're awake," Samuel's husky voice says from nearby, making tingles run down my spine.

"What's up with the bright lights?" I groggily ask.

"You're in the infirmary. You got shot. Don't you

remember?"

The memories begin to flood my brain. At first, I have a hard time separating what's real and what was part of the dream I just had. Most importantly, I don't know if the great wolf did indeed show up for me when I was facing off with the hunters.

"Yeah, now I do." I touch the place on my shoulder, finding a bandage there.

Samuel grabs my hand, lacing our hands together. He smiles at me, but the gesture doesn't reach his eyes. My heart twists inside my chest, and I fear dark times await me.

"What is it?" I ask.

"You can't seem to go a day without causing trouble, can you?" He tries for levity, but I'm not buying it.

"Samuel, what did the alpha say?"

"I could lie and say you have nothing to worry about, but if I did, I'd be doing you a disservice."

"You're scaring me." I squeeze his hand, wishing he would just spill it already. "Is he going to kill me?"

"Not for the time being, but he wanted to, Red. If we hadn't defied him and gone after you, you would already be dead."

I close my eyes, thinking how my strange compulsion to save that black wolf put the Wolfe brothers in deep trouble with their father. From the little information I gathered, I'm aware that going against the alpha's orders can be punishable by death. And yet, they did it for me.

"Why would you risk your lives like that?" I open my eyes again, needing to see the truth on Samuel's face.

He touches my temple, then run his fingers down my cheek. "Because you're important to us."

The door to the infirmary bursts open. Dr. Mervina comes in, followed by Tristan and Dante. Their somber expressions put me on high alert.

"How are you feeling, Amelia?" Dr. Mervina asks.

"Like shit."

"You're really ought to stop ending up here." She lifts the bandage off my shoulder. "You're almost healed. That's good."

"What's going to happen to me? Is the alpha going to kick me out of the pack for forfeiting the challenge?"

"Don't worry about Anthony for now." Dr. Mervina watches my face closely before continuing. "Tell me what happened at the clearing, Amelia."

"I-I'm not quite sure. I got a vision of the black wolf. He was hurt, and being pursued by dark-clad hunters."

"How many were there?" Tristan asks.

"Three. One of them got away."

"Fuck." He begins to pace in front of my bed, and I can honestly say I've never seen him look so frazzled. His usually properly styled hair is messy, and he hasn't shaved in a while.

"I got one of them before I was shot. I'm not sure what happened to him."

"We brought him alive to the compound for interrogation, but before we could do so, he killed himself," Samuel answers.

"What? How?"

"Poison," Dr. Mervina says. "He didn't want to be interrogated, which makes us believe they're not your garden-variety hunters."

"They all had the same tattoo on their necks. A raven," I say.

I catch the worried glances Dante and Tristan share, so I ask, "Does that mean anything to you?"

"No, but if they're branded like that and they carry poison on them, then we're dealing with a highly organized and extremely dangerous organization," Tristan replies.

"We can talk about that later," Dr. Mervina chimes in. "I'd like to discuss the other phenomenon that occurred in the woods—the great wolf apparition that you summoned."

"You've seen it, too? I wasn't imagining things?"

"I saw it through Dante's eyes. By the time we arrived at the clearing, he was already gone."

"How do you know I summoned it?" I ask with a hint of suspicion. Can the woman peer into my thoughts, too?

"Because I've dreamed about it. I've seen you use your

powers to bring forth the Guardians of Wolves."

"Guardians of Wolves? What's that?"

Dante, Samuel, and Tristan are all staring at their mother now, watching her with extreme attention.

Dr. Mervina takes a deep breath, looking at her sons as she does so. "They're the spirits of past wolf warriors, the consorts of the Mother of Wolves. They vowed to protect her even after death."

"Mom, not again with this Mother of Wolves nonsense." Tristan says, exasperated.

"I had a dream, just now," I say. "The great wolf appeared for me again, and he spoke to me. He called me Mother of Wolves. What does that mean? Am I her reincarnation or something?"

Dr. Mervina shakes her head, wriggling her hands together. "I don't know."

"That changes nothing. Amelia can't stay here. It's not safe." Tristan speaks to his mother as if I'm not in the room.

"Why am I not safe? Where am I going to go?" It's futile to hope they'll let me return to Chicago, not after everything that happened. And to be honest, I don't want to go. There are too many unanswered questions about my new existence, and I can only find the answers here in Crimson Hollow.

"To my place in the city." Tristan stares hard in my direction, the tight set of his jaw telling me there's no room for arguments.

"Why can't I stay with Dante?"

"My studio is too close to the compound. We need to get you out of our father's sight."

"What about your place, Samuel?" I plead. I don't want to stay under the same roof as Tristan—not for one second.

"I tried, Red, but the band practices at my place. We really don't want other supernaturals to know what's going on."

Other supernaturals? I assumed everyone in The Howlers were wolf shifters, but truth be told, I hadn't seen any of the other band members around. I'm curious about them, but not enough to ask questions. I have more important things to worry about.

"How about I just stay here, then?" I ask stubbornly.

"No. Absolutely not," Dr. Mervina almost shouts, and then it finally dawns on me. A rift has been created between the alpha and his sons, and I'm right smack in the middle of it.

"Okay." I turn to Tristan, who is openly glaring at me. "But if you treat me poorly, I'll be on the first flight out to Chicago."

It's a meaningless, empty threat, and he knows that. He doesn't take the bait. "I promise I'll be on my best behavior. Now, let's get you out of here before Dad changes his mind again."

I catch the small wince from Dr. Mervina, and the sadness that clouds her eyes. Something is definitely going on with the alpha, and I have a feeling it's not only related to me.

CHAPTER 25

RED

The ride to Tristan's apartment is filled with heavy silence. He seems to be just as displeased with the arrangement as I am. Sure, we shared a moment of truce right before my fight with Rochelle, but now it seems we're back to the status quo. Him hating my guts for the sole reason that I exist.

His apartment is on the main square street, above Wolfe Corp's office. The place itself is not as big as I imagined. Judging by the width of its front, I'd say maybe a hand full of employees could fit in there. I don't think it deserves the tag 'Corp' in the title, but I bite my tongue and don't say anything. Antagonizing Tristan right now when I have to stay at his place for an indefinite amount of time is not the smartest idea.

In front of his office, I peer through the window. There are a couple of people working there, but no one pays any attention to my snooping. Tristan bypasses the entrance to his office, and unlocks the door next to it instead. I glance at the intercom, noticing there's no name on the tag. Either he doesn't want people to know he lives here, or there's no need to disclose that information because it's common knowledge.

A flight of steep, narrow stairs appears once the door swings open. Without waiting, Tristan takes them two at a time. I keep pace, and once we reach the landing, I find an immaculate and roomy apartment with big windows that let plenty of light in. To my right, an open kitchen equipped with state-of-the-art appliances is also in pristine condition.

A massive dark grey leather couch in an L shape takes up most of the living room. It faces a large flat-screen TV mounted above the fireplace.

A bear-pelt rug is placed in front of the couch, which is a surprise. I turn to him with an eyebrow raised. "Interesting choice for a rug."

He gives me a haughty glance. "That was a gift from the alpha of the Thunderborn sleuth. It's a great honor to receive it."

"Wait? There are also bear shifters in Crimson Hollow?"

"Of course. Bears, eagles, coyotes. We even have a few kitsune here. You know, fox shifters."

Crossing my arms in front of my chest, I narrow my eyes. "I know what kitsune means. So basically, most the animals around here could potentially be shifters. Is that caused by the same virus that infected me?"

Tristan shakes his head and swings around, walking down the hallway. I think he expects me to follow him. "I don't know if that's true, but I don't think so. You'd have to ask my mother about that."

He disappears inside the first room to his left. I stop at the door, only sticking my head inside. It's a small bedroom with a queen-sized bed covered with a light blue bedspread, no frills. The furniture is modern, all white and sleek. There are two nightstands, one on each side of the bed, and a dresser with a mirror above it.

"You have your own bathroom. There are towels in the cupboard." Tristan turns to me, making room so I can enter.

My gaze darts around, but only because I want to look at anything but him. I hug my middle as a sense of uneasiness takes hold of me. So many life-altering moments are happening in such a short period of time that I barely have time to process everything.

"How long am I going to stay here?"

"As long as needed. I promise you'll barely see me."

I finally glance at him, furrowing my eyebrows a little. "You defied the alpha, your dad, to protect me. I don't get it."

Tristan doesn't say a word. Instead, he keeps staring at me with his intense grey eyes that seem to be brewing a storm in them. Fiery energy unfurls in the pit of my stomach as I fight the incredible pull that's urging me to take a step closer. My heart flutters inside my chest, as if it were a hummingbird instead of a muscle. My mouth goes dry, and I feel a little dizzy. Holding on to the doorframe is a necessity to keep standing upright.

"What's going on with me?" I whisper.

"You're feeling it, too, aren't you?"

"Yes. What is this? I felt the same with Dante before…" My eyes widen at the same time I cover my mouth with my hand. "It can't be. Is this…" I take a deep breath, trying to control my emotions. "Is this imprinting?"

"Probably."

"I don't want to imprint on you!" It's almost a whine. I hold the doorframe tighter, leaning against it as well. I feel suddenly feverish.

"You don't want to imprint on me, but you have no problem imprinting on Dante or Sam?" Tristan's voice sounds more like a growl.

"They weren't assholes to me when I had barely turned into a shifter." I rest my face against the cool wall, needing some relief.

"Tell me how you feel right now? Sick?"

I nod, unable to speak.

Tristan closes the distance between us, and all the muscles in my body tense. I suck in a breath when he touches my face, my mind and my heart starting a war with one another. I want to give in to the overwhelming feeling that's demanding I accept Tristan's proximity, but my mind won't let me.

"That's how I felt for the longest time, but maybe not as

bad as you." His thumb caresses my cheek, and I let out a whimper.

"You don't like me; you never did. And now there's this weird bond between us. How is this fair? Where's the free will to walk away?"

"I never said I didn't like you." His eyes drop to my lips, and my tongue darts out without me willing it do so. Fuck, now my entire body is betraying me.

"I don't want to feel this way. How can I make it stop?"

"Don't fight it," he breathes out, his voice rough, needy.

"You mean give in?"

"Yes, would that be so bad?" Tristan's eyes have turned molten, filled with raw lust. And I'm not immune. There's a sudden throbbing between my legs now, and I feel like the worst person in the world that I'm willing to toss away my pride for a taste of him.

"Yes, very bad." I take a step closer, and Tristan takes it as a sign that I'm done fighting.

With a gentleness I wasn't expecting from him, he brings his lips to mine, just a soft brush at first, before his tongue pries my mouth open. I let go of the doorframe to clutch his steely arms, feeling his strength down to my bones. With a groan, he deepens the kiss, taking proper possession of my mouth. Liquid fire surges from within, spreading through my body at the speed of light. The dizziness is gone, but my head is still fuzzy for entirely different reasons.

Tristan's hands run down my spine until they're resting on my butt cheeks. When he squeezes them, I jump, my legs going around his trim waist. I let out a moan of delight when my core presses against his erection, and then it's game over for me. My mind is still rebelling a little, but I shove those pesky thoughts to a dark corner and forget them for now. I'm letting my body take control.

Tristan takes a few steps back. Before I know it, we're toppling over onto the bed with him between my legs. I don't know what's making me hungrier now—his hands exploring my body or his mouth devouring mine. There's tugging and pulling until there are no barriers left between us. I have no clue how we managed to get rid of our clothes without breaking our kiss. It's almost like we're too afraid that if we break the connection, reality will come and ruin this moment for us.

There's definitely a sense of urgency between us, as if we've been denying our cravings for far too long and now it's do or die. There's no hesitation on Tristan's part when he plunges fast and deep inside of me, his wide girth filling me completely. We don't need foreplay. I arch my back and cry out, loving the sensation of him, the sure away he takes possession of my body.

"Fuck, Amelia. You're so tight," he says between kisses and grunts.

In answer, I squeeze my internal walls. As impossible as it sounds, I feel Tristan getting even larger inside of me. Then he hits my G-spot, and my body simply melts under his. I scratch his back with my nails, then I bite his lower lip until I taste blood on my tongue. The pain only spurs him on, and he keeps pumping faster and faster without saying much besides incoherent words. I honestly can't think of anything to say either, not since my brain has turned into mush. All it can process right now is the amazing tension that's building between my legs.

With a loud roar, Tristan's entire body tenses before his warm seed fills me. That sends me over the edge as well, and I end up howling as I come hard and fast.

It takes a few minutes for my breathing to return to normal after such an earth-shattering orgasm. Tristan has rolled off me, and he's now lying by my side, staring at the ceiling and breathing hard.

Without the lust and the crazy impulse to jump the guy's bones, I'm run over by an intense sense of shame. Heat spreads through my cheeks, and without being aware of doing so, I make a disgruntled sound in the back of my throat. I attempt to get out of bed, but Tristan touches my wrist, holding me in place.

"Wait." He rolls onto his side, and I face him. "Was I too rough?"

The muscles around his mouth are tight, and his eyebrows are furrowed as he watches me closely. I don't squirm under his scrutinizing gaze; on the contrary, I stare deep into his eyes as well. The angry storm is gone from them. In its place, I read genuine concern there.

"No, you weren't."

His eyebrows furrow deeper, as if he doesn't believe me. "I tried to go easy, but…" He shakes his head. "It was so damn hard. I never imagined it would it be like this."

"What would?"

"Mating."

Guilt sneaks into my heart swiftly as reason returns with a vengeance to the forefront of my mind. Groaning, I throw my legs to the side of the bed, then rest my elbows on my knees, hiding my face between my hands.

"What's wrong?" He touches my back, and the pleasure it gives me only works to double my guilt.

"I can't believe I did this to Dante."

"Ah, so that's what this is all about. You're still attached to your human monogamy traditions."

I shoot a scathing glare at him from between my fingers. "Wolves are monogamous. At least that's what I thought."

Tristan leans on his elbow, watching me with the hint of a smile on his lips. I don't want to feel anything more than annoyance for him right now, but my heart has other ideas. It beats out of sync, giddy as hell. Tristan's post-sex looks are not helping either. His hair is a wild mess, and his lips are red from all the kissing. He's never looked sexier, and I have to fight the urge to kiss him again.

"True, but haven't you realized yet that you're not a regular wolf?"

"So now you're also buying the Mother of Wolves theory?"

I ask, suppressing a shiver when I remember the dream. What if I am her?

"You've imprinted on Dante, me, and my guess is also on Sam. If you weren't different, we would be at each other's throats because, like you said, wolves don't share."

"So, you're saying if I went and slept with Dante or Samuel, you wouldn't mind?"

Tristan watches me for a couple of beats without saying a word, then he reaches over and runs his fingertips down my arm. Goose bumps break out all over my skin. "As much as it surprises me to admit it, no, I wouldn't mind. Does that mean you're the legendary Mother of Wolves? I don't know. I've never believed in that story."

"And what are your thoughts regarding the great wolf apparition in the forest? You saw it too, right?"

He nods, then glances down. "This is Crimson Hollow; there's a lot of weird shit in this town."

"Weirder than shifters?"

He raises his head. "Yes, much weirder. Speaking of which, I need to see one of those characters."

"Who?"

Tristan hops out of bed. He doesn't answer me right away, so I press him. "Tristan?"

He bends over to grab his boxer shorts from the floor, pulling them on as he answers. "Zeke Rogers. He owns the—"

"Zeke's Sweet Treats, the bakery shop," I finish his sentence. "Are you saying he's something *other?* I used to go there with Grandma all the time."

"Yes, he's something '*other*' all right. But you should rest a bit. I'll be back soon."

I jump out of bed as well. "No way, Jose. I'm coming with you. I'm done being kept in the dark."

CHAPTER 26

RED

I couldn't go out in public after my sexy time with Tristan without showering first, even though I had cleaned up the remains of our 'mating'. So I took the quickest shower known to man, afraid Tristan would just leave without me. Surprisingly, he waited, but the hard set of his jaw told me he wasn't happy I was coming along.

"So, what are we now? Mated?" I ask on our way to the bakery. Then I immediately pretend interest in the people nearby us. Zeke's establishment is on the other side of the square, so we're walking there instead of driving.

"Yes."

"Am I mated to Dante, too?"

"Yes."

"Are you going to only answer my questions with monosyllables now?"

"I'm all about efficiency." He doesn't glance my away, but at least the corners of his lips twitch up.

"Are mated wolves like married couples?"

"In a sense."

"So it means we tell each other everything, right?"

Tristan stops, shifting toward me. "Where are you going with this?"

Crossing my arms, I glare at the man. "What exactly is Zeke

and why don't you want me to tag along?"

Tristan runs his hand over his head. "It's not that I don't want to tell you what he is, Amelia, but Zeke is, well, I don't want him to know about you."

"Why not? Is he dangerous?"

"He's an imp, okay?" Tristan says, a little exasperated. At least he didn't bark at me like he used to.

"An imp?" My eyebrows arch. Shit, there is a lot of weird crap in this town for sure.

"Yes, an imp, the lowest type of demon there is. They're tricksters who usually prey on the weak. Most supes dismiss them of no consequence."

"But you don't." I narrow my eyes.

"Nope."

"Why exactly are you going to see him? Is this about the hunters or the wolf apparition?"

"The hunters. I'd never mention the apparition to anyone, and you shouldn't either."

Biting my lips, I look around me. That entire episode still freaks me the hell out, and the last thing I want is to discuss it with anyone.

"I don't plan to," I say. "So, what do you want to know about the hunters? Do you think they weren't regular humans?"

"I don't know. We found a small device embedded on the rogue who attacked you. I showed it to your friend Peter."

"Oh?" I can't help the surprise in my tone. "I didn't realize you knew Peter from before."

Despite the current subject and the gravity of the situation, there's a hint of amusement in Tristan's expression.

"It's safe to say I know most of the inhabitants of Crimson Hollow. Perks of being born and raised here."

I pinch my lips before I reply, "Well, you didn't know me."

"Touché. Anyway, Peter has helped me before with computer stuff, so I knew there was a chance he could help me identify the type of object we found."

"And did he?"

"He thinks it's something used to control small animals."
My heart begins to drum faster inside my chest. The ramifications are terrifying. If what Peter suspects is true, no shifter is safe. Tristan's somber expression tells me he feels the same way.

"How does Zeke fit in all this?"

"My father wants to be certain there's no trace of magic in the device."

My mind is going at a hundred miles an hour. Hunters in possession of high-tech controlling devices, weird magic going all around. Why would Grandma not stop me from moving here? Why couldn't she let me live my life in Chicago, blissfully unaware that mythical creatures and monsters exist?

Because apparently, I had a destiny to fulfill. Bitterness pools in my mouth when I think that she most likely faked being sick. I'm not sure I'll ever be able to forgive her, even when I'm used to my new supernatural life.

"Okay, let's go then." I take a step forward.

"Oh my God! Red, you're alive!" Kenya stops in front of me, appearing out of nowhere, then proceeds to engulf me in a bear hug. Her arm grazes the bandage on my shoulder, making me wince a little. It's strange I had forgotten all about my bullet wound when Tristan was buried deep inside of me.

"Kenya, what are you talking about? Of course I'm alive."

She eases back, still clutching my shoulder, to peer into my eyes. "I've been calling and leaving messages, but you seem to have forgotten about me."

I rack my brain, trying to remember when the last time I spoke to her was. She turns her attention to Tristan, who's standing a little stiffly next to me.

"Oh, hi, Tristan. Long time no see. How are you?"

"Very well, Kenya. I trust you and your mother are also well?"

"Oh, very much so."

Kenya looks at me, then back at Tristan. "Hmm, were you guys going somewhere?"

I open my mouth to say yes, but Tristan beats me to the punch. "Not at all."

"In that case, do you mind if I steal Red? I'm meeting a few of our friends at Jerry's diner."

"Kenya, I—" I start.

"You should go, Amelia. I'll catch up with you later." He waves goodbye and quickly crosses the street, unware of the glare I'm throwing at his retreating back. I can't believe he just ditched me.

Kenya grabs my arm and swings me around. "Red, are you hooking up with Tristan Wolfe?"

"Uh..." I feel the blush rush to my cheeks, and Kenya doesn't miss a thing.

She claps her hands together. "Oh my God. You *are* sleeping with him. You have to tell me *everything*. How did you meet? When did it happen? No wonder you weren't answering my calls. I'd pull a disappearing act as well if I had that hunk in my bed."

Shit. Lying is futile, but I can stall. "I'm not going to dish out the dirty details of my love life out here on the curb."

"Fine. We're already late anyway." She laces her arm with mine. "That's why I was calling you in the first place."

"So, who's going to be there?" I'm glad that for now, Kenya has dropped questioning me about Tristan.

"You know, the usual suspects. Leticia, Sonya, Paul, Felix."

"Not Peter?" I ask, hoping the answer will be negative. He's the last person I want to see right now. I can't deal with his unrequited love while I'm juggling three men already. Plus, I know he'll have a thousand questions about my fake job at the compound.

"No. He had to work. He did say you were working for Dr. Mervina now. Was that how you met Tristan?"

"Yes, that's how we met."

"Funny. I never pegged him to be interested in college students. I've always heard he preferred older women."

Kenya probably didn't mean her comment to be malicious,

but jealousy grabs my heart in a vicious hold and won't let go. I can't deal with the image of Tristan hooking up with any other women. But at the same time, a great sense of insecurity drops over my shoulders, making them sag with the weight. I'm not the most experienced lover. Had he thought I sucked? I've only slept with three people my entire life. Ugh, and let's not dwell on the fact that the second person was his brother. It will take me a long time to get on board with this crazy idea of sharing the bed of more than one man.

"I know nothing about his past conquests," I grumble.

"Hey, girlie. I didn't say that to upset you. Those old hags have nothing on you."

She laughs. Despite the turmoil in my chest, she even gets a giggle out of me. I've missed my best friend and her contagiously happy disposition. We're still laughing when Kenya pushes the door of the diner open. She waves at the big group sitting all the way in the back in the biggest booth the place has.

"Look who I found." Kenya points at me.

"Hey, it's the runaway birthday girl." Felix laughs, raising a milkshake glass in my direction. Jerry's doesn't serve alcohol, but they have the best burgers in town, so it's a good trade-off.

"I didn't run away. My stupid dog did." I slide in next to Sonya, noticing for the first time that there's a new face in the group.

An attractive guy with coal-black hair and equally dark eyes is sitting opposite me. His high cheekbones are sharp enough to cut glass.

"Hey, Martin. You made it." Kenya sits next to me, and I suddenly find myself in the middle of a human sandwich. "Red, this is Martin. I met him this morning when he came over to introduce himself to my mother."

"I've always thought it was smart to let the local authorities know who you are, especially in small towns." Martin flashes Kenya a grin, but his eyes don't have any warmth in them. If the sun wasn't out, I'd think he was a vampire. He certainly has the looks.

"Yeah, very smart." Kenya bobs her head up and down in emphasis. It's like she lost her ability to make intelligent comments.

"And how did you meet Martin, Kenya?" I ask.

She waves her hand, throwing her long hair off her shoulder. A total Kenya move when she's interested in someone. "I was lucky to be standing next to my mother when he came over."

"And she was kind enough to invite me to meet her friends." Martin smiles at Kenya, full of teeth now, but it's even more chilling than his toothless grin from before. Why am I having such a strong reaction to this guy?

"He just moved into the old Miller's home," Kenya continues, unaware I'm watching her new friend intently.

"Oh? That's a fix-upper, isn't it?" I ask.

He shrugs. "I don't mind. I like to use my hands."

Kenya and Sonya sigh simultaneously, reminding me of the girls who were in love with Gaston in the *Beauty and the Beast* movie. Okay, I get it. He's pretty enough to be on the cover of a magazine, but there's something off about the guy that I can't quite place.

"Where are you from, Martin?" I start to play with the salt and pepper shakers on the table to keep my hands occupied.

"Milwaukee, originally, but I lived in Chicago for the past ten years before deciding I needed a change."

"Red is from Chicago, too," Sonya says, and I wish she hadn't opened her mouth.

"Oh yeah?" Martin stares at me, curiosity shining in his eyes. "What brought you to Crimson Hollow?"

"Family." I don't elaborate. His intense stare is giving me the creeps.

Leticia, who is sitting next to him, touches his arm to get his attention. Next to me, Kenya stiffens. I do the same. Kenya is getting tense because she has competition. Adrenaline is spiking in my veins for entirely different reasons. Martin has a tattoo on his neck, the exact same raven the hunters in the forest did. My blood turns cold. It's just too much of a coincidence. Hunters invade our forest... and now this guy shows up sporting the same tattoo? He must be one of them.

"Kenya, could you please let me out? I need to use the restroom."

"Yeah, sure."

Out of the booth, I make a beeline toward the restroom, pulling my cell phone out of my bag. Then, like an idiot, I remember that I never exchanged digits with Tristan, or any of the brothers for that matter. Oh my God, I'm such a dimwit.

"Hey, having phone trouble?"

I jump, finding Martin standing right in front of me.

"What?"

"You were looking at your phone like it had insulted you or something."

"No, nothing of the sort." I hastily put my phone back in the bag, wincing a little when the brusque movement jolts the wound on my shoulder. Come to think about it, why is it not healed yet? All the other times I got hurt, it hadn't taken more than a few hours for the wound to knit back together. I file that realization away, intending to ask Dr. Mervina later.

"Are you hurt?" Martin asks.

Damn it. He's too observant, but considering he's probably part of a sadistic group hell-bent on killing my people, it's not surprising.

My people. I've never thought of the wolves as such until now.

"I pulled a muscle while I was at the gym. Nothing major."

"You have to be careful. Always warm-up before workouts." There's an easygoing smile on his lips, but I can see clearly as day the hint of danger in his eyes. No wonder I was getting bad vibes from him from the get-go.

"For sure. I have to go." I edge around him, my heart beating so fast there's a chance it might leap out of my mouth.

At the door, I wave at Kenya, trying to catch her attention. She frowns when she sees I'm about to head out. I make the sign that I'll call her later, then I bolt. I have to find Tristan.

CHAPTER 27
TRISTAN

Why would an imp choose to run a bakery? The smell of sugar and vanilla immediately assaults my senses the moment I enter his busy shop. There are two girls working at the counter, both one-hundred percent human. I wonder what they would think if they knew they worked for a demon. The youngest of the duo, a teenager with red hair and freckles all over her face, beams a smile in my direction.

"I'll be right with you, sir."

"I'm actually looking for Zeke. Is he around?"

"Yes, he's in the back."

A door behind the counter opens, and out comes the owner of the place, the infamous Zeke Rogers. With light blond hair and baby-blue eyes, he looks more like an angel than the opposite. But all that's needed is a cursory glance into his eyes to see the glint of malice and mischief there.

"Tristan Wolfe, to what do I owe the pleasure of your visit? Come looking for a special cake?" The imp smiles, knowing full well I didn't come for cake.

"May I have a word with you in private?"

Zeke raises both eyebrows, and the cunning in his gaze becomes even more acute. I have to be on high alert here. The imp is notorious for trying to trick people into bargains that only benefit himself.

"Naturally. Come with me." He motions for me to come behind the counter, then I follow him to his back office. The smell of sweet treats becomes even more unbearable as we get near the kitchen.

"How can you stand the smell?" I cover my nose.

"Trust me, my friend. After centuries trapped in a cell in the bowels of an underworld dungeon, the sweet scent of sugar, cake, and chocolate is absolutely divine."

Well, he has me there. Not that I know from experience what such a place must smell like, but I can't imagine it's anything pleasant. With flourish, Zeke opens the door to his office, which looks like it was decorated by a five-year-old girl. It's an explosion of pastel colors, bright and cheery, fully capable of blinding me if I stare at them for too long.

"Good Lord," I say.

Zeke sits behind his glass desk, motioning for me to sit on a chair that's painted in silvery glitter with a fucking unicorn horn sticking out of its back. "You're joking, right?"

"What? Unicorns are lovely creatures. Very docile. They also taste delicious." Zeke smirks, amusement dancing in his eyes.

"Well, I don't want to take up too much of your time. I've come about something I'd like your opinion on."

Zeke leans back in his chair, folding his hands together. "My demonic opinion?"

I grunt, shifting slightly. "What other opinion would I need? Cake frosting?"

"Well, you know I left the dark side a long time ago. What are you willing to offer in exchange?"

"How about I don't kick your sparkly ass?"

"Such violence. And I'm the biggest supporter of the pack."

"You don't support anyone if it doesn't suit your interests." I narrow my eyes, contemplating what I can give the imp that will satisfy him. Then I decide to give him a bit of gossip, knowing full well he's worse than the old church ladies in town.

"We've had trespassers—hunters—in our area."

Zeke's spine goes taut as he sits straighter in his chair. "We haven't had hunters in Crimson Hollow since the time following the Thirteen Days of Chaos."

"I know."

"I take it you haven't told anyone about it, not even Mayor Montgomery."

I scoff. "She's the last person I'd bring this issue to."

Zeke rubs his chin, peering at me through narrowed eyes. "True. I've heard she's giving you a hard time. Some land dispute with the Shadow Creek pack."

"How do you—never mind. What I have to show you relates to the hunters."

"Okay, okay. You've got me intrigued. I won't ask you for a return favor. Show me what you've got."

I pull the device we found on the hunters from my pocket, then place it in the middle of the desk. Zeke grabs it with eager hands, turning it from side to side, examining every corner of the small silver box. "I'm sorry, but what am I looking at here?"

"We believe it's some kind of mind-control device, but we're not sure."

"Dude, no offense, but I'm not an expert in electronics. Have you tried that guy from the hardware store?"

I don't bother telling Zeke I've already gone to Peter. "I know you aren't a techie guy. I want to know if you sense any traces of magic in it."

"Nope. I sense *nichts*, nothing, *nada*."

He hands the object over, but it's too soon for me to feel any type of relief. I pull the other device, the one we found on the rogue from Shadow Creek, out. "How about this one?"

Zeke takes the device from my hand, and I immediately know it's different with this one. His blue eyes change into an electric purple, and the irises start to swirl. His skin tone changes as well, acquiring a greenish tint. I realize I'm seeing his true demonic form.

My nostrils flare, and my gums begin to ache as my canines elongate. Sensing a malefic energy whoosh from the device and spread throughout the room, I jump out of the chair, ready to shift if necessary.

"What the fuck is going on?"

"Did the hunter also have this?" Zeke doesn't take his eyes from the device.

"No."

With a shudder, he drops the device on his desk. It clinks against the glass surface, the evil presence I felt dispersing.

"What the hell happened here, Zeke?"

Breathing hard and with eyes as round as saucers, Zeke keeps staring at the device as if it's going to come to life. At least his skin is no longer green, and the electric purple irises changed back to blue.

"Something extremely evil and powerful touched that thing." The imp shudders.

"A demon?" I ask.

"Not any demon. An archdemon."

Not wanting Zeke to touch the damned object again, I remove it from his sight, shoving it in my jeans pocket. To say I'm not a little afraid to carry it now would be a lie. I fucking hate demons.

"What are you going to do with that?" Zeke asks.

"I don't know."

"I'll give you a piece of free advice." His tone is solemn, unusual for the guy, and it has my undivided attention. "Destroy it. Burn it with sacred fire."

I clench my jaw because the only supes with the power to summon sacred fire are the witches. And I'm not going to them for help.

"I'll keep that in mind."

CHAPTER 28
DANTE

"Mom, what's going on with Dad? He hasn't been the same since he returned from his trip to Vancouver."

She has her head down, busy writing in a small notebook. She glances up with eyes full of sadness. "I don't know, Dante. At first, I thought his strange behavior was due to my revelation. I should have never told him I saw his death." She sighs, her shoulders sagging. "But he was going on that trip to Vancouver, and I was afraid something was going to happen there. I wanted him to be prepared."

"But he said the meeting was fine. Even Valerius, the new Shadow Creek alpha, was on his best behavior."

Mom rests her head in her hands. "A fact that's strange and suspicious by itself. The Shadow Creek wolves are notorious for creating trouble during those alpha meetings."

"Dad was always so centered and fair. I honestly don't recognize him anymore. The alpha I knew would have never forced Red into that challenge with Rochelle, or be willing to kill her without knowing what happened in the forest."

"You haven't seen anything in your visions?" There's a hopeful tone in Mom's voice, and I hate that I can't give her what she needs—peace of mind that Dad will be okay.

I shake my head. "No. I haven't had any visions since the one about Red."

Mom lets out a shaky breath. "The sight has deserted me, too."

"Have you tried calling to it?" Mom has the power to do it, to call upon visions instead of waiting for them to happen spontaneously. I've never been able to summon the sight at will.

"Yes, many times. All I see is a big void."

The door to Mom's office in the clinic bursts open. Dad comes in, practically foaming at the mouth with the veins on his forehead bulging. "Where is she?"

His body is shaking, and his hands are balled into fists by his side. Blind rage seems to have overtaken him.

"Who? Amelia?" Mom asks in confusion.

"Who else? I told Seth to go fetch the girl, but he just informed me that she has left the compound with Tristan."

Mom and I trade a worried glance before she stands, resting her open palms on her desk. Leaning forward, she narrows her eyes. "We spoke about this, Anthony. You agreed to let Tristan take Red away until we can do a proper investigation of the events in the forest. Her presence here might incite some of the more restless wolves."

Incredulity takes over Dad's expression. His scowl turns into something akin to embarrassment. "I don't remember agreeing to that."

There's a moment of silence. Mom is clearly speaking to Dad mind to mind. The tension slowly leaves his body. Not wanting to bring his anger back with my presence, I slip out of Mom's office. There's nothing I can do for him that Mom can't do better. She's his mate after all, and has the strongest connection to him. My chest feels unbearably heavy as I leave the alpha's manor. I fear a big shift is coming, one I didn't foresee happening any time soon.

In my distraction, I fail to notice Lyria's approach until she's right in front of me, blocking the way. Rochelle is behind her, her posture saying she doesn't want to be there. Other than that, she seems fine, no side effects from her challenge with

Red.

"What do you want?" I snap at Lyria.

"I want to know what the fuck is going on. Why did Tristan take that bitch with him after the stunt she pulled during the challenge?"

Clenching my jaw hard, I bite my tongue so as to not literally bite Lyria's head off.

Rochelle switches her weight from foot to foot in a fidgety motion, keeping her gaze glued to the ground.

"That's none of your concern," I say, trying my best to keep my voice down.

"None of my concern? I'm still the pack's beta, or have I been demoted without being informed? With the way things are going in this pack, I wouldn't be surprised."

"If you were a true beta, your biggest concern right now would be to secure the area and make sure there aren't more hunters around, not to worry about who Tristan is with."

Lyria takes a step forward, baring her sharp teeth at me. "How dare you question my position in the pack? While you were busy doing God knows what, I dispatched our enforcers. They've found no trace of any hunters."

"Good. Now get out of my way. I have better things to do than waste my time with you."

Lyria narrows her eyes, nostrils flaring. "You think you're so special because you have your mother's gift. But your days of privilege might be coming to an end."

"What's that supposed to mean? Are you threatening me?" I take a menacing step toward her. Beta or not, if she doesn't back the fuck down, I'll make her do it by force if necessary.

"Why don't you use your special powers to find out?" The woman sneers, then swings around and strides away.

Good. Walk away, Lyria.

Rochelle watches her go. Only when Lyria disappears inside the building across the courtyard does she look in my direction. "Lyria feels her position in the pack is in jeopardy."

"She's not wrong," I say, but immediately berate myself

for letting that statement slip. We don't need more gossip circulating. I know the wolves are restless. With Dad acting so out of character, fights will erupt soon enough and mayhem will commence. Wolves need a strong alpha at the realm.

"Is Red the Mother of Wolves?" Rochelle's question catches me off guard.

I watch her more closely now, even daring to nudge her mind, trying to get a peek at her thoughts. I stop short of forcing my way in. I'm not a cad. I don't sense any malice from the enforcer, but I'm still on high alert.

"What? Where did you get that from?"

"When we were fighting, I sensed her power. She would have won the fight if she hadn't been plagued by that warning."

"What do you know about her warning?" I take a step in her direction, suspicion bringing forth the aggressive nature of my wolf.

"For a moment, I saw what Red did. I felt the pain of the fallen wolf. That's why I collapsed during the challenge. I don't know how she did that, but my grandmother used to tell me stories about the Mother of Wolves. She brought peace to the shifters in the New World."

"I know about the legends, but what makes you think Red is the Mother of Wolves?"

"She connected with a wolf outside our pack. I know she wasn't changed by one of us, but she was able to link mind to mind with us, the same way she was able to hear the dying wolf's pleas from across a great distance."

The enforcer widens her eyes as her tone of voice becomes more and more excited. She truly believes Red is the Mother of Wolves, a truth I can't share with anyone yet. Rochelle is lower in rank than Lyria. If that odious woman asks her what she knows, she won't be able to keep the truth from the beta.

"The Mother of Wolves is a legend, Rochelle. Nothing but a legend."

CHAPTER 29

RED

I blindly cross the street without looking for incoming traffic, adrenaline and fear mixing in my veins. Tires screech, followed by the sound of a loud horn. Somebody yells at me, but I don't acknowledge them. I have to find Tristan. I must look like a deranged woman, running across the peaceful square like the devil is after me. Just as I reach the other side, about to play chicken with traffic again, Tristan exits Zeke's Sweet Treats.

I call out his name so loudly he looks startled. He glances at the street before crossing it with long strides. Worry creases his features by the time he's standing in front of me. "What happened?"

"I met one of the hunters."

His eyebrows meet his hairline before his expression turns into one of fury. "Where?"

"At the diner. Kenya introduced me to him. He just moved to Crimson Hollow. His name is Martin and he has a tattoo of a raven on his neck, just like the hunters in the forest."

Tristan grabs my arms, squeezing them a little as he peers intently into my eyes. "Go back to my apartment and wait for me there."

"What? No! I'm coming with you."

"Please, Amelia. Do as I say. Things have just gotten a

helluva lot more complicated and dangerous."

"I don't care. If I'm in the middle of this mess, I have the right to know all the details."

"And I don't want to worry about your safety more than I already do," Tristan shouts, making me wince. His eyes soften while he cups my cheek gently, in stark contrast to his outburst of a second ago. "Please, Red. Do this for me."

Something shifts inside of my chest, and my resolve begins to crumble. It's not his touch that's doing it, but the way Tristan's voice broke just now. His tough-guy armor cracked a little, and he didn't try to hide it.

"Fine. I'll wait for you at your place. Please be careful."

Tristan's eyes flash with ember while he watches me as if in wonder. I don't know what to make of that stare. I'm so used to contemptuous glances from him. I don't have time to react before he slides his hand to the back of my head, pulling my face to his for a crushing kiss. His tongue darts inside my mouth urgently, demanding, leaving me completely breathless. He eases back just as fast, his chest rising and falling rapidly. My head is a little fuzzy, so it's no surprise I remain rooted to the spot, dazedly watching Tristan stride away across the square toward the diner.

It takes me a minute to realize that he totally manipulated the hell out of me. Fuck! Now that we're mated, does he have some sort of influence over me? Clenching my jaw hard, I have every intention of following him, but my legs give out from under me as a crushing headache hits me out of nowhere. Holding my head between my hands, I grunt in pain as another warning comes to me. Billy and Rochelle, surrounded by hunters and vicious wolves. My entire body begins to shake, and the ache in my gums tells me I'm about to shift. Frantically shaking my head, I take in my surroundings, my sight already changing to the wolf's. Damn it! There are way too many people here; I can't shift into a wolf in broad daylight, but I'm not sure if I can stop it from happening.

I spot a cluster of shrubbery a few yards away. If I can get to it in time, it will offer enough cover. But my legs won't cooperate anymore; I can't stand. So I get on my hands and knees and crawl. My joints snap, my muscles beginning to stretch. If anyone glances in my direction, they will see something grotesque—me in mid-shift. Making terribly slow progress, I finally reach the protection of the shrubs, finalizing the shift.

My muscles are coiled tight with tension. The wolf is ready to sprint toward those in need, but I must act with caution. The sight of a wolf running in the middle of town will surely cause a commotion, and the last thing I want is the citizens of Crimson Hollow to think they have a wolf problem. I slowly stick my head out until I find the quickest route out of the busy square. If I run fast enough, people might mistake me for a random dog.

The booming voice of someone speaking on a megaphone echoes in the square. I glance toward the sound, finding Zeke Rogers, the bakery owner, dressed in the most outrageous unicorn costume ever, calling out for people to try a free sample of cake. The crowd in the square flocks to the front of his shop. His perfectly timed appearance just gave me the opening I need to make a run for it. I prepare to bolt when his gaze finds mine from all the way across the street. Then he winks at me.

The imp is helping me, but there's not time to dwell on how he knew I needed help. My wolf has had enough with delays, and it takes over. My paws hit the soft grass fast and hard, and my surroundings turn into a blur. I don't stop for traffic, but weave between cars like a mad speeding bullet, aiming for the dark alley between two shops. It leads to a flight of narrow stairs. At the top, it opens to a residential street. The mountain and the forest are right behind the row of quaint little houses. I don't stop until I leave the human world behind and enter wolf's territory. Letting my senses lead the way, I go where the pull is taking me. I don't get any more visions of Billy and Rochelle, but I know with the dead certainty that I'm going in the right direction.

I can't keep track of the time, but the sound of fighting eventually reaches my ears. Propelled by the noise, I manage to run faster, until I'm in the thick of the battle. A dark-clad hunter is taking aim, but the noise of my paw snapping a twig makes him turn around. He's not fast enough to avoid my attack, though. Snarling, I leap through the air, aiming my sharp teeth at the soft spot between his neck and shoulder. The impact sends us barreling to the ground, and I'm suddenly trapped in the wolf's blood lust. Muscles are torn, the metallic taste of blood filling my mouth. I don't stop the vicious attack until the man quits moving under me.

"Red, over here!" Rochelle's voice echoes in my head. I lift my face and sniff the air, catching her scent almost right away.

Running to her location, I dodge bullets that zip too close past me. I jump over a boulder, landing hard on the slippery ground on the other side. When I lose traction, I begin to slide down the incline until my rear paws gain leverage. Not too far from where I stand, Rochelle and Billy are surrounded by three wolves. They're moving in circles, taunting my pack members until they're ready for the attack.

I barrel forward, ready to take on all three wolves at the same time if necessary. I'm not sure where this bravery is coming from, especially since I caved when Lyria and her friends picked on me during my first run. These wolves are bigger and sound much more savage than my pack's beta.

"We're with you. You can do this." The voice I recognize as the one belonging to the great wolf sounds in my mind. It could be my imagination, but it gives me confidence and determination. Even if I die today, I won't let my friends perish.

I tackle the wolf closest to me, catching him in mid-jump. We roll on the ground several times, snarling and trying to get a bite of each other, until I manage to clamp my jaw around the soft tissue of his shoulder. The beast lets out a whine, but the wound I inflicted does nothing to weaken him. He dislodges me before sinking his teeth into my back. I shake from side to side, bucking and kicking until I dislodge the wolf, who hits a boulder nearby. The blow slows him down, and I take that opportunity to glance in Rochelle and Billy's direction.

Billy is having trouble fending off one of the wolves. Rochelle jumps in between the two, engaging the enemy to take her on instead. Billy moves out of the way. He's limping, and I catch a whiff of his blood.

"Go back to the compound, Billy. Get some help!" I send the thought out, hoping I can get through to him.

Glancing in my direction, he shakes his head. *"I can't leave you two alone."*

I feel a presence behind me, turning to find the spirit of the great wolf shimmering in the distance. This time, it hadn't used twigs and rocks to take shape. *"We'll not interfere,"* it says in my head. *"You need to win this fight on your own."*

The wolf I was fighting before stands again; he'll be on me in the next moment. With the last second I have left before I'm jumped, I shout at Billy again. *"Go, you, fool. Go!"*

I'm not sure if he heeded to my command before I have to deal with the crazed wolf coming my way. Only this time, he brought a friend, a darker and meaner-looking wolf. A jagged gray scar runs from the middle of this forehead down to where his left eye should be. When he peels his lips back to growl at me, rose-tinted saliva drips from his foul mouth. It's blood, either from Rochelle or Billy.

Red-hot fury bursts through my veins, and I feel a surge of energy erupt from the ground, spreading through my limbs. *"How dare you attack my wolves."* I take a step forward, my muscles coiled tightly, ready to spring into action.

I hear static in my head, then a faint but constant command. The voice is robotic, and it repeats the same thing over and over again. Maim, don't kill.

There's no time to dwell on who that could be. I attack, seeing nothing but fur, limbs, and my mark—the soft skin of my enemy's neck. I slash without mercy, shaking my head from side to side, until his body becomes limp. I don't have the luxury to rejoice in my victory before I'm shoved hard against the boulder nearby, and the scarred wolf is on me. He goes for my exposed side, biting so hard the pain almost makes me faint. I don't whimper. Instead, I howl before using the little bit of strength left in me to push him off.

I sense them before I hear them howling in the distance. Dante, Tristan, and Samuel, plus the other wolves in the pack. The enemy wolf retreats right before a gunshot echoes in the forest, and Rochelle falls to the ground with a whimper.

"No!" I jump to my paws, but my legs are unsteady and fold with the first step I take.

A hunter comes running down the hill. He stops next to Rochelle's limp form, then hoists her body over his shoulder. He pauses to glance in my direction. Even though he's wearing a ski mask, I recognize his dark gaze. It's Martin. He must have left the diner soon after I did. He narrows his eyes as if in recognition as well, then bolts up the rise. He's followed by his minions, the scarred dark wolf and the second one who was fighting Rochelle.

I want to give chase, so I rise again and will my legs to move. The howling gets louder and louder, until Dante's panicked voice explodes into my mind. *"Red! Where are you?"*

"Don't worry about me. He's getting away, and he took Rochelle with him."

Dante's wolf breaks through the woods, a blur of white fur, but instead of going after the hunter and Rochelle, he barrels my way.

"What are you doing? Go after the bad guy!"

"You're hurt."

Samuel and Tristan follow close behind. Suddenly, they're surrounding me. Fuckers. *"Stop fussing over me. Go after Martin. He has Rochelle."*

My command falls on deaf ears. It's like they can't even hear me.

"I asked you to stay in my apartment," Tristan grumbles

before he licks the wound on my shoulder.

I shove him off. *"I'm going after Rochelle."*

Limping, I follow the scent of the enemy wolves, but I don't get far. Another threat appears, blocking my way. The pack's alpha. He doesn't attempt to speak to my mind…

He simply attacks.

CHAPTER 30
SAMUEL

I'm frozen to the ground as I watch my father, the great alpha, attack Red out of the blue. She got hurt defending members of our—*his*—pack, and he attacked her. He attacked *my mate*. The shackles of submission that bind me to him break at that precise moment. It's one thing to disobey his orders; it's quite another to no longer recognize him as the highest-ranked wolf in the pack. And that's exactly what happens to me. I jump on his back, tackling him off Red, who had curled into herself to protect her vital spots.

Howling resonates all around me, but I can't discern individuals in that call, nor can I tell who is with me or against me in this fight for power. As it should be, my mind is blocked to my father's invasion. He can no longer enter it, not even by force.

I'm not sure if I caught him by surprise or not, but he's on to me. Trying to overpower me with his muscles, he jumps as he bites, pushing me to the ground. If I fall, he'll show no mercy and quickly end this fight. That's what happens when a beta challenges the alpha. There's no greater betrayal, so the only possible outcome is death.

I manage to keep upright, but Dad's claws have left their mark on my side. The wound stings, but it's nothing compared to what'll happen if I falter and let him sink his teeth into me. My human side wants to check on Red, see if she's okay, except if lose concentration now, it's game over for me.

We keep at the dance of attack and retreat, circling each other until one of us makes a fatal mistake. Dad finally gets tired of it, faking an attack to the left only to jump at the last minute to the right, trying to grab a hold of me. I was prepared for it. He'd taught me that move when I was little, and I came to see it as one of his trademark attacks. Few wolves are fast enough to switch course last minute, though, and I barely escape unscathed this time. Dad loses momentum. I take the opportunity to hit him with a clawed paw, scratching him on the side. Throwing his head back, he howls in pain, then he turns on me with so much hatred in his gaze that he resembles a rabid wolf, a rogue.

Realization hits me then. Dad is somehow being controlled, just like that rogue wolf who attacked Red was. But how? I don't see anything protruding from the back of his head. My moment of hesitation is my doom. Dad barrels into me, sending me careening across the ground until I reach a patch of rocks. Pain explodes up my spine, and then nothing. I can't feel my legs. Can't move. All I can do is watch Dad stalk me, teeth bared and growling. This is it. He's going to end me.

A blur collides with him—another wolf—and it only takes a moment to recognize Dante. Dad forgets about me to take care of his other traitorous son, but it seems that whatever is controlling the alpha has also equipped him with more than his normal strength. He's stronger than us, but he's not showing any signs that the fight with me has affected him at all. Then Tristan joins the fray, attacking Dad without holding back. The scene is vicious and heartbreaking. Sadness takes over me. That's not our father. It's something else, but to the wolves, it doesn't matter. I feel a nudge on my side, swinging my muzzle around to see Red. She's still in wolf form, covered in blood.

"Are you okay?" she asks.

"No." The sound of a loud whine makes me shiver, and I hide my face under my paws. My wolf has weakened, and

that has allowed my human emotions to take over. *"I can't look."*

Red rests her jaw over my head. *"Me neither. I'm so sorry, Sam."*

The sound of fighting abruptly stops. Without raising my head, I ask, *"Is it over?"*

"Yes."

One by one, the members of the pack begin to howl, until the sound combines into one voice—one harmony. It's the mourning signal. Removing the paw covering my eyes, I survey the battleground. Dad is lying on his side, not moving. His pelt is covered in blood, but there's a slow rise and fall to his chest. He's not dead, and my heart jumps at the knowledge. Scanning farther, I take in the condition of my brothers. They've sustained wounds, but they're standing upright, unlike me.

Tristan glances in my direction, his gaze falling on Red first before switching to me. *"We couldn't kill him, Sam. We simply couldn't."*

His statement is loaded with meaning. It's clear now that Anthony Wolfe is no longer fit to be alpha, but without a clear victor from the challenge, who will take his place?

CHAPTER 31
DANTE

The reality of what my brothers and I just did doesn't hit me until Mom changes back into human, kneels next to our father, and cries in gasping sobs. An immense sense of guilt presses against my chest, almost caving it in. But when I saw our father attacking Red, reason fled from my mind. True, Sam reacted first, but it was only Tristan keeping me in place that prevented me from joining the fight. When Dad hurt Sam badly, Tristan finally let me go. We both finished what our younger brother had started.

Tristan had the opportunity to end it all. He'd had Dad by his throat; all he'd had to do was sink his teeth deeper and slash the skin open. If he'd done so, he'd have been the new alpha, but he couldn't go through with it. Because of that, the pack now has no leader. Mom, as the female alpha, could take on the role, but it wouldn't be long until some young pup challenged her authority or tried to force her into mating.

Red leaves Sam's side, trotting with a limp to where Mom is standing. Lyria lets out a growl, leaping into Red's path. She's daring her to take another step farther. I want to move in front of Red, protect her from the pack's beta, but now is not the time to play the bonded male role. Sinking my paws deeper into the ground, I lock my muscles tight and fight the instinct. A quick glimpse in Tristan's direction tells me he's fighting the same battle.

Despite her injuries, Red bares her teeth, taking a step forward. The fur on her back is standing on end. She won't submit to Lyria. Pride fills my chest; Red has finally stepped into the role she was born for. She snarls at Lyria, inching forward a little more, unafraid of the beta.

They stay locked in that aggressive stance for a moment until Lyria retreats, an outcome I wasn't expecting. Maybe she smelled Tristan's scent all over Red, then figured out he and Red are mated. How long until the enforcer and the rest of the pack discovers Red is mated to all three of us? I can't imagine that going well. Lyria returns to the group of enforcers, still eyeing Red with hatred, but for now, I don't have to worry about her.

Mom turns to me. "We need to get your father back to the infirmary as soon as possible."

I'd nod if I was human. As a wolf, I simply do what she asked and shift back. I won't be able to carry Dad otherwise. My body is scratched and bleeding in several places. Dad got me good a few times. If Tristan hadn't joined the fight as well, I'd be in similar shape to Sam—hurt so badly I couldn't get up.

I should have intervened sooner.

Shaking my head, I kneel next to my father, pressing my fingers against his throat. His pulse is weak, and he's lost a lot of blood. I also take the time to inspect the back of his head, searching for a clue as to why he acted so crazed, just like the rogue wolf who attacked Red had. There isn't a controlling device attached anywhere, but I do find a patch of puckered skin. Looking more closely as I part the fur, I see a light pink scar there. Dread trickles down my spine as suspicion takes hold of me.

"What is it?" Tristan asks telepathically.

"Not good news." I pick Dad up, hating the feel of his limp body in my arms. A great lump lodges in my throat. Before he was the alpha—before he went mad—he was our father. He

never let his position in the pack interfere with our upbringing. Always found the time to be around my brothers and me. He was kind and patient, a truly devoted dad.

There's no time for sentimentalities, though. Clenching my jaw hard, I run back to the compound with my father in my arms, not looking to see who is following me. A few seconds later, I sense a wolf at my heels—Mom. She changed back, and not because she's faster on four legs, but because she doesn't trust the other wolves at the moment. Leadership instability is a dangerous thing in a pack.

※

℞ED

I'm so sick of the ways things are done in this pack, so when Lyria jumps in front of me, blocking my way, I don't think twice before I'm challenging her. My body is sore in more places than I can count, and I'm not sure how I'm still able to stand on four legs, but there's a new fire burning inside of me that's giving me strength. I know without a doubt I can take her if she decides to step up to the challenge. I'm ready. Oddly, she backs down, returning to her group of friends with her tail between her legs.

Dante changes back to human form. He checks his father's vitals, before searching for something on the back of the former alpha's head. Frowning, he turns in Tristan's direction. I know they're speaking telepathically the same way that I sense Dante found something. Tristan throws his head back and howls, a sound filled with so much sadness that it makes my eyes sting.

He goes to Samuel, who is still in the same prone position as before. Tristan nudges his brother on the side, but all Samuel does is shake his head.

"What is it?" I ask, hoping I'm doing this telepathic communication thing right. I must be, because Samuel answers.

"I can't feel my legs."

Tristan's gaze collides with mine after his brother's announcement. *"Red, I have to shift back to human to carry Sam back to the compound. I'll need you to guard our backs."* I don't detect a shred of doubt in him about my ability to do so. He doesn't even ask if I can do it. He just trusts that I can.

"I'm on it."

Billy separates from the rest of the pack to stand by my side. His brother Seth growls at him, but the omega ignores the warning. To me, he says. *"I've got your back."*

"Thanks, Billy."

"What about Rochelle? We need to organize a rescue mission," he says.

"Fuck!" Tristan's reply is loud in my head. *"Let's get Sam to the infirmary first, then we can talk about it."*

Tristan shifts back. Without another word, he lifts Samuel into his arms. I make a disgruntled sound in the back of my throat when I catch all the cuts and bruises on Tristan's body his fur had hid. My throat goes dry as my heart clenches painfully in my chest. The alpha was able to inflict all that damage while fighting three wolves at the same time. If the brothers had not intervened, I'd be dead.

Tristan takes off with Samuel, running faster than a regular human could. I'm not sure if it's because he's a shifter or if he's been fueled by the emergency of the situation. I don't waste time thinking about it, just leap forward to keep up, wincing with every step I take. Billy is close behind me. In the distance, I can hear the other wolves running after us. No one pulls any shady attempt to attack us, which gives me a little bit more hope that the pack will survive this.

Within minutes, we reach the edge of the compound, the familiar wired fence looming in the horizon. Tristan aims for the gate, which is hidden behind thick shrubbery. Up until this point, I hadn't even known it was there. It swings open automatically. As I cross the threshold, I see the mounted security cameras on top of it. Those measures don't comfort me, though. The hunters who attacked us and kidnapped Rochelle were well equipped with high-tech weapons. Plus, they were controlling wolves, using them as their attack dogs. How are we going to fight them?

Tristan makes a beeline for the infirmary building. Before I venture in, I shift back. For the first time since I became a wolf, I don't give a rat's ass about walking naked out in the open. Tristan enters the first room to his right, a generic examination room with a single bed and a cupboard with medical supplies, very similar to the one I occupied when I was brought into the compound.

Still in wolf form, Samuel whines when Tristan lays him on the bed. "You have to shift back, Sam."

"But it hurts too badly," he says, not blocking me from the conversation.

I come into the room, stopping next to the bed. After I touch the side of his face, I lean down and press my cheek against his. "You can do it, Sam."

Feeling his body shake, I ease back, but keep my hand on his shoulder. He growls as his muscles begin to spasm and change shape. It takes longer than usual for him to complete the shift, and I can feel the agony he's going through deep in my bones. When his beautiful face turns to mine, its twisted into a grimace.

"Red..."

I touch his forehead with the tips of my fingers. "Please don't speak, Sam."

"I have to."

Tristan grunts on the other side of the bed, catching my attention. "What is it?"

Shaking his head, he says, "Nothing. I'll wait outside."

Once Tristan closes the door behind him, Sam says, "He's sensing our bond, that's all."

"What?"

Sam throws his head back, closing his eyes and moaning through clenched teeth. My eyes roam over his body, noticing patches where the skin is already turning purple. There's an angry gash just underneath his right thorax that has mercifully stopped bleeding. It seems to be knitting back together. Even so, he's in really bad shape.

"We need to take you to the hospital."

He chuckles as he opens his eyes. "You can't take me to a hospital, Red. One close look at my blood and they'd be able to tell I'm not human."

"There aren't supernaturals working there?"

"Yes, of course, but most of the staff is human. Besides, Mom is the best doctor around."

"What? I thought she was veterinarian."

"That, too." He grimaces again, and I feel bad for asking stupid questions.

"What can I do to help?"

His electric blue gaze connects with mine. For a moment, it's clear of pain. Instead, a fiery and intense emotion shines in his eyes, waking up radioactive butterflies in my stomach. A shiver runs down my spine. The room seems like it's spinning out of control, and the only stable thing in that vortex is Samuel. Gasping, I finally understand this crazy emotion is the mating bond taking place. I also felt similar intense feelings with Dante and Tristan. And now Samuel. How can one person be equally connected to three men?

"Lie next to me?" he whispers.

"Won't I hurt you more?"

"No."

I hesitate for a moment, glancing over his many injuries. He needs medical attention ASAP, but it seems only his mother can help him right now. In the end, I can't deny his request. My body yearns to be near him, so I do as he asks, extremely aware of every part of my body that touches his, which is almost everything in this tiny bed. I lie on my side, facing him, but he remains on his back.

"How are your legs?" I ask, almost in a whisper.

"I can feel them now, but I almost wish I didn't. They hurt like a mother."

A sense of relief—albeit small—spreads over my chest. If he can feel them, then he's not paralyzed.

"Can I get you anything for the pain?"

"You know what would make me feel a little better?" He smiles a little.

"What?" My gaze drops to his mouth, and I feel like the worst person in the world for being aroused by our proximity.

"A kiss."

"Sam…"

"Please? I would ask for more. Shit, my body definitely wants more…" He grabs my hand, guiding it to his erection. "But I don't want our first time to be like this. When we finally sleep together, it will be epic."

Desire spreads like wildfire through my body, even though I can't entertain the idea of sexy times right now. Not with Sam mangled like this. Pulling my hand from his cock, I bring my fingers to his lips, running the tips over them. Sam parts his mouth, sucking my index finger into it. My breathing catches as pure electricity wakes up every cell in my body. The feel of his warm tongue is so intense, so erotic, that he'd be able to make me come in no time just by doing that. Rubbing my legs together, I try to ease the sudden ache between them.

I pull my finger away, then lean closer until my lips are brushing his. In this new position, my breasts press against his arm, turning my nipples into tiny pebbles. His tongue darts out, teasing my lips open. At the same time, he places his hand on the back of my head, tangling his fingers in my hair. Moving like that must be hurting him like crazy, but for now, he doesn't seem to mind.

Guided by him, I deepen the kiss. Just like I expected, it's nuclear, an explosion of senses. He tastes like he looks: exotic, intoxicating, delicious. But his kiss is not wild; it's precise. Samuel knows exactly what to do to give the most pleasure possible. I feel awake, more alive than ever, and my entire body begins to tingle. He makes a sound in the back of his throat that's all male, and I have to fight the instinct to roll on top of him for a ride.

As intense as the kiss is, I don't let it override my good senses. Samuel is hurt, we don't know the fate of his father, and we need to rescue Rochelle. So with reluctance, I ease back.

He smiles, his eyes at half-mast. "Best first kiss ever."

"You're a rascal even when you're half dead."

"I'd be a rascal even if I was completely dead." He chuckles, but then the amusement vanishes from his eyes. He must be thinking about this father.

I slide off the bed, missing his warmth immediately. "I'll go check on him."

"Okay."

I'm at the door when he says, "Red?"

"What is it, Sam?"

"I don't want you wasting your time coddling me. Rally the wolves. Go after those bastards who took Rochelle, then make them pay."

CHAPTER 32
DANTE

There are some moments in life that no matter how many years pass, they'll never be forgotten, not even the tiniest details. This is one such moment. My mother hovering over Dad, her body as tense as a coiled spring, her hands shaking as she examines him while he lies still on the bed. His face, which once had a warm honey hue, is now washed out. It has the sickly color of death. From where I stand, the incision points on Dad's neck where Tristan held him with his teeth are evident. But those small wounds aren't where my mother's sharp gaze is focused. She's pressing her hands with care over his abdomen, where great purple patches take over most of the skin.

"Mom?" I say.

"He has internal bleeding. We need to operate."

"I'll call Zaya."

Without looking at me, my mother nods. Zaya is the head nurse at Crimson Hollow's hospital and a supernatural. Her powers are a mystery to me. No one knows for sure what kind of supe she is, only that she has affinity with water. From time to time, she vanishes to an unknown location, but always comes back.

When I take a step toward the door to go in search of a phone, the sound of Dad moaning makes me stop in my tracks. I return to his bedside in time to catch him slowly open his eyes. His face twists into a grimace. Extreme regret is in his gaze when he takes me in.

"Dante, my son." He raises his arm, reaching out for me.

Wrapping my hand around his cold fingers, I squeeze. "Dad, please don't talk. Save your energy. We need to get you patched up."

"There's no time, Dante. I need to tell you..." He closes his eyes, taking a deep a breath.

"Anthony, you have internal bleeding. We have to operate." Mom touches his forehead.

"Mer, my darling." Dad looks at her. "I'm so sorry."

"Sorry for what?" Mom's voice trembles, a choke I can feel deep in my heart.

"For not taking your words seriously. For not being extra careful."

"What are you talking about, my love?"

"At the alpha's meeting..., something happened to me. I went out to dinner with some of my closest friends, and I can't remember how the evening ended. All I know is I woke up the next morning in my room with a terrible ache in the back of my head."

"The scar," I say. "Dad, you have a small scar there."

"Yes. I know."

"Why didn't you tell me this sooner?" Mom asks.

"Because my mind wasn't the same. Honey, whatever was done to me, it changed my thought process. It completely controlled my emotions."

Rubbing my face, I start to pace. "Who did you have dinner with that night?"

"The usual suspects. The two alphas from the biggest packs in Canada, and Simon from the London pack."

"Not that new alpha from Shadow Creek?" Mom asks.

"No. Nobody likes him."

"It doesn't mean he isn't involved somehow," I say. "We need to let Tristan know."

In that precise moment, Tristan walks in. "Know what?"

"How is Sam? Is he going to be all right?" Dad asks, and I notice his voice is getting weaker and weaker.

"Sam will be okay. Don't worry about him," Tristan replies.

I sense the lie immediately. Sam is not okay, but there's no point in telling Dad that right now. With tears in his eyes, he motions for us. "Come closer, my sons."

My blood runs cold when I see a great shadow hovering above Dad's bed. The Grim Reaper. "No," I whisper, not sure if I said the word out loud or only in my head.

The shadow takes the shape of woman as it lands right next to Mom. I can tell she senses the otherworldly presence by the shivers that runs down her spine, but I'm the only one who can actually see the agent of death.

"Please, don't take him," I beg.

A strikingly beautiful woman with skin so pale it's almost translucent stares at me. Her fiery red eyes are a stark contrast against her white skin and dark hair. *"His time has come, and no one can cheat death."*

She raises her hand over Dad's chest. At that precise moment, Dad begins to cough. A trickle of blood escapes the corner of his lips. Mom wipes the blood off while tears stream down her face.

"Dante?" Dad asks.

I finally force my legs to move, trying my best not to stare at the wraith who came to take my father away. My vision is blurry, and there's a terrible weight pressing down on my chest.

"Yes, Dad?"

"Please tell Sam I'm so sorry for what I did to him. You know I'd never hurt one of you on purpose."

"We all know, Dad." Tristan places a hand on our father's shoulder.

"And the girl, Amelia, she's terrific. I couldn't have hoped for a better mate for my sons."

Of course Dad would know right away if any of us was

bonded to a wolf. He turns to Mom.

"Please don't cry, my love. It will all be okay."

"Don't say that. This is not okay. I'm not ready to let you go," Mom says with a choked sob, covering her mouth.

"It's only a temporary separation, Mer. We'll meet again." With great effort, Dad lifts his arm to touch her face.

In turn, she leans down and kisses Dad's lips. I shift my attention back to the Grim Reaper. For a fleeting moment, I catch sadness in her gaze. The emotion is gone as fast as it came, replaced by cold detachment. A swirl of energy begins to emerge from Dad's body at the same time he begins to convulse.

I look away, not able to witness death suck away my father's life energy. Mom lets out an anguished cry. Soon after, Tristan punches the wall, leaving a hole in the shape of his fist behind.

Sudden light in the corner of the room grows brighter and brighter, until a man with short golden hair who is dressed in all white appears. The glow surrounding him makes it impossible to mistake what he is. An angel.

"It is done," the Grim Reaper says.

"So I see," the angel replies with a nod of his head. "I'll have him now." He lifts his hand, palm up.

With a furrow of her eyebrows, the reaper sends the swirling ball of energy she acquired from Dad in the angel's direction.

"I didn't think you'd be the one to come," she says.

"I asked to."

"Why?" Surprise laces the reaper's voice. Despite my grief, I can't help but to feel morbid curiosity about the scene unfolding in front of me.

Dad's life force is now hovering over the angel's hand.

"Because I've missed you, Valeria."

"Don't say that, Gabriel." Her neutral expression changes to something of incredible sadness. It's in that moment I see a thin, almost unsubstantial energy thread linking the Grim Reaper and the angel. Bonded—they were bonded once upon a time. Despite being on different sides of the afterlife spectrum now, their connection remains.

The sound of my mother's inconsolable cries over my father's dead body pulls me back to my reality. Before the angel vanishes, I ask, "Where are you taking my father?"

Gabriel looks at me with a small smile on his lips. "To a place where all the great souls go. And one day, I'll come for you, Dante."

The glow surrounding the angel expands, becoming brighter and brighter until it swallows him whole. Then it's gone, and so is my father.

CHAPTER 33

RED

When I leave Sam's room, Tristan is not outside. The hallway is silent, and I have no idea where Dr. Mervina has taken her husband. I stop for a minute, listening carefully. Seconds tick by until I'm hit with a pain in my chest so sharp that I almost double over. Pressing my hand over my sternum, I try to massage the pain away to no avail. Then I hear Dr. Mervina's anguished cry down the corridor, and I know the worst has happened. The alpha is dead.

I choke on a sob while my legs falter. To stop from crumbling to the ground, I lean against the wall while the greatest grief I've ever known hits me like a cannonball.

Billy bursts through the door down the corridor, his young face twisted in an expression of terror and disbelief. "Red, what happened?"

"The alpha. He's gone."

The omega stops in his tracks, lowering his gaze to the floor. His hands are balled into fists at his side, his chest rising and falling rapidly. I want to reach out to comfort him, but a new sense of urgency overrides the compulsion. I stand straighter, letting the unknown strong force take control.

"Where are the enforcers?"

"Everyone is assembled in the mess hall."

"Let's go then." I stride toward the exit, not waiting for

Billy.

"What are you going to do? Shouldn't we wait for the betas or Dr. Mervina?"

"No. They're grieving, and they should be allowed that moment. Unfortunately, we cannot wait. The longer we delay a rescue mission, the less chances we have of finding Rochelle."

I march across the quad with purpose. My mind is made up, my body ready. When I enter the busy mess hall, it's with squared shoulders and chin high. The conversation ceases the moment my presence is acknowledged. Seth, Billy's brother and one of the most experienced enforcers, takes a step forward.

"The alpha is dead."

It's more of a statement than a question, but I answer anyway. "Yes."

Loud murmurs erupt in the room, and I can sense all the conflicting emotions within the pack. Some are shocked, others are sad, but a great many are angry and blaming me.

"Who is the new alpha, then?" a younger man at the back of the room asks.

"Anthony Wolfe is dead, but his mate, the female alpha, is still very much alive." My voice is loud and hard. I don't want any of the most volatile wolves to start getting fancy ideas.

"What do you want?" Lyria stands up, glaring at me.

"We need to organize a rescue party, or did you already forget that one of our own was taken today?"

"I didn't forget." Her gaze turns to slits while her lips become a thin flat line.

"Good."

"What are we going to do?" someone asks.

Lyria opens her mouth to reply, but I cut her off. "We'll return to the place where Rochelle and Billy were ambushed, see if we can pick up a scent."

"Who the fuck do you think you are?" Lyria breaks away from her group of friends, striding in my direction with purpose. "Do you think that just because you fucked Tristan, it automatically grants you authority?"

"This has nothing to do with authority," I say through clenched teeth.

"You're nothing in this pack; you don't tell us what to do. I'm the beta. I'm the one in charge."

"If you are in charge, then why the hell were you sitting on your ass doing nothing?" I take a step forward, ready to punch the bitch in the face.

"I don't have to explain myself to you. You're nothing but a lowly omega."

"We need to get moving. The longer we wait, the harder it will be to find Rochelle," Billy says.

"Shut your trap, Billy. You forget your place." Seth rises, glaring at the young man.

"Billy is right. We need to act now," I say. Finally, I see some heads nod.

"And I say we wait until a new alpha has been picked," Lyria growls, making me see red. Is she for real?

Seething, I ball my hands into fists at my sides as my entire body begins to tremble. The wolf is begging to be set free again.

"I can't believe this. You'd rather wait to deal with pack politics than save a life?"

"You know nothing about what it's like to be a true wolf. If I had been the one who found you in the forest, I'd have let you bleed to death."

Everything happens in a blur. The shift occurs so fast I don't even feel it this time. One second, I'm standing on two legs; the next, I'm jumping at her in wolf form. She falls with me on top of her, but I'm not a coward. I won't attack her while she's still human, so I leap off and wait for the bitch to change.

Lyria rolls on her hand and knees, snarling even before her transformation is complete. Her wolf is larger than mine with more muscles, but size is not everything. She attacks with lips peeled back and the clear intention of ripping me to shreds.

I jump to the side, missing her sharp sheep teeth by a hair. Before she can recover from her miss, I'm on top of her, my teeth sinking viciously into a soft spot on her shoulder. She howls in pain, then tries to shake me off. I hold on to her for as long as I can, but when I feel myself losing leverage, I leap off. I can't let her get the advantage.

Knowing I won't be an easy target, she doesn't come at me again. Instead, she lowers her body, eyeing me. We begin to circle one another. I feel a maligned presence in my head, scratching the protective wall I have in place. She's trying to break through, no doubt to taunt me and make me lose my concentration.

Imagining a laser-sharp weapon, I send my own message to her. *"Back the fuck down, or I'll humiliate you in front of the pack."*

She growls harder, which tells me she heard me loud and clear. Since my side of the conversation is closed off, she has no option but to show me her evil intentions with actions. She attempts another attack, vicious but sloppy. I dodge with ease, light on my paws, but conscious we're wasting time with this fight. I need to end it.

Summoning all my strength, I jump on her once more. This time, I'm aiming to bring her down. She manages to scratch my face with her claw in the process, but the pain only propels me farther. Lyria is finally down, and I have the advantage. She's still putting up a fight, her pride not allowing her to submit. When she turns her muzzle in an attempt to bite my shoulder, she leaves her throat exposed. Without hesitation, I take my chance, sinking my teeth into the soft spot and feeling her accelerated pulse on my tongue. Blinded by rage, she continues to struggle, so I send her another message.

"I don't want to harm you, but I'll kill if you don't yield."

"I'll never submit to you. You're a filthy mutt!"

I press harder, tasting blood. *"Stop! This is my last warning."*

My voice, even in my head, sounds different. It's like several people spoke all at once. A shiver runs down my spine as my senses expand to encompass my surroundings. I feel a great awareness of combined shock from the audience of shifters who can't do anything but watch their beta and a newcomer fight. Some thoughts are filled with malice. They think I'm an impostor, or worse, a spy. I shut those negatives thoughts off to focus on Lyria, who is finally ceasing to struggle.

"Are you going to stop this nonsense?" I ask.

"Yes," she hisses, and I can imagine the woman doing so with a defiant gaze.

I let go of her throat and back away, still wary this might have been a ploy. But she doesn't attempt to strike again after she gets up. Instead, she howls, and her call is answered by all the wolves present.

What the hell is going on?

Billy stops by my side, nudging me on the shoulder.

"Why are they howling like that?" I ask him.

"They're acknowledging what was pretty clear from this fight's outcome."

"What?"

"That you just replaced Lyria as the pack's new beta."

I don't reply for several beats. My brain is too busy comprehending what Billy just told me. Part of me wants to rejoice with pride, but there's a small part that wonders if the reason I was able to win against the enforcer is because I'm mated to the Wolfe brothers. Maybe the magical bond gave me some kind of special strength?

My spine goes taut when I sense the pack's alpha approaching. That sensation was reserved solely for Anthony Wolfe, but now that he's dead, Dr. Mervina is emanating the same energy that makes us aware of her presence. I turn in time to see her enter the mess hall, followed by Tristan and Dante.

They're all dressed already, and the grime from the fight has been scrubbed clean. Lacerations are still visible on their solemn faces. Neither Dante nor Tristan looks in my direction; they don't attempt to talk to me mind to mind either. The indifference on their end feels like a sucker punch to my gut. Even though the logical side of my brain tells me they must have their reasons, the pain in my chest is real.

On the other hand, Dr. Mervina's gaze does stop on me for a moment. I don't see any disapproval in her eyes before she turns her attention to the assembly.

"My husband and soulmate, the alpha of the Crimson Hollow pack, is dead," Dr. Mervina announces.

Her voice is strong and clear, her posture that of a leader who understands that despite experiencing great loss, the show must go on. Even so, her eyes carry unbearable sadness. Inevitably, I think about Dante, Tristan, and Samuel. If anything were to happen to them, if I were to lose one, my heart would be breaking into a thousand pieces. Is that what being in love is like? This is the first time I think about our strange relationship in this light. Love had never entered the equation before. Suddenly, I don't know if what I'm feeling is real or if the power that bonds me to them is the cause.

"And by the custom of this pack, which has been in place for generations, I'll fill his role as leader until a new alpha can arise."

"What about her?" A dark-haired guy I don't recognize points in my direction. "She's the reason the alpha is dead."

My spine goes rigid as I watch the man. It seems I still have a long way to go before I can gain the pack's trust. A growl comes from Tristan's direction, but when I look at him, he's as still as a statue, emotionless. Did I imagine the sound?

"She's the new beta. Watch your mouth, Deacon," Billy, who has shifted back into human, says.

His brother Seth doesn't reproach him this time, but I don't miss the narrowed gaze. I wonder how much trouble Billy will get into from being so outspoken about his support of me.

Dr. Mervina glances at me again, but her expression remains neutral.

"Amelia Redford is part of this pack. If she's earned her place as beta, I expect everyone to respect it. I forbid any new challenges until we deal with the bigger threat to the pack."

"Are we going after the hunters who took Rochelle?" Billy asks.

"No, we're not."

If I were in human form, I would be frowning.

"I've requested assistance from our allies, the Thunderborn sleuth, since the hunters ran toward their territory. Until we hear from them, I want everyone to retire and rest. We'll honor the fallen alpha tomorrow at sunset."

CHAPTER 34

RED

I wait until everyone leaves the mess hall to make the trek back to the alpha's manor. It's only when I cross the threshold of the big house that I shift back. My entire body aches since I still haven't had time to recover from the injuries I sustained during the fight with those rabid wolves. Now, thanks to that bitch Lyria, I have a scratch on my face to add to my battle scars. I must be quite the sight, but at this point, my appearance is the least of my worries.

I thought I was doing the right thing by going after the hunters, but now I feel like a fool. Lyria is right; I know nothing of pack business, and maybe I should stop pretending I do.

My shoulders hunch forward as I enter the manor with my gaze lowered, so I'm caught by surprise when a pair of strong arms wrap around me. Dante's scent fills my nose while my body relaxes against his automatically. It's like I was born to be in his arms, and I wish I could mold myself to him.

"I knew you had it you," he whispers in my ear. "Congratulations."

I ease back, tilting my head up so I can look into his eye. "That bitch had it coming. Dante, I'm so sorry about your father."

Dante watches me for a moment, his green eyes brighter

than usual, before he leans forward and kisses my forehead.

"Me too, but I know he's okay."

"Do you know what happened to him? Why he attacked me?"

"Yes. We believe my father was betrayed during the alphas' conference in Vancouver. Someone from his inner circle must have slipped him a sleeping pill. During the time my father was passed out, a chip was implanted into his brain."

"A chip?"

"A controlling chip much more advanced than the device we found on the rogue who attacked you."

"Why would anyone do that?"

"We don't know. But the first device was embedded with a demonic energy, so this goes beyond despicable humans."

"Was that the reason your mother didn't want us to go after Rochelle?"

"Yes, among other things."

Realizing that maybe I hadn't screwed up so badly makes me feel a little bit better, but not by much. I don't notice I'm biting my lower lip until Dante frees it by pulling my chin down with his thumb. Then he kisses me, a rubbing of lips first before his tongue darts into my mouth. Holding on to his biceps, I let him take control and make me forget, for as long as the kiss lasts, all the challenges ahead of us.

A throat clearing behind us interrupts our moment. Dante and I break apart to find Tristan watching us with an undecipherable expression on his face. His arms are crossed in front of his chest, which anyone who has ever studied a little bit of body language knows is the equivalent of a shield. Heat surges to my cheeks as mortification takes over. I don't think I'll ever get used to the fact I'm in a relationship with all three brothers, and none of them seem to mind.

"I-I should go to my room and shower." I take a step toward the grand staircase's direction.

"Are you okay?" Tristan asks.

"Yes. Why do you ask?"

"A lot of things happened in a short of amount of time. It would be okay if you weren't."

"I'm fine, Tristan. For real. How is Sam?"

"His body will mend."

"And his mind?" A lurch inside of my chest makes me stop.

Tristan looks away, rubbing his face in the process. "You should go to him after you're done. He needs you more than we do."

Without waiting for my reply, Tristan strides in the opposite direction, to his old office is my guess. I turn to Dante with a question in my gaze.

"Don't worry about Tristan. He'll be okay. We're all coping with what happened in a different way. Knowing Tristan, he'll bury himself in work."

"And you?"

Dante gives me a sad smile. "Maybe I'll paint something. Don't worry about me. Tristan is right. Sam needs you the most right now. Go to him."

He walks out of the front door, leaving me in the empty foyer. It takes me a few seconds to get out of my paralysis. It seems that both Dante and Tristan need me, but they're playing tough in favor of Sam, which makes me even more worried about his condition.

I run back to my room. Despite all the grime caked on my skin and my hair, I take the quickest shower known to man. I'm out of my room in ten minutes flat, almost running back to the infirmary where my instinct says Sam is. The link between us becomes stronger and stronger as I get closer to his quarters.

Not wanting to invade his privacy, I knock on the door first. "Sam?"

"Come in, Red."

Opening the door, I find Sam propped against a pillow, his arm now hooked to an IV. He looks a little bit better, but the hollowness of his eyes tells me that Tristan's assessment was correct. Sam is not well. Even so, he smiles at me. "I was waiting for you."

"You could tell I was coming?"

He nods. "I could sense your presence getting closer. It will be like this with us now. We're linked, Red."

I shift from foot to foot, not knowing what to do. We kissed, but that was before I knew his father had passed. Does he regret coming to my rescue?

"Why are you standing all the way by the door? Come here." He pats the little area next to him on the mattress.

I do as he says, sitting on the bed and taking his hand. It's so cold. "Sam, you don't need to pretend with me."

"I'm not pretending, Red. I just don't want to think about it. If I do, then I have to feel, and I don't want to feel anything right now."

I touch the side of his face, and Samuel closes his eyes for a moment. "What I can do?"

He looks deep into my eyes. "I said before that I didn't want our first time to be here, in a hospital bed, but I've changed my mind. Please, let me make love to you, Red."

My heart lurches inside my chest. Make love. This is the first time the word has ever entered a conversation between me and any of the brothers, and even though it doesn't mean he loves me, my stupid heart can't tell the difference.

"Are you sure that's safe?" I glance at the IV.

Following my gaze, Sam rips the tube from his skin. "Problem solved."

He captures my lips with his. I couldn't have put up a fight even if I wanted to. Sam's kisses have the power to melt any resolve I might have.

"You smell different," he says.

I tense, thinking he's referring to Dante's scent on me.

"What do you mean?"

"You smell like a beta."

"I didn't know that ranking affected one's scent."

"Oh, it does. It's subtle, but the difference is definitely there. You'll learn to notice." He buries his nose in the crook of my neck, taking a deep breath. "I fucking love it."

Samuel licks my neck up until he reaches my earlobe, biting it a little, while his hand grazes my side, then the underside of my breast. Heat ignites, making me squirm closer to his hot and very naked body. I remember the size of his cock the first time he shifted in front of me, and a phantom ache pulses between my legs. I want him inside of me so badly I could almost shout the command, yet something holds me back. This isn't right. How can I be thinking about having sex with Samuel when his father has just died?

"Sam, maybe we should wait." My voice has no strength, no true conviction.

Without words, he slides his hand underneath my shirt, leaving a trail of goose bumps as he moves closer to the edge of my bra. "Your skin is so soft and warm. I'd crave a taste even if you weren't my mate."

Oh my God. He's using his rock-god sexy voice, and I'm melting through the sheets.

"The first time I saw you on that stage, I couldn't look away. You had me ensnared even though I was never into cocky rock stars before."

Samuel's throaty laughter makes me giddy, filling me with warmth. I lean on my elbow, so I can look at his face. He's such a beautiful man, and it's almost impossible to believe he's staring at me with such hunger. I trace his face with the tips of my fingers, committing to memory all his edges and angles, his chin dimple, his full mouth. His eyes, despite the laughter, remain sad, so I do the only thing I can think of—I kiss him hard. He answers in kind, plunging his demanding tongue into my mouth with the eagerness of a starving man. Using his deft fingers, he unhooks the front clasp of my bra and takes possession of my breasts, kneading as he goes.

"I really hate clothes on you," he says between kisses.

"I'm wearing a skirt."

As if I issued a challenge, Samuel lets go of my breast to transfer his hand to my ass. "What kind of underwear do you like, Red? Are you a white cotton or black lace kind of girl?"

"It depends on my mood, but sometimes I don't wear them at all."

To illustrate my point, I roll on top of him before remembering he is still recovering from his injuries, then stop. "Is this okay?"

His eyes narrow to slits at the same time he grabs my hips, bringing them forward a little. The motion makes my clit rub against his erection, and we hiss at the same time. "Is that answer good enough for you?"

I rotate my hips, making Samuel dig his fingers harder into my skin.

"Fuck. I think I'd still enjoy this even if every single bone in my body was broken," he rasps out.

"I promise I'll be careful."

Wrapping my fingers around his shaft, I guide it to my entrance. The feeling we shouldn't be doing this when everyone else is in mourning is still present, but Samuel wants this, he needs this, so I'll give it to him. I'll give everything he wants.

I lower my hips, impaling myself on him slowly, making Samuel let out a string of curses. When I try to keep the pace easy, gentle, he won't let me. With his hands on my hips, he takes control, making me fuck him harder and harder. I'm not sure he saw the worry in my gaze, but he manages to say, "Stop worrying, Red. You're not hurting me, but I might die a little."

Leaning forward, I capture his face between my hands and kiss him. Then it happens, the blissful, overwhelming, earth-shattering orgasm that breaks me and then puts me back together all in the same breath. I cry out, but the sound is muffled by Sam's tongue. Not much later, I feel him expand inside of me, then it's his turn to make undiscernible sounds with the back of his throat.

Everything slows down until we stop moving altogether. I roll off him with my heartbeat still erratic and my breathing matching the crazy tempo. Resting my hand on his chest, I close my eyes while I wait for the world to stop spinning. We don't speak for several minutes until Samuel begins to shake. Alarmed, I open my eyes in time to catch his face twist in the worst anguished expression I've ever seen on a man. He covers his mouth with a fist to suppress a loud sob, then turns to me, hiding his face in the crook of my neck.

"He's dead, Red. He's dead, and it's all my fault."

I run my fingers through his hair, murmuring, "No, it wasn't your fault, Sam. It wasn't your fault."

My reply goes unanswered, and I don't know if he even heard me. He continues to cry, harder and louder with each breath he takes, so I do the only thing I can. I hold him tight while he releases all his grief.

CHAPTER 35
RED

I couldn't leave Sam alone after he broke down like that, so I spent the night. However, I can't say that I slept. I was up the whole night, thinking about the problems within the pack, the dangerous, unknown enemy we'll have to face, my complicated relationship with the brothers, and worrying about my future. What's going to happen to me? How do I fit into the puzzle? That painting Dante did comes back to haunt me. I still don't know what it means.

I'm watching Sam's face, glad to see his relaxed expression, when the door opens and Dr. Mervina comes in. Mortification rushes to my face, making it hot. I pull the sheet all the way up to my chin, even though I'm still wearing my clothes.

Dr. Mervina ignores my reaction, moving straight to Sam's side of the bed to check on him. "How was he during the night?"

"Good. He slept like a baby."

She places a hand on his forehead, then her gaze shifts to the IV that's no longer attached to his arm. With a tsking sound, she proceeds to find another line. I decide I should give her room to do her thing, so I slide off the bed.

"I'm going to check on Dante and Tristan," I say, not knowing why I feel compelled to tell her.

"Tristan went into town, but Dante is in his studio."

"Okay."

I stop for a moment to take Dr. Mervina in. Her eyebrows are furrowed in concentration and she has her professional mask on, but I wonder how she can function like that. I'd probably be a blubbering mess if I'd lost my mate.

"How are you holding up?" I ask.

"I don't know yet." She glances at me. "For now, all my focus is on discovering who betrayed Anthony. My mind is set on retribution."

"Do you think it was someone close to him?"

Dr. Mervina doesn't answer. Instead, she returns her attention to Samuel. "You should go check on Dante. I'm sure he'd want to see you."

I know a dismissal when I hear one. "Okay. Would you tell Sam I'll be back to check on him?"

"Of course."

I don't go to Dante right away, veering to my room first, wanting to shower and change clothes. I'd feel weird going to him still having Sam's scent all over me, and I'm not sure if that's ever going to change. By the time I take the path that leads to his studio up the mountain, it's already midmorning. The bright sun shining through the canopy of trees feels a little out of place when there's so much darkness going around.

I'm halfway there when I hear someone approaching. I turn around, finding Lyria coming in my direction. My entire body tenses up. If she wants a repeat of yesterday's showdown, I'd be more than happy to oblige.

"What do you want?" I ask.

"Relax, I'm not here to fight with you."

"Then what?"

"You're the beta now, and as such, you have the alpha's ear."

I cross my arms, watching the enforcer. "So?"

"You need to dissuade Dr. Mervina from waiting to hear back from the leader of the Thunderborn sleuth. We need to go after those hunters now."

Suspicion sneaks up my spine. "You were more than happy to wait around yesterday. Why the sudden hurry now?"

"The pack's leadership has been established. That's all I wanted. Now it's foolish to wait for a report that might take days to come through. Bears are not as reliable as Dr. Mervina thinks. They also have their own agenda."

"You should bring your concerns to her yourself."

Lyria lets out a humorless laugh. "She won't listen to me. She never liked me when I was the beta, but she couldn't deny me an audience due to ranking. But now that the title has been stripped from me…"

The woman doesn't need to continue. I get the gist, but I don't believe for a second her motivations are true. She's planning something. No sooner does the thought enter my mind than a shiver runs down my spine and the small hairs on the back of my neck stand on end. But the warning comes too late. There's a zap, then a prickle on my neck, which immediately makes my skin numb.

"What the hell?" I pull a dart from my skin, staring at it for a second before my legs vanish from under me.

My body is suddenly on the ground, but I don't feel the fall. The world around me is quickly becoming fuzzier and fuzzier.

"What have you done to me?" I ask.

My heart sinks when Seth emerges from his hiding spot carrying a tranquilizer gun. This was a trap.

Lyria moves closer, then crouches in front me, pulling my hair back. "Do you seriously think I'd let a lowly Shadow Creek mutt take my rightful place in the pack?"

"Lyria, quit wasting time with her. We need to deliver her to Valerius before the Wolfe brothers realize she's missing."

"Seth, why are you doing this? I thought you were Tristan's best friend."

The blond man's features twist into a scowl. "Do you think I'm betraying him? I'm saving him from your clutches."

Lyria lets go of my hair, only to roll me over and press my

face against the ground. My entire body has gone numb, and I can't even feel my wolf anymore. The edges of my vision begin to darken, but I manage to ask one final question. "Where are you taking me?"

"To where you belong," Seth answers before my entire world goes dark.

⚜

Dante

I awake with a start, the sharp pain in my chest making it almost impossible to breathe. Something terrible has happened. I throw my legs to the side of the bed, and practically jump from it. My studio is shrouded in darkness. Only a few rays of sunshine manage to penetrate the blinds, but I know it must be midmorning already. Without bothering to find a pair of shoes, I hurry out barefoot, wearing only the loose sweatpants I fell asleep in.

The sense of foreboding doesn't ease up; it only gets stronger and stronger the farther I get from my studio. Before I know it, I break into a run, heading straight to the alpha's manor. I must have made the five-minute trek in less than a minute, zooming down the mountain like the devil himself was after me.

I make a beeline to Sam's room in the infirmary. Before I reach his door, he rushes out naked as a newborn baby, looking frantic. Mom is right behind him, urging him to return to bed.

"What happened?" I ask.

"Something's not right," he says. "You feel it, too, don't you, Dante?"

"Yes. Where's Red?"

"She went to see you," Mom answers.

Dread drips down my spine. Locking gazes with Sam, I

know he's thinking the same thing I am. Something happened to Red.

"Did you look in her room?" Sam asks.

I shake my head. "She's not in this building. As a matter of fact, I can't sense her at all."

Sam stares at me without blinking for a few seconds before he replies, "Me neither."

The door down the hallway bursts open. Tristan explodes out like a bulldozer ready to raze a building to the ground. "Where is she?"

"We don't know," Sam and I answer in unison.

"Your bond is strong enough that you felt something was off all the way from town?" Mom asks incredulously.

"I was already on my way back when the feeling hit. I couldn't breathe for a few seconds."

"The same thing happened to us," I say.

Mom's scrutinizing gaze falls on each of us before she speaks. "She's definitely not a regular wolf, and neither is the bond you have with her."

"What good is this magical bond if we don't know what happened to her or where she is?" Sam throws his arms in the air.

"You don't know that you can't locate her. I'll get the enforcers available to start a search party. Meanwhile, get ready." Mom begins to hurry toward the exit, her shoulders squared as if she's preparing to go to battle.

"You don't think she ran away, do you?" Sam's eyes shine with lingering fear. Maybe if he had asked me that questions a few days ago, I would have told him it was a possibility, but not now.

"No. She didn't run away, and I'm afraid her disappearance is linked to what was done to Dad up in Vancouver," Tristan replies.

Sam's eyes widen a fraction before he whispers, as if he's afraid the walls are listening, "If that's true, then it means we have a traitor in our midst."

"Yes, we most certainly do." And I have a nagging suspicion I know who it is. But I can't make accusations without proof, not when the person in question is Tristan's best friend.

CHAPTER 36

RED

I'm plagued by weird images, a darkness that keeps reaching for me while I run without direction in an unknown forest. There's a hollowness in my chest that freezes my veins, vanquishing any joy I have ever felt in my entire life. My face is ice cold because I'd been crying and the tears have solidified, giving me a glacial mask.

A lonely wolf howls in the distance, and the sound is so sad and filled with anguish that it makes me want to cry even more. I see a river ahead, its serene waters bathed in moonlight. If I can cross that body of water, the darkness won't be able to reach me. Hope propels me forward. I'm only a few steps away from salvation when giant claws made from black smoke appear on my arms. At first, they have no substance until they clamp around my limbs, sharp talons digging into my skin. I let out a cry as the hands of pure evil yank me back a second before I was ready to jump toward salvation.

With a start, my eyes fly open, but the tendrils of the nightmare remain, clutching my chest in a vicious hold. My accelerated heartbeat makes it hard to draw air in, and when I don't recognize my surroundings right away, my panic seems to double. I try to sit up, but I find that my arms and legs are restrained. I'm trapped.

What the hell happened to me?

Memories of an encounter with Lyria and Seth comes to the surface. They drugged and kidnapped me, but where am I? I pull at my restraints, trying to break free, but the bindings are strong and my body is still not completely recovered from the tranquilizer.

"Stop fussing. You're not going anywhere," a voice says from a dark corner of the room.

"Who's there?" My heart begins to beat faster while sweat breaks out on my forehead.

A man with long, straight black hair emerges from the shadows. His face is all sharp edges and angles. In a cruel way, he might even be considered beautiful.

"Forgive me my manners. My name is Valerius Locklear, and I'm the alpha of the Shadow Creek pack. Welcome home, Amelia Redford, Mother of Wolves."

TO BE CONTINUED

ABOUT THE AUTHOR

USA Today Bestselling author M. H. Soars always knew creative arts were her calling but not in a million years did she think she would become an author. With a background in fashion design she thought she would follow that path. But one day, out of the blue, she had an idea for a book. One page turned into ten pages, ten pages turned into a hundred, and before she knew, her first novel, The Prophecy of Arcadia, was born.

M. H. Soars resides in The Netherlands with her husband and daughter. She is currently working on the *Love Me, I'm Famous* series, and the *Crimson Hollow World* novels. She also writes SciFi and Fantasy under the pen name Michelle Hercules.

Join M. H. Soars VIP group on Facebook:
https://www.facebook.com/groups/mhsoars/

Connect with M. H. Soars:
Website: www.mhsoars.com
Email: books@mhsoars.com
Facebook: https://www.facebook.com/mhsoars
Twitter: @mhsoars

Printed in Great Britain
by Amazon